Copyright 2016

Lars Emmerich

Polymath Publishing and Consulting, Inc.

All rights reserved.

The Incident

Reckoning

Part 1

Chapter 1

Six corpses and a bomb.

It had been a shitty week. And though it was Friday, there was no end in sight.

Special Agent Sam Jameson emerged from Homeland Security Deputy Director Tom Jarvis' office and walked quickly down the hallway toward the elevators. She was on her way to her office in the bowels of the country's third largest bureaucracy.

Brock followed in Sam's wake. She was still overcome with relief at her discovery of the coincidence that had falsely associated her lover with a brood of very bad people, who Sam suspected were responsible for as many as five of those corpses.

Maybe the bomb, too. It was hard to say.

It was good to have Brock back in her life. Now, they could try to stay alive together, instead of trying to stay alive apart.

She wasn't quite sure why the cops had it in for her, and she hadn't gotten much help from her two bosses at Homeland.

Tom Jarvis was a douchebag bureaucrat, and Francis Ekman was a milquetoast sycophant, and she was still uncertain why they'd withheld a key piece of information: the name of the guy who had probably dropped the bomb in the front yard of their very expensive Alexandria brownstone.

If Fatso Minton had indeed dropped that bomb, karma had already delivered its comeuppance. Sam was certain that the gruesome imagery of Fatso's mutilated body would add itself to the regular rotation of macabre horrors in her dreams.

Sam and Brock moved like a phalanx through the sea of Homeland clerks milling about in the hallways. Dan Gable hustled to keep pace.

Frank Ekman, Sam's newly-appointed human shield, brought up the rear. There was a strong chance that Homeland was compromised, and a strong chance that Ekman and Jarvis were themselves the problem, but Sam and Brock had been forced to bring this particular enemy close. It was necessary to reduce the number of variables in their world. It was tough to run from both the good guys and the bad guys at the same time.

"Wait here, Frank," Sam said as they passed Ekman's office. Sam's boss did as she told him. Sam had him over a barrel.

Ekman peeled off, nodded at his secretary, and shut the door to his office.

"Will you please call me right away if he goes anywhere?" Sam whispered to the secretary, who gave her a puzzled look in response. "We have plans," Sam explained. The secretary nodded.

The pencil pushers averted their eyes as Sam, Brock and Dan approached the elevator lobby. The kind of people who were content to sit in dark cubicles writing memos harbored a natural aversion to alphas, the kind of people who caught spies and flew fighter jets. The clerks cleared away.

They also whispered amongst themselves. There had been rumors that Sam was somehow tainted by involvement in unsavory activities, rumors likely started and perpetuated by the bureaucrat whose office Hurricane Sam had just left.

She had left Tom Jarvis red-faced and with his mouth agape. It hadn't mattered much that he sat two rungs above her on the organizational chart, and just two rungs below The Man Himself. What mattered was that Jarvis was no match for Sam, and his decades of office work hadn't stacked up well against her years in the real world.

She pushed the button and waited for the elevator. She smiled at a few of the staring cubicle dwellers, who immediately looked away. Dan and Brock watched with amusement.

They held their conversation until they were alone in the elevator, when Dan spoke up. "I'm glad you're here in person. A few things have come up that I'm glad we don't have to talk about by phone."

"I imagine," Sam said. "It's been a hell of a week for you, too. I appreciate all of your help. You've been a godsend."

"No sweat. How's the remodeling going?" he asked with a twinkle in his eye.

"Great. We saved a ton of money on the demolition," Sam quipped.

The elevator dinged, and they made their way to Sam's office, with its million-dollar view of Capitol Hill in one direction and the Washington Monument in the other.

Sam sat behind her desk, drew a long breath, rubbed her eyes, and blew the air out slowly. "What a grisly scene," she said, referring to the pictures Dan had brought into Jarvis' office minutes earlier.

In addition to the human tragedy, Fatso's death was wildly inconvenient. Sam had planned to return to Fatso's home in Dayton to ask him a few more pointed questions.

One pointed question, really: why did you drop a goddamned bomb on my goddamned house?

"So we're back at square one?" she asked Dan.

"Fortunately, no. That's what I wanted to talk to you about." He sat in a chair adjacent to the couch in Sam's office. "Who's the one guy you'd love to have a conversation with?" he asked.

"Dibiaso," Sam said without hesitation. "Jarvis apparently knows him as Martinson."

"Exactly. His burner phone was active for roughly two weeks, and he made several dozen calls."

Brock shook his head. "What are the odds that he and I rode together twice in the same damned carpool?"

"Stranger than fiction," Sam said.

"Here's the deal," Dan said. "I have no idea how Ekman and Jarvis learned Dibiaso was using that particular burner phone. I haven't found anything confirming it, and neither of those clowns are talking."

Sam shook her head. "That's a problem."

"It *sounds* like a problem," Dan said, "But it may not really *be* a problem. Here's why. The phone's user – maybe Dibiaso, maybe someone else – spoke with roughly a dozen people. I accessed those phone records via the trapdoor—"

"You got a warrant?" Sam interjected.

Dan laughed. "You're joking, right? Who needs a warrant in

the digital age?"

Sam shook her head. "I didn't hear that."

"As I was saying," Dan went on, "I looked at those records. All of them were burners, little prepaid phones that weren't in use for much more than a few weeks."

"Not helpful," Sam said.

"Right," Dan said. "Definitely not ideal for our purposes. They're easy to track geographically, but it's really tough to associate those accounts with any particular person. You have to have some other information, like the phone's location data overlapping with a person's known address, or credit card information used to purchase the phone."

"Do you have that?" Brock asked.

"No. We have nothing at all, on anyone who used any of the phones that Dibiaso – or whatever his name is – spoke with using the burner number that Ekman gave us. Those phones were all bought with cash and used in public places."

"Doesn't sound like good news," Brock said, looking glum.

"No, but it's very telling," Sam said. "These dudes were more than investment bankers cheating on their wives."

"It does have a pro vibe about it," Dan said. "But there's one thing that jumped out at me."

Sam nodded, hoping to accelerate Dan's dramatic pause.

"One of the phones subsequently popped up in a foreign country. Any guesses?"

"California?"

Dan frowned. "Venezuela."

Sam nodded thoughtfully. "So that improves our confidence that whoever used this phone – who I think signed the Pentagon visitor log as Avery Martinson, and Ekman and Jarvis refer to as Arturo Dibiaso – is somehow relevant to the Bolero investigation."

"That sounds interesting, but inconclusive," Brock said.

"And not very helpful, really," Sam said.

"Right, but the thing is, we got lucky twice," Dan said. "Whoever ventured down to Venezuela with that phone was a bit sloppy. They turned the phone off twice in front of one particular address, and turned it on a couple of times in the same spot."

Sam sat up. "Almost like they turned it off while they were home, and turned it on again when they left."

"Exactly," Dan said. "Didn't want to give away where they were staying. Except they weren't smart about it."

"So you got the address, then?"

Dan handed her a slip of paper.

Sam looked at Brock. "Ever been to Caracas?"

"I'll brush up on my French."

"Spanish."

"Guten Tag, Fräulein."

"You're a natural."

Chapter 2

Peter Kittredge picked dirty underwear off the floor of his Caracas apartment.

He found himself in a rough spot.

While the Agency-inflicted wounds on his back were healing, Kittredge wasn't certain whether he would ever fully recover from the wounds his participation in a CIA assassination had inflicted on his conscience.

And he had nothing to wear. Someone had ransacked his apartment, and he wasn't finished picking the broken glass out of his carefully tailored ensembles. Plus, he hadn't done laundry in almost two weeks.

It was funny how the small things got to a person. Putting on a pair of unwashed underwear was symbolic of the mayhem that had taken over his entire life.

He selected a reasonably clean white tee from the pile of dirty clothes still strewn about the bedroom floor and pulled it free of the mess.

As he draped it over his head, he heard something clatter on the hardwood. It had a hard, plastic sound.

Several seconds of searching ended the mystery: an old-school cell phone. Nothing smart about it. It had a tiny display, actual buttons, and a stubby antenna sticking up from the top.

Kittredge had never seen it before.

Charley. You cheating bastard.

Theirs was an open relationship. They could have sex with whomever they wanted, whenever they wanted. The only caveats were not to play coy about it, and not to get emotionally attached.

Burner phones were a far more dangerous sign in an open relationship than in an exclusive one. In the latter, there was the chance that it was just casual sex. In the former, it was the kiss of death. It meant emotional attachment.

Or a parallel life. In Charley's case, that seemed extremely likely. That parallel life may have included another serious relationship, or maybe not. Kittredge wasn't sure whether he cared to know.

He was certain that he should have felt something, but he didn't. He was numb. His VSS acquaintances had intimated that there was much more to Charley Arlinghaus than he knew. And Kittredge certainly had misgivings of his own regarding his boyfriend.

Ex-boyfriend, maybe. He wasn't sure.

Charley had sort of nudged Kittredge into spying for Exel Oil. It had happened so slowly that Kittredge almost hadn't noticed until he was already a long way in, probably too far in to get out.

And El Grande, the VSS guerrilla-looking guy who'd taken Kittredge under his wing, had claimed that Exel Oil and the CIA were really the same thing, working by various means to muscle in on the vast crude reserves under Venezuela's lush jungles. The Venezuelan government had long ago thrown out the gringo oil vultures, as El Grande occasionally referred to them, but America's otherworldly oil lust was nobody's secret.

Sonuvabitch, Kittredge thought. *A fine mess I dove into.*

But it was better than dying of boredom in his modest embassy office, grinding through hopelessly uninteresting economic reports, he thought.

There was a reckless, wild, adventurous soul hidden beneath the sterile mountain of buttoned-down behavior and even more buttoned-down economic data that, before his exciting but ill-fated adventure spying for Exel Oil, had been the extent of his daily reality.

I'm well and truly screwed, Kittredge thought with absolute certainty, *and this will definitely end poorly.*

But I probably still wouldn't change much if I had it to do over again.

He craved the rush, the ride. Even the abject fear was delicious in its vibrancy.

Sometimes.

Other times, it was just abject fear.

Kittredge turned on the burner phone. It took forever to time in. It wasn't password-protected. Its call history was empty, and there were no voice or text messages.

He sighed. It would have been great to learn something about what Charley had been up to, but it occurred to Kittredge that at the moment, he probably already had all the excitement and intrigue he could handle.

As if on cue, his own phone buzzed.

Quinn. "Wear something nice, that shows off your broad

shoulders." Delivered with a fake lisp.

"Go to hell, Quinn."

"Peter, my boy, life's nothing without a sense of humor."

Kittredge didn't respond.

"Anyway, good chat," Quinn said. "Hurry down. I'm illegally parked at your curb." Quinn hung up.

Kittredge finished dressing in dirty clothes and left his apartment.

* * *

"Super-Agent Kittredge, how the hell's it hanging?" Fredericks clapped him on the back.

Kittredge winced, his scabbed-over skin howling in protest.

"Still a little tender back there?" Fredericks leaned in conspiratorially. "Quinn goes overboard sometimes. He's afraid to admit that he likes torturing people."

"Well, it does make him a certifiable psychopath," Kittredge said, taking a seat in the US embassy's first-floor conference room next to an embassy coworker.

Kittredge had been surprised to learn from Quinn during the short drive from his apartment to the embassy that the morning's festivities would be attended by none other than Ambassador Wolfe himself.

"Does he know?" Kittredge had asked.

Quinn had played dumb. "Does who know what?"

"You know what I mean. Does the ambassador know what you're doing?"

"We." Quinn had corrected. "What *we* are doing. Partners

forever, remember? Says so on the paper you signed."

"I'm serious, Quinn. Is he in on this?"

"No questions, little buddy. Those are unhealthy. Just play your part, speak your lines, and everything will come up roses."

The ambassador arrived late, as was customary, hurriedly breezing in after everyone else had settled into their seats. It was an old trick used to solidify the pecking order. Everyone else in the room stood up at his arrival, as if he was a military general. It grated on Kittredge, just like it always did.

Maybe that was one of those little things that had driven Kittredge over the edge.

Fredericks spoke. "Mr. Ambassador, thank you for your time. I'm Jeff Santos, from the State Department Economic Policy Directorate."

Kittredge was taken aback by the outright lie.

His face must have betrayed his shock, because Quinn was looking daggers at him. It felt like Quinn's crazy, mismatched wolf eyes were boring through him. Kittredge shuddered. *Pure evil in there,* he thought, working hard to restore passivity to his own expression.

Fredericks' nasal voice droned on. "We're thankful that Mr. Kittredge has volunteered to brief the economic data during our meeting this afternoon."

What the hell? Kittredge hadn't volunteered to brief anything to anyone.

All eyes in the room turned to him, and he felt his face flush. He managed a wan smile and a small, nervous wave.

"He's one of our best," Ambassador Wolfe said, a mostly-genuine smile on his face. "Pete, let's go over the data afterwards."

It's Peter, you ass. You've only known me for three years. "Sounds great, Mr. Ambassador."

Fredericks continued. "Really, the point of the whole thing is to show the economic benefits of the scale our companies can bring to the oil extraction operation here in Venezuela. We think the Venezuelans will ultimately be receptive, once they see how much they stand to gain through increased efficiency. And the infrastructure benefits go without saying."

Kittredge would never have guessed that Fredericks could have conjured or even memorized such a statement. Perhaps the hard-boiled gumshoe routine and the gruff exterior were just an act, meant to disguise a much sharper intellect than Fredericks had revealed during any of their earlier interactions.

Impressive.

Spooky.

Just like Quinn. The giant of an agent could change in a flash between his bumpkin and philosopher affectations, and the vacillations between his normal-guy and murderous psychopath personas were lightning fast.

The meeting at the embassy concluded uneventfully, though Kittredge suddenly found himself obligated to attend a mid-afternoon appointment with the ambassador to cover the materials for the briefing with the Venezuelan Economic Development Consortium. The consortium met at four thirty. *Nothing like off-the-cuff diplomacy. Maybe that's why it always seems to end up in violence.*

Kittredge was none too pleased at the prospect of preparing and delivering a briefing, as there wasn't much emotional or intellectual space in his life at the moment to accommodate such a large responsibility on such short notice, but he reasoned that he eventually had to dive back into his life as an economic advisor to the ambassador. *Might as well be now,* he thought as the meeting broke up.

Quinn shook his hand on the way out. "Pleasure to meet you this morning, Mr. Kittredge," he said loudly.

Kittredge looked askance at the feral-eyed assassin. In truth, Kittredge had met Quinn just shy of a week earlier, when the giant sociopath had taken a belt sander and a bag of salt to his lower back to extort what amounted to an oath of lifetime fealty to the Agency. Before Kittredge could voice the biting sarcasm that popped to mind, Quinn's grip tightened like a vice around his hand.

Kittredge took the hint. "Pleasure to meet you. And *Mister Santos*, too," he said with an edge to his voice.

Quinn winked and joined the flow of embassy functionaries and CIA operatives moving out the conference room door.

* * *

Kittredge had a solid afternoon of work ahead of him preparing for the briefing he was apparently on the hook to deliver. He still had no idea who his audience might be, other than it comprised a vague collective the embassy people referred to as the Venezuelan Economic Development Consortium.

There was something else on his mind, too.

I've got to warn El Grande.

He knew that the CIA wanted to kill someone in the VEDC, a person they called El Cucaracha. Kittredge had no idea who that might be, although during a recent conversation, Fredericks had thrown out a first name: Hugo.

There were probably half a million Venezuelans named Hugo, so that wasn't a terribly specific clue. And as far as Kittredge could tell, membership on the VEDC was a revolving door kind of thing on the Venezuelan side, with random local luminaries making haphazard cameo appearances at various events.

None of that information had helped him narrow down who Fredericks' target might be.

To make matters worse, Quinn and Fredericks had revealed absolutely nothing about the method of assassination, other than to say that there wouldn't be any violence. Puzzling. Not to mention contradictory by definition, Kittredge thought.

This was all of more than passing interest to Kittredge, beholden as he was to each of the involved parties.

No drama there, he thought wryly.

He made his way through embassy security, and wound out onto Calle los Estanques, toward the unfortunately-named Cafe Ole. It was a long walk for lunch, particularly given the mediocre cafe fare, but lunch was only a peripheral purpose. He would have preferred to summon a taxi, but doing so would have signaled a different thing entirely.

He ordered patacones, or fried green plantains, and a creamy lasagna known as pasticho Venezolano. Far too rich for an afternoon of intellectually involved work, Kittredge realized with a sigh, but El Grande's contact instructions had been very clear. La Tizanda, a sickeningly sweet fruit smoothie, rounded out the order.

As he took the order, the waiter spoke the magic words: "I hope you enjoy this meal very much, Señor."

Kittredge delivered his scripted reply. "I have no doubt that I will."

The waiter nodded, then disappeared into the kitchen.

He returned moments later with Kittredge's order. Tucked beneath the small plate of patacones was a small slip of paper. It contained an address, which Kittredge guessed would take five minutes to reach on foot.

He ate quickly, feeling the rich, starchy foods expand in his belly. He'd have to talk to El Grande about a healthier order next time. He paid cash and left, walking as quickly as the gut bomb would allow.

Kittredge reached the specified apartment building, and took the stairs to find the right apartment number. He knocked four times.

He heard footsteps within, then a frail female voice: "Are you the television repairman?"

It was the question he expected to hear. "No, but I passed him on the way up," he said.

The door opened to reveal an old Venezuelan lady, hunched at the waist and again just below the neck. She waved him in with a bony hand, tottered over to a radio, and turned the music on to cover their conversation.

Kittredge cringed. He had always thought that Latin music was a caricature of itself, and being constantly subjected to omnipresent, droning beats beneath melodramatic wailing was one of the few things he truly hated about living in Venezuela.

The old woman motioned him toward a chair. He sat. She pulled a second chair close to his and settled slowly next to him, leaning her ear toward him. He spoke slowly and clearly into her ear, suppressing his revulsion at the stale, senescent air that surrounded the ancient woman. "For El Grande: Agency planning unknown action against codename El Cucaracha, first name Hugo, during VDEC meeting today," he said.

She repeated his message three times, perfectly each time. He had no idea who the woman was, but her mind was in far better shape than her gnarled body.

It was all very simple. Treason usually was. Uncomplicated, but definitely not easy. While the Central Intelligence Agency had encouraged Kittredge to maintain an ongoing relationship with the Venezuelan Special Services, Fredericks and Quinn had warned him in no uncertain terms about divulging operational details. Routine check-in, he would tell Quinn. It would have looked suspicious if he hadn't gone. Something along those lines.

"El Grande thanks you," the old woman spoke into his ear.

He nodded. "Give my regards to Maria."

The woman gave him a knowing smile. "Of course."

Chapter 3

"Caracas, then," Brock said. "Any chance we can pack a few things first?"

"Better to buy what we need than risk a trip back home," Sam said. "Now that we've put our cards on the table with Jarvis, we have to watch our backs even more closely. Either we've cleared the air or doubled our exposure, depending on how big a bastard he is."

Dan grunted his assent, and Brock nodded.

"I'll get us booked," Sam said.

Dan protested. "Not a good idea to leave transportation trails back to you, boss."

"I agree," she said. "That's why this particular trail will lead back to our new human shield."

Dan nodded with a knowing smile.

Sam sent Dan back to his office with a task: hack into Jeff Jensen's computer account. She wanted to know what Jensen may have discovered before his untimely death a few days earlier.

Then she got to work. She inserted her government ID card into her desktop computer's Common Access Card receptacle. She typed in her personal identification number and watched the blue whirly disk spin on the screen while the ancient Dell paperweight shuffled electrons around inside at glacial speed.

No fewer than seven warning panes popped open, ranging from threats of dire consequences for attaching portable storage media to the government system, notices that use of the computer system implied consent to search, notices of an overdue flu shot, and even a high-wind warning from Wednesday.

Sam shook her head. She had no idea why a windowless building full of clerks needed real-time warning of gusty winds. Each inane announcement required her acknowledgement, after which the spinning blue asshole, as she called it, returned again to mock her impatience.

I hate this freaking place, she thought for the thousandth time.

She stayed at Homeland because it was on a very short list of places where she could pursue her calling without getting thrown in jail. She loved hunting down the world's bastards. It was okay when justice involved a jail sentence for them. It was also okay when it involved a more permanent solution.

Sam clicked around until she found what she was looking for: Francis Ekman's government travel credit card information.

In what was universally regarded as a sweetheart deal struck between the bankers running the credit card companies and the ex-bankers running the federal treasury, all government travel expenditures were to be accomplished using a commercial credit card. Individuals were personally liable for all expenses until the government got good and ready to reimburse them, and may the gods help you if you didn't fill out your forms properly.

It was a huge hassle, and Sam didn't blame Ekman for sloughing the task off on her for several of his recent trips. She had resented playing travel agent on his behalf, and had given him an earful, but she had exacted instant revenge by storing all of his information for a rainy day.

Like today.

She booked three one-way trips to Caracas on his card. One was for a man and a woman pulled from the inactive alias list in the Homeland database. The unused legends had the names Thomas Brownstein and Tricia Leavens. Thomas was to fly to Caracas via Charlotte, while Tricia's reservations were for a direct flight from DC.

She booked Francis Ekman's ticket as well, using his own name and following the same itinerary as Tricia's. She placed Ekman in the seat directly in front of hers. Better to keep an eye on him.

She didn't book him under an alias for a simple reason. She wanted to advertise his presence, either as deterrent or invitation to any bastards lurking within Homeland's ranks. Sometimes you had to stir things up in order to get them to settle down.

It took well over half an hour to book the flights, the unfortunate consequence of a bespoke multimillion dollar travel system commissioned by Homeland. The system had half the functionality of the online tools already available to consumers, and it worked at a tectonic pace, when it wasn't down for weekly maintenance. It was one more reason Sam disliked the lumbering, incompetent, insipid government she served.

By the time she had finished, Brock was snoring on the couch in her office. She printed the tickets, then nudged him awake.

She picked up her phone and punched the hot key for Ekman's office. "Hi, Patty. Just wanted to let Frank know that we're leaving in an hour."

Brock heard Patty fuss in the background.

"Sorry, can't say where we're going. Security and all."

More fussing.

"Sorry, Patty, I also can't say whether he'll need an overnight bag." Sam made some sympathetic noises, then hung up.

She led Brock back to the elevators. They went down to the building's dank basement, and wound their way through the warren of dark cement hallways to what Homeland agents euphemistically referred to as the Travel Agency.

Its formal name was the Field Documents Branch, and it was one of the few government offices that knowingly employed convicted criminals. Forgers, to be exact. They'd all served their sentences and subsequently chosen to use their powers for good rather than evil. Or, as they often joked, they wanted to work where they could do some serious damage to humanity.

"Hey, Ron," Sam said as she recognized a familiar face. "Got a few minutes?"

"Anything for you, Sam," he said.

"It's not Sam today. Meet Tricia Leavens," she said. Then she looked at Brock and said, "This handsome fellow is Thomas Brownstein. We just need you to work your magic for us. And I'll apologize in advance that we're in a bit of a hurry."

"Everyone is," Ron said. He cross-checked the aliases in the database of unassigned legends, then checked Brock's military identification card.

"Pretty unusual for a military guy to get a Homeland alias,"

Ron observed. "Usually some extra paperwork involved."

Sam smiled. "Usually," she said with a wink. "But there's not always time for that."

"Right," Ron said. "Sometimes you gotta get out there and crack skulls, and catch up on the trivia later."

Sam loved her occasional interactions with people like Ron, people who understood the bigger picture. Without them, nothing at the Department of Homeland Security would ever get done.

Ron motioned Sam and Brock toward the camera, and they took turns posing for their ID photos. Twenty minutes later, they each had a driver's license, passport, library card, credit and ATM cards, miscellaneous receipts to stuff in their wallets for authenticity, and a fact sheet detailing their fake lives.

All of the items looked worn and used, an extremely important touch often overlooked by amateurs.

The fact sheets were made out of a strange paper that felt thin and brittle.

"The usual routine," Ron said. "Study the legends until you can recite them in your sleep. Then you can either burn the paper or eat it. But probably not both."

Sam chuckled. "Thanks, Ron."

"And I'm required to harass you with the usual warning that you'll have to account for all of your expenditures at the end of the op, blah blah blah."

Sam smiled. Ron's healthy perspective on the bullshit was not unexpected, given his background.

"You're also supposed to turn in your personal credentials to me," he said.

"Yeah, silly us. We must have left them in our other pants," she said.

Ron winked. "I know how that goes. Never know when you'll find yourself with a strong need to be someone else. If there's an audit this afternoon, I'm sure I'll think of something."

Sam gave Ron a hug and thanked him, and she and Brock left the field documents office.

"I love this spy shit," Brock said. "Where do we get our ninja stars and exploding pens?"

"Sorry," Sam said. "We spend all our money hiring people to write emails to each other."

They rode the elevator back up to her floor, and made their way to Dan's office. They found him hunched over his computer keyboard, glancing quickly between his two large screens at windows full of what looked to Sam like machine language.

"Can you see the Matrix?" Brock quipped.

"I like the blonde," Dan said. Esoteric movie quotes were apparently a universal guy thing, Sam thought.

"Hate to interrupt the fraternity boy handshake," she said, "but have you made any progress working on the Jensen thing?"

"Sure have. It was actually pretty easy. I was able to convince the network administrator that I had a legitimate need to see Jeff's files."

"Unheard of," Sam said.

"Well, I also bribed her. She's a big chocolate lover. Emphasis on *big*."

"Good work. Learn anything?"

Dan described how Jeff's coworkers had slowly taken over his crime scene investigation case work since his death, and how one of them had commented on a set of partial fingerprints. The other CSI had received the results, but was unable to decipher the origin of the partial prints.

"Gotta be the partials from the music box at Phil's," Sam said. Dan nodded. Sam had illegally lifted the music box from Phil Quartermain's apartment moments after discovering that the DC Metro investigator's throat had been slit. Homeland CSI Jeff Jensen had agreed, after Sam applied the right leverage, to run forensic tests on the music box outside of normal channels.

Jensen's examination had produced a set of partial prints that couldn't be immediately matched, but Jensen had apparently entered the partials into the database for further analysis. The mainframe did in a matter of days what it would have taken several million man-hours to do manually: overlay the fingerprint fragments in hundreds of different locations and orientations on top of every individual fingerprint in the database, until it found a match within a reasonable confidence. It was a grueling process that took enormous computing power, and it didn't always result in a match.

In this case, Dan explained, the computer had found a match. "Unfortunately," he said, "the record is sealed."

"Balls," Sam said.

"That was my reaction, too."

"So we're dead in the water? I mean, opening sealed records requires months of haggling with lawyers and other bottom feeders."

Dan looked offended. "I thought you held me in higher regard than that," he said with mock indignation. "You seem to have forgotten that I did juvie time in high school for hacking. Let me see what I can do."

"Thanks, Dan. I'm glad you're on my team."

"Can you fix my parking tickets?" Brock asked.

"For a small fee."

A pensive look crossed Dan's face. "Listen," he said, "something has been bugging me."

"I apologize for whatever I've done," Sam said.

"Not that. It's been bothering me how quickly Jensen was killed after you enlisted his help with the music box evidence."

Sam nodded. "It would make sense if they had been tracking me. They could've easily figured out that we spent time together, which might have been the kiss of death for him. But I haven't seen hide or hair of anyone, DC Metro guys included, since right after Quartermain's murder on Monday."

Dan looked pensive. He scrunched his face and scratched what would have been his neck, if he had a neck. Instead, he had one giant set of shoulders with a head stuck on top of them. He was built like a bodybuilder, which seemed an unlikely frame to house the mind of an investigative computer genius with the temperament to sit in front of a computer monitor for weeks at a time in order to solve difficult cases. He complemented Sam's tenacious fieldwork perfectly, with equally tenacious network ops. It was increasingly a cyber world, and Dan was among the very best.

"You found a CD ROM in the music box, didn't you?" he

finally asked.

Sam nodded. "It had the financial data linking Abrams and Cooper to Executive Strategies and JIE Associates."

"And you used Jensen's computer to access the data?"

"I did."

Dan asked for the CD ROM, which Sam happened to have tucked into her pocket.

"You're setting a bad example, walking around with crime scene evidence up your sleeve," he chided as he took the computer disk from her and dropped it into a waiting tray on his own computer.

He opened several more windows full of what looked like alphabet soup. It had an old-school computer aesthetic, nothing but a black background behind undecipherable code made up of ugly green font. But it seemed to make sense to Dan.

He scratched his chin, typed, mumbled, nodded his head, and typed some more.

"Care to let me in on the secret?" Sam asked.

"Here's the deal," Dan said. "Ever heard of an outfit called Hack Team?"

Sam shook her head, but Brock piped up. "Spyware guys? I saw a documentary a while ago."

"That's right," Dan said. "They produce some of the world's best spyware and sell it exclusively to governments, mostly the kind who can't afford to write their own."

"Seemed like they did business with some shady people," Brock said. "Though you can't always believe what you see in a documentary."

"In this case, it's pretty accurate. Don't tell anyone I told you this," Dan said with a conspiratorial air, "but the federal government is actually ten times shadier. It's just that we're much quieter about it."

Brock nodded. "Figures."

"But Hack Team sells their stuff all over the world," Dan went on. "They even have a slick little video sales pitch. Their software is supposed to be untraceable, but they're too vain not to bury a signature line or two inside the code. It's plain as day, if you know what you're looking for."

"What does it do?" Sam asked.

"Nothing much. Just records your position, your keystrokes, any ambient audio in the room, and even takes video, if your laptop has a built-in camera, all without alerting the user that anything funny is going on. They can also hack any passwords to bank accounts, social media sites, you name it."

"Jesus," Sam said. "That's dastardly."

"And then some," Dan agreed. "It's the dictator's perfect tool."

Brock nodded. "Actually," he said, "I think using something like that pretty much turns *any* government into a de facto dictatorship."

"It's a brave new world," Dan agreed. "Anyway, politics aside, it's pretty easy for whoever put the Hack Team software on this disk to set up an alert. As soon as the user accesses the data, they'll have instant access to everything on that laptop, and instant access to everyone who uses it."

Sam shuddered. "So they watched me look through the data."

Dan nodded grimly. "I'm surprised they didn't find you, Sam." He looked concerned. "You don't still have the laptop, do you?"

She shook her head. "I dropped it off back at Jeff's," she said slowly.

Her face darkened and her eyes moistened. "I got him killed. He had rounded the corner. He was beating his drug habit, getting his life back together, and I got him killed."

"Bullshit, baby," Brock said, draping an arm around her shoulders. "You're not responsible for someone else's crime."

"I should have been smarter than that."

Dan shook his head. "It's not like you had many other options."

Brock's watch alarm beeped, interrupting Sam's self-flagellation. "If we're going to Caracas today, we need to roll," he said.

"Can you find me a list of countries we suspect of using Hack Team software?" Sam asked on the way out of Dan's office.

"Sure thing," Dan said. "It won't be one hundred percent accurate, because that kind of stuff is hard to track, but our guys keep a pretty close watch on it. It'll be a long list though."

"I have a specific country in mind," Sam said.

Chapter 4

El Jerga turned down the volume on his rented sedan's radio. He was approaching the city from the west, and he needed the mental bandwidth to navigate while dodging traffic.

His highly enjoyable and lucrative trip to the Midwest was a pleasant, glowing memory. His target hadn't survived as long as El Jerga had hoped, but it had been long enough for the demons inside him to run amok. The skinny man's otherworldly howls of agony fueled their frenzy.

If he was a deviant, El Jerga rationalized, his environment certainly shouldered some portion of the culpability. Venezuela's overly politicized society demanded muscle of all sorts, and a man of his particular brand of eager proclivity was almost infinitely useful to innumerable would-be masters.

El Jerga had picked and chosen his affiliations carefully, always aligned with the interests of his beloved uncle, may El Señor have mercy on his soul, and always furthering the cause of the little guy. His father had died in one of the thousands of oil field uprisings, fighting for livable pay and less deadly conditions, and those values had taken on a talisman's import for El Jerga as he came of age under his uncle's tutelage.

Because his enemies were still strong, El Jerga had an ideologue's zeal. An untested philosophy is always easy to support, because its shortcomings aren't yet as painfully obvious as those of a sitting government. Governing a society is a messy, involved, and invariably ugly process, and El Jerga's self-evident truths were thus far unsullied by the welter of pragmatic politics.

That made his ideology a convenient justification for the ungodly atrocities El Jerga loved to commit against his fellow man. When he was at work on someone, he relished the way the power of life and death flowed through him. It excited him on a visceral, wordless, precognitive level. It was progeny of some atavistic remnant of the predators from which humans evolved, but from which El Jerga had somehow descended without evolving.

He was more animal than human, and he knew it. He used it shamelessly, not because it was okay in and of itself, but because it was okay in light of his cause. He would still have given himself over to his wanton hunger without the cause, of course, but it was wonderful to have found a community that cultivated and cherished his unique talents.

Match made in heaven.

El Jerga took the exit for Dulles International Airport, automatically thinking of the airport's namesakes, the Dulles family. He had studied their history. They swung the hammer of the gods. They thought they were gods. And godly. They believed that their religion, some apocalyptic good versus evil dogma, should guide their statecraft. So they had decimated the godless. What qualified a race or nationality as godless in the minds of the Dulles brothers wasn't entirely clear, but they certainly had blood on their hands, El Jerga had concluded.

The horrendous hypocrisy in his thinking was hidden from El

Jerga by his need not to see it.

He parked the large sedan in the short-term parking lot at Dulles, shuffled in his slow way into the ticketing area of the large, light-filled airport atrium, and took a seat.

He listened.

He heard many uncomfortably loud announcements, about smoking and unattended baggage and suspicious persons and parking violations and flight delays.

Then he heard what he was listening for. "Mister Palms, Mister Harold Palms, please pick up a white courtesy phone."

He picked up the courtesy phone. "Stand by for your party," the operator announced.

A gruff gringo voice came on the line. "Seven," he said.

"Nueve," El Jerga answered. The code sum was sixteen.

"Hurry," the gringo said. "Thirty minutes. Take the subway to the office. Cleaning crew will meet you. When you're done, use the L'Enfant station for your egress. It'll be sanitized by friends."

"Acknowledged," El Jerga croaked.

He hung up the phone, hustled back to his car, exited the airport after paying the parking fee, and drove more quickly than was wise toward the Tysons Corner park-and-ride complex.

Cutting it close, he thought. Wasn't his fault. He was on time. Wasn't his problem if they didn't have their act together.

Still, he was anxious. And disappointed. A daylight hit at the office would afford him none of the pleasures that he had allowed himself to lust for. He wanted to take his time, to savor his victims. Especially the girl. But he would be forced to work quickly and silently.

Pity.

He looked at his watch again.

He would be lucky either way, he decided. Lucky if he made it to the gringo government building in time to do his duty, because it would mean another impressively large paycheck. His hookers weren't cheap, and he had grown accustomed to the eager favors his wallet garnered.

But he would be equally lucky if he missed them. It would keep his hopes alive for a long, fulfilling engagement. He longed to hear her screams, taste her flesh, draw her blood, revel in his release over her gorgeous, powerless form.

All in the name of the cause, of course.

Chapter 5

"Caracas?" Ekman protested, his angular cheeks flushed. "I'm not going."

"Sorry, Francis. You don't have a choice. Part of our deal with Jarvis, remember?" Sam said coolly. "You're definitely along for the ride on this one."

"This is ridiculous. You have to know I'm not working against your interests here."

"I'll know soon enough, won't I?" Sam said with a smile. "C'mon, we have flights to catch."

Ekman's phone rang. "Special Agent In Charge Ekman, how may I help you?"

Clown, Sam thought. *Even answers the phone like an errand boy.*

Ekman listened for a second, tightened his jaw, and held the phone out to Sam. "It's your deputy. Apparently, I'm answering the phone for you now, too," he said through clenched teeth.

"Thanks, Frank," Sam said cheerily. Brock chuckled.

"Hi, Dan."

"Don't say anything. I got in to that thing we were talking about earlier. Know what I mean?"

"Umm, no," Sam said. "Can I have a hint?"

"That *sealed* thing."

"Ahh, *that* thing." The identity of the person who left the partial print on the CD ROM in the music box. The person's identity had been sealed by executive fiat or court order. Sam had asked Dan to hack into the system to find the data. "I'm with you now. Did we learn anything?"

"You bet your ass I did."

"Leave my ass out of this, please," she said, winking at Brock. "My boyfriend's standing right here."

"Funny. Avery Martinson."

Sweet Jesus. Sam did her best to keep her expression neutral. She didn't want to give anything away to Ekman. *But this is a doozie.*

"Did you hear me?" Dan asked.

"Uh, yeah. Sure, I'll do that, Dan. Thanks for taking care of that for me."

"That was a nonsense response," Dan said. "I presume Ekman's listening?"

"Yes, that's right," she said. "Spot on with your analysis. Let me consider that for a moment."

"You sound ridiculous, you know," Dan said. "You never talk that way. He's going to know you're snowing him."

She ignored him. Her mind raced.

Avery Martinson was the name someone had used to sign in on the Pentagon visitor log at exactly the same time that Arturo Dibiaso's cell phone information placed him at the Pentagon visitor's desk. Sam was certain it wasn't a coincidence.

So in her mind, Avery Martinson *was* Arturo Dibiaso. Or they were working together. Same thing, for her purposes.

And when she had thrown Martinson's name at Jarvis during their showdown an hour earlier, Jarvis had been unable to hide his alarm.

Jarvis knows Dibiaso.

And Dibiaso planted the financial data linking Executive Strategies, JIE Associates, Everett Cooper, and John Abrams.

Smart money is on Dibiaso being a Company man.

That means if Jarvis isn't an Agency goon himself, he's at least in play by the CIA.

"Dan, I need you to look into the Tandem Joint files."

"What?"

"The TJ files, Dan." She noticed Ekman watching her as he stuffed papers and personal effects into his briefcase. She shouldn't be having this conversation in front of him, but she didn't have time to walk all the way back up to Dan's office. Brock would miss his flight.

Dan was silent for a long moment. "Ah. Of course. TJ. Same initials as our esteemed deputy director."

"Yes, that's right. That's the one. Maybe use some of those new software tools you were telling me about earlier. Let me know what you find."

"Holy shit, Sam," Dan said. "Do you realize what you're asking? We'll need top cover and authorizations that we don't have, and that we can never get."

"That's definitely a concern, yes," Sam said, watching Ekman with her peripheral vision. He had stopped watching her and was busily tidying his desk.

"Seriously, Sam. If we get caught–"

"I have every confidence in your abilities, Dan." *Getting caught snooping into Jarvis' personal files would suck,* she thought. *But not nearly as much as getting blindsided by an Agency bastard.* Jarvis was dirty. Sam could feel it in her bones.

"I think right away is best," she said.

Dan reluctantly agreed and signed off with a flourish of profanity.

"What was that all about?" Ekman asked when she replaced the phone on its cradle.

"Nothing. Clearing off some case work that piled up this week."

"I don't believe you," Ekman said.

"Fortunately for me," she said with a smug smile, "what you believe no longer matters."

Ekman reddened, but remained silent. She'd beaten him into submission during their earlier meeting in Jarvis' office, and he was now under orders from Jarvis to accompany Sam.

She couldn't tell for sure, but she thought she detected a hint of superiority in his eyes, a new affectation for Ekman. *I wonder if that little weasel is in bed with Jarvis,* she thought to herself.

Guess I'll know soon enough.

"Grab your man-purse and let's hit it, Francis. Brock has a plane to catch."

"I really, really hate it when you call me Francis."

"Seriously? Why didn't you say something?" Sam gave him a wicked smile.

Brock tried unsuccessfully to stifle his laugh.

Ekman sulked. He tried to follow Sam out of the office, but she waved him in front. "You first. Walk where I can see you."

He gave her a look that said *you've got to be kidding me,* but Sam gave him a look that said *shut your damn pie hole and do as you're told.*

Sam's look won out, and Ekman strode out of his office, with Sam and Brock following two paces behind him.

Chapter 6

El Jerga exited the subway station at L'Enfant Plaza. He was nauseous from the fumes, and from sitting sideways as the train jerked and jolted to stop after stop along the way from the Tysons Corner station. He was amazed that there weren't more accidents in the world's subway systems. They seemed to him like death traps, and he regarded them much like he regarded airplanes, with fear and loathing.

He paused for a long inhalation of relatively clean air, and felt the nausea and fog lifting as he rode the escalator toward daylight.

He ran through the identification challenge-and-response sequence in his mind for what must have been the hundredth time. El Jerga was always careful about making contact, as agents were captured and killed in grisly fashion – sometimes by their own agencies – as a result of relatively minor identification mistakes. Things were easily misinterpreted in a world where no one trusted anyone else.

But he was especially fastidious about leaving nothing to chance this time. He was about to enter the most xenophobic institution on the planet, the gringo government's Homeland Security building.

And if all went well, he would leave two dead people in his wake.

It had occurred more than once to El Jerga that because the

risk was just shy of egregious, such an audacious hit was a strong statement. His handlers were obviously prepared to pay a high cost for such a statement.

It was beyond obvious to El Jerga: he was expendable.

But he resolved not to be expended.

If anything looked even slightly off, he would abort. Easy.

The escalator disgorged its passengers at just below street level, and El Jerga climbed the short flight of stairs leading out of the man-made cave.

His senses were on high alert. Years of training gave him eyes that instantly recognized and processed hundreds of things that average eyes never even noticed.

Like the gringo agent stationed by the tree across the street. El Jerga could tell by the purpose with which the man studied the newspaper in front of his face. Normal men reading the newspaper on their lunch break had a far more desultory air about them. This man was on the job.

El Jerga's highly trained eyes also noticed the unmarked gringo sedan stationed half a block away.

Sure, it was possible that these agents were here for a different purpose.

But it was also possible that they weren't.

His instructions hadn't included any mention of the extra help. And if they had, he would never have agreed. El Jerga worked alone, always and without exception. El Grande knew this, and El Grande knew to make it clear in no uncertain terms to any third parties he chose to involve. This was nonnegotiable.

He crossed the street with the pedestrian light, and ambled unhurriedly over to the bench. He sat down next to the agent, and let a couple of quiet moments pass.

Then El Jerga ripped the newspaper from the agent's hand. "This is your only warning," he croaked.

The man rose and left without a word.

El Jerga turned and waved to the men stationed in the sedan half a block down the street. The big car's engine spooled to life, and the sedan roared past El Jerga. He couldn't see inside the tinted windows as the car passed, but El Jerga was sure that the looks on the men's faces were not friendly looks.

He didn't care. Today wasn't going to be his day to die. A younger, more foolish El Jerga might have been tempted to put up with the uncoordinated changes to the plan, but he was far too wizened for that. One didn't survive over a hundred killings by letting eagerness and zeal win out over solid trade craft.

He spotted the other two agents across the street almost instantly.

He was in a public place in broad daylight, unlikely to be killed or nabbed. And he was curious. So he decided to watch for a while.

El Jerga put on his sunglasses, opened the newspaper in his lap, and pretended to read. He wasn't even looking at the newspaper, though. His sunglasses were fitted with lenses that elevated the sight angle by twenty degrees, so that with his head hunched down toward the paper, he could still see directly in front of his position. His well-trained eyes watched the gringos enter and leave the Department of

Homeland Security like busy bees flitting about their hive.

Now that he had aborted his operation, El Jerga wasn't certain what he was looking for.

But he was certain he would know it when he saw it.

* * *

Agh. This miserable town, Sam thought to herself as she exited the Homeland Security building two paces behind Frank Ekman, her boss. It annoyed her the way nobody ever looked at anybody else when they passed on the street. She wasn't a social butterfly by any stretch, but she believed in giving other residents of Planet Earth – even, gasp, *complete strangers* – the courtesy of an acknowledgement whenever their paths crossed.

But there were times when the outrageously annoying self-absorption of the DC citizenry came in handy.

Because it was unusual for anyone to look at anyone else, catching someone's eyes on you was almost always significant in Sam's line of work.

Like now, for instance. Sam's eyes hadn't even adjusted to the daylight when she felt someone else's gaze on her. It was an energy thing, she had always thought. She could tell when someone beamed the energy of their consciousness her way.

She turned to find out that her intuition was spot-on.

In this case, it was a guy in a cleaning outfit, carrying a tray full of cleaning utensils. He didn't carry himself like a normal cleaner. He didn't ignore her like a normal DC resident. He didn't leer like a normal alpha male.

He looked at her like an agent.

She grabbed Brock's arm and charged into the street, causing cars to swerve and honk.

"What the–" Brock's question was interrupted by a close call with a large automobile. He had to jump out of the way of a taxi cab who applied his brakes a second too late. Brock saw the cell phone in the driver's hand, then the irate look on his face, then felt Sam's strong pull on his arm urging him onward, across the street toward the Department of Agriculture, and east toward the Smithsonian.

* * *

El Jerga watched the other agents watch him. His instructions had been to make contact with a man dressed in cleaning crew garb. That particular agent was still out in front of Homeland, now doing a terrible job staying nonchalant while he tried to steal glances at El Jerga on the bench across the street.

That particular agent wasn't the problem. It was the others that were the problem. They were out in force, poorly disguised and distinguishable even to a casual observer.

It was a mature situation, El Jerga realized. He wasn't sure whether he was the object of all this attention or not. What he knew for certain, however, is that he had thrown a wrench into someone's well-oiled plan. He had aborted his mission in the heart of the gringos' defenses.

It was the only choice he could have made. He would have words with El Grande over this, that much was clear.

A flash of red exiting the building caught his eye. A tall woman, gorgeous legs, flame red hair burning in the sunlight. And her tall, athletic male companion at her side.

Her.

And him.

El Jerga saw the other agents turn as one to look at her. *Amateurs.*

He looked back at the woman, and realized that she had made him. He watched her charge across the busy afternoon street, boy toy in tow, narrowly escaping an early death by automobile.

He pulled the newspaper back up by his face, but it was futile. She knew. He could tell by the way she looked at him.

El Jerga waited until the pair had crossed the street and continued away from him on the sidewalk. Then he rose, folded the newspaper under his arm, and joined the gaggle of agents in pursuit of Special Agent Sam Jameson.

* * *

"Walk quickly but not in a hurry," Sam said.

"What about Ekman?" Brock had lost sight of him in the crowd and confusion.

"Can't risk dragging him along."

"What the hell is going on?"

"We're being stalked. The cleaner outside the Homeland entrance, and that person over there." She nodded her head diagonally and to the left, pointing toward a bench.

"The businessman?" Brock asked through clenched teeth.

"No. The guy with the newspaper."

"How do you know?"

"Just do. One more behind us."

Brock turned to look, but she gripped his hand and twisted his forearm to keep him pointed straight ahead. "Don't look. It's rule number one. Use reflections to see behind you."

They walked past a bus stop, and Sam used the reflective plexiglass to confirm her suspicion. "Kid with a Walkman, eyes boring holes in the back of our heads. Newspaper guy is following, too. Turn left here."

They ducked into an alcove leading to a Department of Agriculture service entrance. Locked.

Sam fished into her wallet for a keycard, which she swiped through the receptacle of the electronic door lock. It beeped, turned green, and unlocked.

"Nice," Brock said.

"Sometimes living in a police state comes in handy," Sam said. "But usually only when you're the police." She shut the door behind them. "Unfortunately, there's now a record of me visiting this building. But that can't be helped now."

They promptly got lost in the labyrinthine building full of clerks. "So this is where they pay farmers to grow inedible corn?" Brock asked.

"And where they pay them to grow nothing at all."

"This place is huge."

"Your tax dollars at work."

"Or not."

Sam stopped a passerby. "Excuse me, sir. How do we get out of this building?"

The man pointed toward a long hallway. "Double doors on the left down there. Go to the end of that hallway, then take a right. Find more double doors on your left about halfway down, and go up the stairs. Two flights. Turn left out of the stairwell, then take the third right after you pass the trades and tariffs compliance unit. Can't miss it."

"Sure. Right. Thanks," Sam said. *No help whatsoever. Guess we'll have to wing it.*

They walked down the hallway and through the first set of double doors. Sam reached into her bag and pulled out a ball cap and sweater for Brock and a scarf for herself. "Rule number two of running for your life," she said, "is to always leave a place as someone different than the person who arrived."

She stooped, rounded her shoulders, and walked with a limp, leaning on Brock's arm. "We categorize people by more discriminators than we can consciously comprehend. It's best to change as many features as possible."

She practiced her gait as they wound their way through the huge, dark office building, and had perfected a consistently inconsistent shuffle by the time they finally found the front entrance.

Daylight assaulted their eyes again, and they turned west, back toward Homeland but one full block north. They headed north across the street, this time at a crosswalk, and found themselves in the long, manicured garden of the National Mall. "Slowly," Sam said. "Gawk like a tourist."

"I'm going to miss my flight."

"Don't worry," Sam said. "Francis will pick up the rebooking fee."

"Besides," she said a few paces later. "If we screw this up, we won't be in any shape to catch a plane anyway."

Chapter 7

The sun hurled angry photons at Kittredge from its late afternoon perch, which combined with the humidity and his nerves to produce uncomfortable pools of sweat on the small of his back.

By his own standards, he had done a poor job preparing for the briefing with the Venezuelan Economic Development Consortium, but it had been good enough for the ambassador. The old politician had seemed distracted, as if he knew the meeting was little more than pretense, and had approved Kittredge's presentation with uncharacteristically few changes.

Kittredge had taken a short, brisk walk around the embassy to calm his nerves, a decision his uncomfortable perspiration caused him to regret. It made his scabs itch, and he would have to change his shirt.

He made his way back to his office inside the embassy, dressed in a clean shirt from the hanger behind the door, straightened his tie, and took several deep breaths.

Showtime.

He faked a confidence he didn't feel as he walked to the embassy garage, an underground parking facility full of the armored cars that conveyed the ambassador and a few select minions around one of the world's most dangerous cities.

Kittredge was surprised to see four large security men with sniper rifles gathered in a tight semicircle near the limousines. And he was dismayed to find Fredericks at the center of the semicircle, issuing terse instructions to the armed heavies.

Kittredge felt a flash of anger. "I thought you said no violence," he said to Fredericks without preamble.

The gunmen looked at him curiously, and Fredericks laughed icily. "I'm sorry, Pete. I must have forgotten to ask for your inputs." The sarcasm was thick. "As a highly trained economist, do you have any further thoughts on the operational arrangements I've made?"

The gunmen sniggered, and Kittredge flushed. "Actually, yes," he said. "I didn't agree to be part of a shootout."

"Let's revisit our arrangement," Fredericks said. "You actually agreed to do whatever the hell I tell you to do. So give your little talk when the time comes, and otherwise, feel free to shut the fuck up. If I decide to put a round through someone's head, that's what's going to happen, regardless of how your inner child feels about it."

Stunned and speechless, Kittredge left. He wandered over to join the group of diplomats and functionaries waiting to be seated in their assigned vehicles.

Quinn arrived seconds later, and pulled Kittredge aside. "You're riding with me, little buddy."

This is going to end poorly, Kittredge thought.

* * *

The motorcade spilled out of the underground parking facility and made its way down the winding road from the US Embassy toward Urdaneta Avenue.

Holy shit, Kittredge thought. *Are we going where I think we're going?*

"What is going on?" he asked Quinn.

Quinn chuckled. "Welcome to the big leagues."

Familiar buildings passed by the windows, and Kittredge's alarm grew as the parade of diplomatic vehicles cruised through traffic. His pulse began to pound and his stomach filled with butterflies as he realized what their destination must be.

El Palacio de Miraflores.

The workplace of the president of Venezuela.

It loomed large at the end of Urdaneta Avenue. The motorcade stopped at the gates of the palace.

Kittredge's mind racing to connect the dots.

El Cucaracha.

Hugo Freaking Chavez?

"What is this? What are we doing here?" he asked Quinn.

Quinn smiled. "Every once in a while, a man has the opportunity to alter the course of history," he said with a twinkle in his eye. "As I said, welcome to the big leagues."

The motorcade remained stopped at the presidential palace's front gate for almost fifteen minutes. Kittredge couldn't see around the vehicles in front to discern the cause of the delay, but he was certain it related to security.

The picture became clearer seconds later. Large men dressed in black, hands cuffed behind their backs, were paraded slowly along the length of the motorcade from back to front by their Venezuelan captors. *The snipers have been arrested,* Kittredge realized. And the Venezuelans were making a show of it.

El Grande knew exactly who the Agency was after. Kittredge's warning, delivered to the old woman earlier in the afternoon, must have been effective.

His heart began to pound anew, and a fresh tsunami of adrenaline hit his veins. *What if Quinn and Fredericks figure out that I'm the leak?* He was certain that they could turn on him in a heartbeat, just like the animals they were.

His mind raced. He felt an almost desperate need to understand whether Quinn suspected him of warning the VSS. "We're blown," he said in a worried whisper.

Quinn's face remained calm and relaxed. "Have a little faith, man. This isn't our first day on the job."

"But the snipers–"

"Seriously. Chill."

Had they planned for this? Perhaps the snipers were *supposed* to be discovered by Venezuelan security personnel. That would mean that his warning to El Grande hadn't been so effective after all.

Kittredge bounced his knee up and down nervously as his mind churned, and the motion shook the large armored Suburban.

Quinn put a huge paw on Kittredge's knee and squeezed in a vice-like grip. "Get ahold of yourself," he said. "You're one of us now, so it's time you started acting like a pro."

There was another uncomfortable possibility, Kittredge realized. "We could be walking into a trap."

"Sure. But probably not," Quinn said. "Governments don't kill each others' ambassadors."

"Last I checked, I'm not the ambassador," Kittredge said.

Quinn chuckled. "Good point. Maybe you're screwed."

"What do you mean, *I'm* screwed? I thought we were in this together."

"Look, Peter. There's nothing to worry about. Everything's working like clockwork so far. Almost boringly predictable."

"Are you crazy? Shouldn't we be turning around and going back to the embassy? They just arrested the snipers!"

Quinn shook his head. "Really, dude, relax. We're going to a friendly little meeting. Stand up and do your dog-and-pony show and click through your slides. Pretend you're the Fed chairman and spew some of that meaningless bullshit you economists are so in love with, then get back in the car and go home. That's it. That's all you have to do."

Kittredge looked up at Quinn, into the huge assassin's feral, mismatched, wolf-like eyes, and felt both calmness and fear. The calmness came from knowing that, on this day at least, he was ostensibly aligned with an eminently competent and endlessly ruthless force of nature. Quinn was an anomaly, a mountain of a man with exquisite training and zero moral compunction, a good man to have on your side in a fight.

But Kittredge was afraid of what his alliance might make him, how it might already have altered him. He knew that his deal with the devil, as Quinn himself had termed it a little under a week ago, couldn't possibly leave him untainted. His physical and psychological injuries at the hands of the Agency might someday heal, but he wondered whether his soul wouldn't be indelibly altered.

He was also afraid because he knew that his partial alliance with both sides made him equally vulnerable to both sides. Either the

VSS or the Agency could suddenly find his services no longer useful. Regardless of which side might make that determination, it was certain to be an unhealthy proposition for Kittredge.

The standstill at the presidential palace gate finally ended, and the motorcade moved forward slowly.

They were, it seemed, on their way to do mortal harm to Hugo Chavez, the president of Venezuela.

* * *

President Hugo Chavez looked much taller on TV. Maybe the camera angle was always engineered to make him larger than life, Kittredge mused during the long, drawn out exchange of official pleasantries that marked the start of the Venezuelan Economic Development Consortium meeting.

Kittredge took his place in the procession of American embassy personnel as they advanced slowly to shake hands with Chavez and his long line of aides and functionaries. Kittredge recognized a few of the faces in the Venezuelan party from his embassy interactions over the years, but he had never before attended a meeting of such import, and he was working hard to keep his nerves under control.

He was acutely aware that his briefing was a collection of almost-truths, assembled to manipulate Chavez and his administration into permitting American oil companies to plunder Venezuelan oil.

One man's almost-truth was another man's blatant lie, and Kittredge mused darkly that Chavez was likely to throw them all out on their ears after just a few slides praising the "added value of vertical efficiencies" and the "game-changing cost savings made possible by a robust global distribution and refining infrastructure."

Pure horse shit. It was almost laughable in its transparent desperation. *We just want your damn oil.*

It wouldn't be the first time that the voracious American energy industry had come pounding on Venezuelan doors, and unlike many of his oil-rich counterparts throughout the world, Chavez was adept at rebuffing gringo overtures. In fact, Chavez was merely the latest in a long line of Venezuelan leaders who had thus far successfully held the northerners at bay.

It seemed that this success was the motivation for whatever Quinn and Fredericks had in mind for the meeting. Kittredge had no idea what might be in store, but he was certain that if the operation was successful, it would bring a heavy cost for President Hugo Chavez, and possibly for his entire country.

Kittredge hoped the VSS hadn't shot their wad arresting the snipers, and had something clever hidden up their sleeves. He found himself rooting for the sworn enemies of his homeland, partially because he was himself a perennial underdog and thus cheered for the little guys as a rule, and partially because he thought Quinn and Fredericks were bastards.

At the same time, Kittredge hoped that, should the VSS actually win this contest of wits and wills, the evidence wouldn't point too directly back to his own participation on behalf of El Grande's guerrilla VSS force. If they connected the dots, Kittredge knew, he would surely die a miserable, painful death, probably at Quinn's hands.

Perfunctories and flesh-pressing complete, the meeting began, and Kittredge soon found himself walking woodenly and self-consciously toward the front of the room, his title slide covering the enormous screen.

He spoke too quickly, he thought, and his meager attempts at humor came off too rehearsed, but no one stopped him with questions or bullshit flags, and his uncomfortable moment in the spotlight came to an end soon enough.

"Thank you, Mr. Kittredge," President Hugo Chavez said. Kittredge had always thought Chavez's voice was equal parts erudite and gangster, and it felt surreal to Kittredge to hear the imposing, menacing voice of Venezuelan defiance to gringo exploitation speak his own name.

"We sincerely appreciate your work on behalf of Venezuelan and American partnership," Chavez said.

Kittredge blushed fiercely. He could have sworn that Chavez had a twinkle in his eye as he spoke. He was certain that Chavez's words and tone held innuendo. *He knows?* Perhaps it was the exaggerated self-consciousness of guilt, but Kittredge couldn't help but think that Chavez was aware of his multiple intrigues.

He felt sweat forming on his brow, and hoped furtively that his discomfort wasn't too evident. *Jesus, what a mess I'm in,* he thought as he took his seat.

"But as I have made clear on many occasions in the past, I do have some concerns," the president intoned, looking pointedly at the US Ambassador.

"Yes, Mr. President, we are aware of your concerns, and hope to address them adequately," the ambassador responded.

"Yes, so you have said many times," Chavez continued, impatience creeping into his voice. "But I am afraid that my concerns are quite fundamental, born of the demonstrated economic, political, and military aggression of which your country has been repeatedly guilty, both on this continent and others around the globe."

The ambassador shifted uncomfortably. "Mr. President, we always strive to create mutually beneficial partnerships with our allies and business partners the world over, and we are proud of our demonstrated commitment to human dignity and the right of self-determination–"

Chavez's harsh laugh cut off the ambassador's response. "Provided this so-called self-determination aligns rather precisely with your own imperial ambitions. The moment it wavers, you abandon your precious democratic principles in favor of the ancient rules of power and coercion."

"Sir, I'm afraid I must vigorously disagree with your assessment–"

"Yes, you must," Chavez cut him off. "Because to do otherwise would be to admit the largest hypocrisy in modern history. Shall we speak of Guatemala? Panama? Cuba? Bolivia? Of the unfortunate accidents that befell their brave leaders when they resisted your greedy advances?"

"Mr. President, there was never any relationship between those tragic events and the government of the United States of America. We are not a rogue nation of spies and thugs. We champion democracy, the rule of law, and the sanctity of individual liberties."

Chavez shook his head and donned a wan smile. "And yet again today, your actions make liars of you."

He nodded at an officer in the back of the room. A door opened, and an armed guard brought forward the four large American snipers Kittredge had seen in the embassy parking garage an hour earlier. Their hands were bound by cuffs, and their ankles were chained together.

"Your men and their sniper rifles were deployed in our beloved city as instruments of peace, democracy, and liberty, I presume?" Chavez crossed his arms and sat back in his chair.

A stifling, uncomfortable silence descended on the room like a heavy, damp blanket. All eyes, American and Venezuelan alike, turned to the ambassador. He looked old and tired.

"I am afraid that our concern for safety has communicated the wrong message," he said slowly.

"I disagree," Chavez said. "Sadly, your actions have communicated a *truthful* message, I think." He rose, and with him, every member of the Venezuelan contingent.

Holy shit, this is coming apart at the seams, Kittredge thought. He looked quickly between the two prominent figures in the room, and couldn't stop himself from turning to Fredericks and Quinn for some clue as to whether this uncomfortable exchange was part of the plan. *Or maybe it was the wheels coming off of the plan.*

The two CIA agents' faces held inscrutable expressions. If they were surprised at the turn of events, they certainly didn't show it.

"Mr. President," the ambassador said, speaking loudly to recapture the room's attention, "may I please extend my personal and official apology for this gross misrepresentation of our intentions and sentiments?"

Chavez turned to face the ambassador, gazing upward to regard the tall American. His eyes searched the ambassador for a long moment.

Then they communicated tacit permission to continue.

The ambassador took the cue. "My tenure here in your beautiful country has included many difficult moments, and to my great embarrassment and chagrin, this meeting has become one of those difficult moments."

Chavez nodded.

"But it is my sincere hope," the ambassador continued, "that this unfortunate misunderstanding might mark an inflection point in our relationship together, a turn toward renewed trust and partnership."

Chavez smiled. "It could certainly be such a turning point," he said in a low tone, "if this were at all a misunderstanding. But I find it to be yet another symptom of an inescapable truth. Your interest is not in our best interest."

Chavez took a step toward the door, and his entourage made ready to follow, but the US Ambassador placed his hand on Chavez's arm.

The Venezuelan president stopped, sizing up the tall American.

The ambassador reached into his pocket, and pulled out a

gleaming, cylindrical object. "Mr. President," he said in a grave tone, "on behalf of the three hundred million men, women and children of the United States of America, may I at least present you with a small token of our gratitude and goodwill?"

The room waited in awkward anticipation while President Chavez considered.

After a short eternity, he nodded slightly, almost imperceptibly, and the beginnings of a knowing smile crept across his face.

Kittredge wondered whether Chavez had something up his own sleeve. Perhaps another result of the warning Kittredge had sent through clandestine channels to El Grande.

Or, perhaps Chavez simply felt he had cornered the Americans, and was relishing the moment. It was impossible to tell.

The ambassador opened his hand to reveal an exquisitely crafted writing pen. "Those are your initials, sir, written in twenty-four carat gold, symbolic of the untarnished and radiant partnership we hope to create together with you and your great nation. May we move forward together toward greater understanding and cooperation."

Chavez hesitated, and looked at his head of security. After receiving a nod of affirmation, Chavez took the pen. He held it carefully, turning it over and examining its craftsmanship.

"I thank you for your generosity," he finally said. "And it would please me greatly if your words prove true. As a starting point, I hope it comes to pass that our two great nations grow to respect each other's sovereignty and dignity."

The ambassador produced a black rectangular pen case from his other jacket pocket, opened it to reveal the empty interior, and pushed it toward Hugo Chavez, holding it in both hands.

Chavez took the invitation and placed the pen in its plush accommodations inside the beautifully crafted pen case, using his thumb and forefinger to snap the pen into its place, feeling the thick, soft fabric as the pen settled deep into its groove along the length of the case.

The ambassador and the president shook hands to a smattering of tentative applause, which grew to a halfhearted clatter before dying out altogether.

Kittredge glanced at Fredericks. Perhaps Kittredge imagined it, but he was certain that Fredericks' face held the beginnings of a smug smile.

Chapter 8

El Jerga watched two of the agents follow his quarry inside the large Agriculture building, pausing to gain access by swiping a badge in front of the electronic lock. He surmised that it would be far too risky to try to follow the gringos inside. He had no badge to get in, and an altercation was likely, which would probably take more time than simply going around the outside.

So that's what he did. But he had underestimated the building's size. It was as big as a city block. He broke into a jog on his way toward the tourist destinations on the other side of the edifice.

He turned his reversible jacket inside out, donned a fedora, put headphones in his ears, and intentionally added a little more spring to each step of his gait. In his mind, he heard echoes of his dead uncle: if you can't change everything about your appearance, you should at least change a few things.

As El Jerga rounded the corner onto Jefferson Avenue, his trained eye took in the mass of tourists, many moving in gaggles behind guides brandishing brightly colored parasols. If the pair had made it through the bowels of the edifice and emerged into the mass of humanity, it would be extremely difficult to find them. The job would be made far easier by the girl's bright red hair, but she would undoubtedly have made adjustments to hide that aspect of her appearance, if she was half as competent as El Grande had said she was.

El Jerga knew that the redhead and her tall male companion had probably emerged from the huge building well before he had made his way around it, and the odds were slim that he would be able to catch sight of them. But he might catch a lucky break. *And I suddenly have time on my hands,* he thought, shaking his head again at the gaggle of amateurish goons running surveillance around what was supposed to be a very quiet operation.

He scanned the length of the mall, putting himself in his quarry's shoes. It would be easy to melt into a group of tourists, but such groups moved very slowly. Their disguises would have to be very good to avoid detection so close to the locus of their initial discovery by the large surveillance team.

No, they would need to move away from the area more quickly than that, El Jerga decided. Doing so inconspicuously wouldn't be all that hard. They would probably move unhurriedly with the crowds while searching for faster conveyance.

Taxicabs were probably out of the question. Hailing a cab drew attention, and it often took many attempts. It would be far too conspicuous.

So they would probably take public transportation. There were two bus stops within three hundred meters of the corner, one on each side of the boulevard, and it looked like maybe a third bus stop was situated further down the mall on the far side of the street.

There was also a metro entrance nearby, just a few steps from the grand, stately entrance to the Department of Agriculture. Too obvious, El Jerga concluded, and they would have to get lucky with the train timing, because the agents who pursued them through the building would undoubtedly try the subway station first.

That left the bus stops, El Jerga surmised. It would again require a bit of a lucky break with the bus arrival time, but it was probably their best option for escape.

But which stop? Each was about equidistant from the large building's front entrance, and none of them appeared any more crowded than the others, so there didn't appear to be an inherent physical advantage to choosing any particular one.

It's down to the timing, El Jerga realized. He made his way to the nearest bus stop, scanning carefully for signs of the pair. Finding nothing but old people and hipsters, he turned his attention to the bus schedule posted on the kiosk wall.

El Jerga studied the routes and time charts carefully. It was tempting to get in a hurry in situations like this one, but El Jerga's experience had taught him that a slow and methodical approach was almost always fastest. After a full minute's study of the schedule, he concluded that the next bus would arrive at the stop across the street.

He didn't cross immediately. Instead, he waited with the crowd on the eastbound side of the boulevard, but studied the commuters at the bus stop across the way, on the westbound side.

They won't be standing together, he coached himself. *If anything gives them away, it will be their focus.*

His intuition was correct. He felt the intensity of her probing eyes from across the street.

She had done a remarkable job of altering her appearance, especially an appearance as striking as hers, but it wasn't enough.

The eyes always give people away. Having made her, he turned away, watching the street corner for the arrival of the bus.

He heard it before he saw it, and studied its movement as it rounded the corner. He judged the speed of the bus, concluding that the light at the crosswalk would align perfectly for his purposes.

El Jerga folded into the throng of pedestrians crossing the street with the light, arriving just in time to join the tail end of the line of passengers climbing aboard the westbound bus.

He hadn't yet spotted her companion, but that didn't concern him.

El Jerga was certain that he was in line directly behind Special Agent Sam Jameson.

* * *

Sam climbed aboard the bus and made her way to the back. She was careful to choose a side-facing seat tucked behind a bulkhead plastered with advertisements, which minimized her exposure to prying eyes boarding the bus.

She was nervous. Not because she was being pursued – that was becoming routine for her. Rather, she was anxious because she and Brock had parted ways for the moment. Traveling together out of the hot zone of surveillance activity raised their profile to an unacceptable level, and they'd made the difficult but necessary decision to take separate routes away from DHS headquarters and the nest of agents into which they'd apparently blundered.

They had known that their trip to Homeland entailed a degree of risk, and the time they'd spent getting their act together after talking with Jarvis was time the opposition had apparently made good use of.

She cursed their bad luck. If things had gone according to plan, they'd have been in and out of the Homeland building in less than half an hour.

But Fatso Minton's grisly murder wasn't part of Sam's calculations, and his brutal death required her to scrap her plan entirely. She'd caught a lucky break with Dan scoring a location hit on someone in Dibiaso's network, but following that late-breaking lead had necessitated a trip to Caracas. Making the Venezuela arrangements had slowed them down, and she had spent far longer inside the DHS building than was healthy.

Still, Sam was surprised by how quickly the net had closed in around her and Brock.

It was tempting to assume that Jarvis was behind the rapid appearance of the surveillance team, but that was just one of many possibilities. Lots of Homeland people had seen her and Brock, and they'd traveled directly from their home, so any of the DC Metro police goons still on the Venezuelan payroll had ample opportunity to pick up their trail. It could have been any one of dozens of different people who called in the spy team.

The surveillance agents were loose and sloppy, and Sam had made them almost instantly. That was a clue into the resources available to whoever was pursuing her, but it wasn't a dead giveaway.

The odds didn't favor it being an Agency team. They were usually sharp. Not infallible, of course, but at least competent.

There were various elements within the eleven agencies that

DHS had recently absorbed which had surveillance and "direct action" teams of various skill levels. But if the team in front of the DHS building belonged to any of those agencies, they had certainly brought their junior varsity to this particular game.

It was almost certainly not anyone from the DHS Counterintelligence unit. She knew them all. And while they weren't all great agents, they were better than the clubfooted team of gawking amateurs she'd just shaken from her tail.

That led her to doubt that it was Jarvis pulling the strings, because as a deputy director, he had access to much better talent. But ruling out Jarvis was a thought she entertained very cautiously. It could very well be that Jarvis couldn't afford to reveal himself in the process of keeping tabs on her. It would have been a dead giveaway if Jarvis were to use any of the top-tier assets on his roster.

These thoughts spun in her brain as she surveyed the patrons taking seats on the crowded bus, using only her peripheral vision.

A short, stocky Latino man strutted down the bus aisle, loud mariachi music blaring from earbuds stuck to his hear, a fedora perched atop his head at a jaunty angle. He had a hideous scar on his neck.

He took a seat next to her as the bus lurched westward on its route. She moved over to accommodate his wide frame.

She pretended to stare at something outside, but she was gathering details out of the corner of her eye. Late thirties. Latin descent, but Sam had no idea from which region. He looked out the window with a vacuous expression on his face, smacking his chewing gum loudly and bobbing his head to the music, both hands in his jacket pockets.

Not an obvious threat, but there were other available seats the man could have chosen. He didn't have to sit next to her, but that's where he'd plopped down without so much as a nod. That wasn't uncommon in DC, but the man didn't look like he was a native or a transplanted government policy douche, so basic human courtesy wasn't an unreasonable expectation.

She decided to play it safe and get off the bus at the next stop.

Above the tinny noise of the loud music in the man's headset, Sam heard a metallic click from the vicinity of his pocket. It was a noise she would recognize anywhere.

As she moved her head to locate the source of the noise, the traffic light ahead changed to red, and the deceleration of the bus caused her body to lean into the stranger's bulk.

She felt his arm tense and move backward toward the seat, and her eyes settled on his midriff just in time to see a shiny streak of metal emerge from his pocket and slice toward her midsection.

Switchblade.

Rather than fighting her body's momentum, she used it to her advantage. She continued to drive her shoulder into the stocky man, using the force of that interaction to scoot her hips away from the arc of the knife. Her ass cheeks slid across the smooth seat cushion.

She felt a searing pain in her side, and a tugging sensation on her clothing.

Sam brought her right hand across her unbalanced body in a lightning strike at the stranger's neck, aiming for his windpipe. She didn't get enough force behind the blow for it to be lethal, and the jostling of the bus and her unbalanced body position hurt her accuracy. Her curled knuckles connected with the tip of the attacker's nose, and she felt the crunch of his cartilage breaking beneath the force of her blow.

Blood gushed instantly from his face, but he had already begun an attack with his opposite hand. It moved with surprising speed across his body and toward her own face.

She continued to twist in her seat until she slid off completely, her knees landing hard on the floor of the bus as her torso flattened underneath the arc of the man's left hand. She thought she caught the glint of a metal shiv as his hand passed inches from her face.

Sam slid backward out of the seat and onto the floor, sprung to her feet, and pounded the emergency stop button below the opposite window as she ran to the front of the bus, shouting at the driver to open the door for her.

As she bounded toward the exit, she turned to assess the situation. Bloodied and pissed off, her attacker sprinted after her.

"Help!" she shouted. "That man is attacking me!"

She didn't wait to find out whether anyone else on the bus would rise to her defense. She dashed down the steps and out the door. She sprinted across the street and down the escalator into the metro station, glancing over her shoulder to see whether her attacker had followed.

He hadn't.

Sam dashed into the subway station women's room and locked the stall door behind her, pulse pounding.

A funny thing happened on the way to the airport, she thought to herself as she lifted her bloody shirt to assess the damage.

She hoped it wasn't serious. She had a plane to catch.

Chapter 9

Peter Kittredge was well on his way to another fine drunk, not at all unlike the impressive state of inebriation he had attained the previous Friday at Festive, the fantastic DC gay bar with the fantastically pretty boy-toy waiters.

That seemed like a lifetime ago. What had started as the beginning of a very promising one-night stand had turned into one hell of a week.

And he wasn't quite sure what to make of the latest development. He didn't know exactly what he had witnessed a few hours earlier during the extremely strained meeting between the US Ambassador and the President of Venezuela, but he was pretty sure that he needed to tell El Grande about it.

His contact showed up somewhere between the beginning and end of his third double vodka.

"On the rocks with a twist?" was the approved opener, which the wiry Latino delivered with a thick accent.

"Is there any other way?" Kittredge responded, already feeling weary and disillusioned with the clandestine games after his ignominious introduction to the less enjoyable aspects of life as a spy. It was fun to have secrets, and it was even occasionally fun to keep them, but as his scabbed and scarred lower back could attest, it could sting more than a little when those secrets were discovered by the wrong people.

"Someone wants to see you," the wiry man said. "Wait five minutes, then leave. Get in a red Dongfeng sedan at the curb."

"How will I know it's the right sedan?" Kittredge asked.

"You'll know."

The man left without another word.

* * *

The red Dongfeng four-door idled at the curb outside the pub, just as the wiry man had said. Its hazards were flashing.

Kittredge approached as nonchalantly as he could manage, fighting his nearly irrepressible urge to look around in search of the inevitable CIA tail.

As he approached the passenger's side door, Kittredge saw the sedan's driver through the windshield, wearing a dark ball cap pulled low. Kittredge didn't recognize who it was until he'd opened the door and sat down in the passenger's seat.

Then his heart leapt.

Maria.

"Look straight ahead," she said as she drove away from the curb, her voice soft despite the terse command it conveyed. She grabbed his hand and squeezed affectionately as Kittredge fought the urge to stare at her stunning profile.

"Two of your friends are out for a stroll this evening," she said. "Maybe they want to enjoy the Friday night life."

"Shocking," he deadpanned. "Really, it's great to see you, Maria. I'm sorry again about the other day."

"I was very pissed off at you, Peter Kittredge. It could have been a big problem."

"I knew better than to call the hospital."

She nodded. "Si. And I knew better than to sleep with you," she said.

He smiled. "I'm glad for your poor judgment. Truth be told, I've been thinking about you."

"You shouldn't."

"What makes you say that?"

"It will end poorly."

"It doesn't have to," he said, realizing that he suddenly cared very little about President Hugo Chavez, the US Ambassador, the CIA, Quinn, and Bill Fredericks.

"I'm too old for hope to triumph over experience," she said.

He nodded. "But too young to quit the game."

Maria smiled. "It is a fun game, no?"

She drove deftly through downtown Caracas, looping around several times to trap their CIA tail. She honked and waved at one of the vehicles in the Agency tracking team, a beat up green pickup truck with two incongruously white men inside. The men pretended to ignore her, but Maria was certain they'd gotten the message.

They changed cars in the relative privacy of an alleyway between two horrendously dilapidated buildings, and Maria drove around until she was certain the Agency tail had given up. Then she took a circuitous route to their destination, driving just insanely enough to blend in with the locals.

Finally, they arrived at a parking structure, one that was unfamiliar to him. It seemed to serve several residential buildings. She parked in a reserved spot on the first floor.

"Won't the car get towed?"

"We have friends here."

They got out of the car, and she took his hand, interlacing her fingers between his. She led him down a dimly lit stairway to the underground walkway connecting the garage to a residential building across the busy street. Graffiti announcing various political and criminal affiliations adorned the puke-green tile and gray concrete hallway, and their footfalls echoed in the otherwise empty corridor.

"Great place to get knifed," Kittredge observed.

They reached the lobby beneath the apartment building and walked into a waiting elevator. Moments later, Kittredge found himself on the tenth floor of a lower-middle class residential tower, Maria's strong but feminine fingers still gripping his hand.

She led him to a nondescript apartment, wedged her hand into the front pocket of her skin-tight jeans, and pulled out a single key that opened the lock and deadbolt. Kittredge eyed her figure as she worked the lock, feeling a familiar tingling in his loins.

Must and mothballs hit Kittredge's nostrils as he followed her inside. She locked and dead-bolted the door behind them.

Without a word, she met his eyes, reached her hand around his neck, and pulled him forward for a deep, passionate kiss. After a long, breathless moment, she spoke. "Against my better judgment, I like you, Peter Kittredge."

"It's possible that for the first time in my life," he said, "I'm in jeopardy of becoming pussy-whipped."

She laughed, her body pressed against his, a pleasant light in her eyes. "There are worse fates, I think."

He didn't disagree.

They moved from the entryway floor to a bedroom, well-appointed but impersonal. It was clearly a safe house, as there were no pictures on the wall or personal items anywhere in view.

They took their fill of each other, then dozed together.

* * *

Kittredge awakened with a start at the sound of the apartment door slamming shut.

Maria was up in a flash, large-caliber handgun in hand and trained at the bedroom door, her naked body bathed in the light of the harvest moon.

Footsteps, then a familiar voice. Rojo.

The handsome older man seemed indifferent to their nakedness as he took in the bedroom scene. Maria seemed equally unfazed, and made no move to cover her exposed breasts or nethers.

An uncomfortable thought formed in Kittredge's mind. Had Rojo had Maria as well? How many others were in her life? Not that he minded in principle, but Kittredge didn't care to meet them all.

I'm hetero and *jealous? I'd never have guessed.*

Kittredge found his own nudity unsettling in Rojo's presence, and felt himself wither a little under the distinguished-looking spy's hard gaze. "At least you know I'm not wearing a wire," he said. He covered himself with a pillow.

Rojo chuckled. His laugh was short-lived. "It was Chavez, wasn't it?"

Kittredge nodded. "Fredericks brought four gunmen. I told him I wasn't okay with anything violent, but he didn't give a shit.

Anyway, the snipers were arrested, so it must have worked out."

Rojo shook his head. "Too clean. Had to be decoys."

Kittredge raised his eyebrows. "Nothing else happened though. I mean, nothing other than the showdown between Chavez and the ambassador. Chavez even had the gunmen paraded in front of us for effect. Like he was showing off. It was tense, but nothing violent."

"Wrong," Rojo said. "A thousand things happened. Handshakes, embraces, gifts. El Presidente is more careful than he used to be, but he is still far too open."

Maria stood and went to the bathroom. Rojo's eye followed her, but Kittredge couldn't read his expression. Any mortal man would have had obvious lust in his eyes, unless he'd slept with her recently.

So, Rojo's slept with her recently.

Maria left the door open. *Such easy familiarity,* Kittredge thought. If Rojo took any notice, it didn't register on his face. More evidence of intimate history between them.

"Tell me everything, start to finish." Rojo spoke with the quiet presumption of a man used to having his demands satisfied and his proclamations obeyed.

"Please."

"Excuse me?"

"Tell me everything, *please*, you mean," Kittredge said. "I'm not your subject or your employee." He wasn't sure where it came from. Probably from the resentment and jealousy of Rojo knowing Maria, or maybe from his discomfort at being naked in front of a sexual rival.

An attractive rival, at that. *I clearly haven't gone totally hetero.*

Rojo's eyes smiled slightly, but his face was otherwise impassive. "Yes. Tell me everything, Peter Kittredge, if you please."

Having made his point as well as a naked man could reasonably hope, Kittredge recounted the day's events, including as much detail as he remembered.

Rojo asked the kind of questions that betrayed a great deal of prior knowledge. Kittredge asked in several places about whether Rojo had been present during the proceedings, but the handsome older man never even acknowledged the questions, and didn't come close to answering them.

But Rojo's knowledge had an interesting side effect on Kittredge. If Kittredge had had any doubts about the VSS' access to the upper reaches of Venezuelan power, he harbored those doubts no longer. It was clear that Rojo was plugged into the illuminati of Venezuelan society. Probably El Grande, too.

And, vicariously, so was Kittredge.

He liked that.

He relished the unlikely juxtaposition: beleaguered mid-level embassy econocrat by day, international power player by night.

He wasn't yet *the guy,* but at least he was in the game.

Climbing ladders and sleeping with girls. What has become of me?

A more sobering thought: *What would Charley think of me?*

Charley probably wouldn't be surprised at anything, Kittredge realized. At least, if what he'd heard from the VSS people, and what he'd surmised from the CIA people, was anywhere close to correct, Charley Arlinghaus had a ton of explaining to do the moment he awoke from his coma.

"What do you think today was all about?" Rojo asked.

In spite of himself, Kittredge felt flattered at Rojo's question. It felt good for a distinguished heavy like Rojo to ask Kittredge's opinion.

But he had no idea what the day's events might have signified, or what Quinn and Fredericks' participation might portend. "I agree that it's a little suspect the way the snipers were found and arrested so quickly. But if that was a diversion for something else, I sure as hell don't know what."

Rojo nodded.

Maria returned, still nude, and perched on the edge of the bed facing Rojo, who still stood near the doorway. The distinguished-looking fifty-something glanced briefly at Maria, then abruptly turned to leave. "Enjoy yourselves," he said as he walked from the bedroom. "I'll show myself out."

They heard footsteps, then the door opening, shutting, locking.

Chapter 10

Sam walked quickly through security at Reagan International Airport, grateful for the uncharacteristically light foot traffic and uncharacteristically efficient TSA crew.

She patted her side, feeling the shred of cloth she had torn from her bloodied shirt and wrapped around the entire circumference of her torso to stem the bleeding from the long, nasty cut. Had her reflexes been any duller, she'd certainly have bled out. The attacker's expert thrust was sure to have punctured her solar plexus, on an upward vector toward her heart.

It wasn't quite accurate to say that she was lucky to be alive, but she was certainly lucky that the attacker had chosen to open his switchblade within earshot. It was this audible warning that had put Sam's senses on alert, which gave her the advance warning she'd needed to jump and squirm out of the way of the razor-sharp knife.

She'd changed into her only spare shirt, and cut the bloody one to ribbons for use as bandages.

The cut in her side was more than superficial, but as far as she could tell, nothing critical had sprung a leak. But it was extremely painful, and she'd certainly need stitches. For the moment, however, the bleeding seemed to be under control.

She passed the last TSA agent on her way through the security checkpoint. The agent looked at her breasts and her ass, but otherwise ignored her. It was a huge relief. She had half expected to be detained for further questioning, a consequence of having the local cops and a few Homeland officers breathing down her neck. And maybe a foreign intelligence service. It was tough to tell.

Tricia Leavens, her passport read. Along with an equally new and equally inauthentic driver's license, it had sufficed for TSA purposes, and she walked past the gate for her Caracas flight, looking carefully but surreptitiously at the people waiting in the lobby area in front of the airline kiosk.

Nothing jumped out at her as abnormal in the gate area. She wasn't relieved – it didn't mean everything was in order; it just meant that anything untoward was well disguised.

Sam walked several hundred feet past her gate, pondering. She hadn't seen Ekman since she'd spotted the surveillance team right outside the DHS front door.

More importantly, she hadn't seen Brock, aka Thomas Brownstein, since they'd taken separate buses to get away from the hot zone around Homeland.

It took a great deal of discipline not to worry herself sick about whether Brock's bus ride was anything like hers had been, complete with a switchblade-wielding thug waiting to slash through her left ventricle.

They'd become separated before she could replenish her stock of burner phones, so she and Brock had no means of communicating with each other.

He's a big boy, she reminded herself. Brock was a decorated veteran of a hundred combat missions, and he'd used wits and guts to get himself out of all sorts of unhealthy situations over the years.

But flying jets in harm's way wasn't nearly the same thing as employing sound trade craft to keep from getting kidnapped or killed, and Sam knew that Brock had another potential snag ahead of him: rebooking the flight he'd missed as a result of having to shake free from the surveillance team.

There was nothing Tricia Leavens could do to help Thomas Brownstein. And any kind of meddling would only highlight a connection they were working hard to hide.

But there was something Sam could do to help understand what they might be facing.

She set out for the bank of pay phones at the end of the international concourse. Unlike many airports, Reagan still had the ancient and archaic communication devices, mounted to a far wall.

Sam picked up a receiver, dropped in a few quarters, and dialed Dan's office number.

"So, let the record reflect that I was wrong," Dan said after their brief exchange of pleasantries.

"How so?"

"I said that Jarvis was too stupid to be involved in anything other than bureaucratic buggery."

"He's dirty, isn't he?"

"Pretty sure. I dropped the Hack Team goodies into his boot file. He must not fully appreciate the power of the digital age, because it took me less than fifteen minutes to rack up enough shit to justify asking for an arrest warrant."

Sam let out a low whistle. "Can you give me the highlights? I'm boarding soon."

"Sure. Four Tor accesses in the past two days," Dan said.

"Not smart for a government employee," Sam said, "but not illegal."

"Right. But here's the kicker. He used Tor to access a chat room, which he used to plug into a SATCOM link, which he used to link up with a specific computer. I don't know yet precisely where that computer was, or who owns it, but the satellite connection Jarvis used makes me ninety-nine percent confident that the other side of that conversation was in South America."

"Any chance there's a logical explanation?"

"If so, it hasn't yet occurred to me," Dan said. "Any legitimate business wouldn't have required Jarvis to try to mask his IP address by using Tor."

"Unless he wanted to disguise his status as a Fed," Sam said.

"That's a possibility. But he's a manager, not an investigator, so he really has no business dabbling in trade craft. Plus, Homeland's jurisdiction doesn't extend to South America. That's Agency territory."

"I'm sure he'd testify to something that sounds plausible," Sam said. "He'd maybe get dinged for the extra-jurisdictional foray, but it doesn't prove he's a spy."

"I've typed up a search warrant," Dan said.

Sam pondered that for a second as she scanned the airport for signs of Ekman, Brock, or assholes with shivs.

"A warrant is a big step, Dan. Are you sure we're ready for that?"

"No. But if Jarvis is crooked and we didn't take any action, we'd be rolled up in the blowback when he gets caught. They'd crush us for sitting on our suspicions. And judging from his horrible computer security discipline, it's only a matter of time before he gets caught doing something stupid."

"Solid point."

"Besides, it's a cyber warrant. He won't even know we're snooping until it's too late."

"You mean we're going to ask permission to do what we just did?"

"I don't know what you're talking about," Dan said, a smile evident in his voice. "Not my problem if Jarvis can't keep foreign malware off of his computer."

"Okay," Sam said. "Go ahead with it. Post results to the secure site in case I can't reach you from down south."

"Sure thing, boss. One more thing before you go. That cell phone hit in Caracas?"

"What about it?"

"It's active. The phone has been on for a few hours now. No calls, and it's just sitting there. Huge mistake on someone's part."

"Nice. About time we caught a break. What's the address?"

Dan told her.

She wrote it down, thanked him, and signed off.

Motion caught her eye, a familiar gait, topped by a shock of curly black hair. Ekman. If he'd spotted her at the pay phone bank at the end of the concourse, he gave no indication. He veered from the main walkway into the gate area for the Caracas flight, disappearing behind a vendor selling overpriced sunglasses.

Sam ducked into a convenience shop next to a currency exchange kiosk. She bought two burners, and paid for two international SIM cards. She knew from Dan's news about Dibiaso's network of burners that US phones apparently worked in Venezuela, but she wasn't sure about the neighboring countries. Might have to make a hasty exit in a different direction than the one you arrived from, she reasoned, so it was important to have options.

She hadn't allowed herself to worry about Brock, but she wasn't able to put those thoughts off any longer. She emerged from the convenience store and scanned passersby, searching for telltale signs of him.

In the end, Sam looked right past him. He was walking with stooped shoulders, leaning forward a bit at the waist, wearing sunglasses and a hipster hat, bouncing jauntily off of his right foot with each step.

He walked right up to her. "If I didn't know you, I would want to," he said.

Recognition took a second. "Holy smokes, nice work on the disguise!" she said, suddenly self conscious of her own. If Brock could recognize her easily, so could someone else.

"Pretend you're making a call," she instructed.

He complied.

"Ekman's here. By our gate," he said, getting a nod in reply. "Any problems after we split up?"

"It was memorable," she said. "I'll fill you in later."

An announcement interrupted their conversation: *Would Mr. Brownstein and Ms. Leavens please report to gate D 22 immediately.*

"That didn't take long," Sam said. A worried expression crossed her face.

Brock hung up the phone and started toward the gate, his mouth pressed into a grimace.

"Wait a bit," she said. "Let's not go up there together. Go grab a coffee or something, and I'll see what's up."

Brock considered, then nodded reluctantly and headed toward the nearest instantiation of a ubiquitous coffee shop brand.

Calm and steady, Sam reminded herself, breathing deeply and walking confidently to the counter at gate D 22, pretending not to notice the two TSA agents hovering nearby.

"I'm Tricia Leavens," she told the agent.

The agent eyed her closely. Not a friendly look, Sam noticed.

"These agents requested to speak with you," the ticket clerk said, gesturing toward the overweight security guards.

"Step this way, please, ma'am," one of the guards said.

Sam looked at them carefully. Flabby bodies and slack expressions. *Not professional muscle,* she concluded. *Probably real TSA agents.*

"What is this about?" she asked.

"This way, please. My partner and I will explain." He waddled out of the gate area. Sam followed reluctantly, hearing the gate agent announce the start of passenger boarding.

"This had better be quick," she said. "My flight is boarding."

"We'll go as quickly as we can, ma'am."

The portly TSA agent led her down the concourse, past several shops and the restrooms, and used his magnetic badge to gain entrance to an unmarked door. Sam followed, and the second TSA agent brought up the rear, closing the door behind him.

They had entered what was clearly an interrogation room.

"What is this about?" Sam repeated, annoyed. "I've already passed security, and my flight is boarding now."

"Ma'am, we've been asked to detain you and your traveling companion pending the arrival of our supervisor."

Shit. Jarvis? Ekman? Had to be one of them, she thought.

"Asked by whom?" Sam asked.

"By our shift chief."

"Give me a name, please."

"Officer Tirpak."

Sam pulled her DHS badge out of her handbag and held it close to the portly guard's face. "Please let Officer Tirpak know that he's interfering with a federal investigation."

The guard blinked twice. Uncertainty descended.

"Ma'am, I'm sure your credentials are valid, but I'm afraid I can't let you go without my supervisor's approval." He motioned toward a seat.

Sam remained standing. She smiled. "I can sympathize with your position. But I'm going to leave this room and board my flight. Mr. Brownstein, the other individual you've been asked to detain, is my associate. He will be boarding that flight as well."

The guard shook his head, fat jiggling on his neck. "I'm afraid I can't let you return to the gate area until you've been cleared by a TSA supervisor, ma'am."

She held her badge up again, her forefinger pointing to a

particular spot. "Read those words out loud," she said.

"Ma'am, I'm sorry, but–"

"Humor me."

"You're Special Agent Sam Jameson, chief of the counterintelligence investigations division."

"At which agency?"

"Ma'am, really, I have my orders, and–"

Sam raised her voice. "At which agency?" Her sharp tone visibly startled the guard.

"Homeland Security."

"That's right. Can you guess who the head of the Transportation Safety Administration reports to?"

"Homeland Security," the guard repeated.

"Right again. So you see where I'm going with this?"

He opened his mouth as if to speak, but Sam beat him to the punch. "You really don't want to gum up an active Homeland investigation. If my associate and I miss our flight, you, Officer Tirpak, and the seventeen other layers of middle management between you and the TSA director will all have the opportunity to visit us downtown and explain yourselves."

He swallowed, considering.

"Here's what we'll do," she said. "I am going to return to my gate. If Officer Tirpak arrives before I board, he and I will have a conversation. If not, you'll write down my badge number and hand it to him at your convenience, and you can sort out your misunderstanding on your own time. Sound reasonable?"

The TSA agent was conflicted. She could tell he wanted to

stand on procedure and exert authority, but she could also tell that he didn't want the trouble it would cause.

She was tempted to push him along by asking how he'd like to be responsible for another bomb attack on US soil, but she reminded herself that it was best not to sell past the close.

Her patience paid off a few seconds later. "Special Agent Jameson, I'm very sorry for the inconvenience. I'll straighten this out with my supervisor, and I'll find you at the gate if necessary."

Sam thanked him on her way out.

She walked quickly to the gate, arriving as the last few passengers were boarding.

Brock had waited for her. He followed her down the jetway.

"Ekman?" she asked when they were clear of the gate kiosk.

"Already boarded. I don't think he saw me. What was the TSA thing all about?"

"Someone's screwing with us. But it was stupid and lazy of them to page us using our aliases, because it tips their hand. It has to be someone in the fake ID shop, or someone with enough authority to force the ID guys to give up the aliases."

Brock considered. "My money's on Jarvis," he said.

"Mine too."

They approached the line of passengers at the airplane door.

"Are we really going to spend five hours on a plane with Ekman, after all that's happened?" Brock asked.

"Yes. But it's going to work out perfectly," Sam said. "We're going to take turns punching him in the balls until he gives us a straight answer."

Part 2

Chapter 11

Peter Kittredge awoke disoriented, his brain reeling to recall his body's current location, struggling for context in light of the week's ridiculous events.

Maria's soft breathing provided a welcome clue, as did the scent of her, wild and beautiful and slightly musky. She slept next to him in the safe house bedroom.

He rose, hungry, having chosen frolic instead of dinner, and having slumbered afterwards in a pleasant post-coital languor.

He walked slowly out of the unfamiliar bedroom, taking care not to walk into the furniture and glancing at the alarm clock along the way: 10:22 p.m. No wonder his stomach was growling.

Kittredge padded softly to the kitchen, opened the refrigerator, and squinted while his eyes adjusted to the light.

"Not much to choose from," said a voice behind him.

Kittredge jumped, alarmed and suddenly very alert.

"Who the hell is that?"

He heard a familiar laugh. "You are lucky we are friends. I could have gotten the drop on you, as you Yanquis like to say."

A reading lamp clicked on in the corner of the sitting room, illuminating a rugged, handsome, familiar face. El Grande sat comfortably in a plush reading chair, legs crossed, wearing a friendly smile.

"You scared the hell out of me," Kittredge said, heart

pounding.

"My apologies." El Grande eyed Kittredge's naked frame. "I see you and Maria have found each other again, no?"

Kittredge didn't know what to say. There wasn't much to be said on the subject, and he could certainly think of nothing constructive.

Plus, he was stark naked in the presence of a VSS authority figure for the second time in the same evening, and he realized that he felt aggravated by what seemed like another intrusion on his private moments.

But he also realized that he and Maria were stealing moments together while holed up in various VSS safe houses, so his expectation of privacy wasn't entirely rational.

"Let me grab my clothes," he said.

"There is no need. I have a simple request, and I'll be on my way."

Kittredge waited.

"Inform us before your next Agency meeting," El Grande said.

"I can't always predict when they'll show up. Those guys are a long way up my ass, and they watch me pretty consistently."

"I understand. But when you can, when there is time and you have details, you will inform us, no?"

"Perhaps. Depending on the timing. I can't always sneak away to contact you."

"Si. I am not asking for you to tell us about every meeting. Just the next meeting they happen to plan in advance."

Kittredge cocked his head. "Why?"

"We have our reasons."

With that, El Grande rose and walked to the front door of the apartment, using the fisheye to scan the hallway for passersby before quietly opening the door.

"Please give my regards to Maria," he said. Then he disappeared down the dark hallway.

Sure thing, Kittredge thought, wondering how the conversation might go. *Hey Maria, another one of your ex-boyfriends wishes he was still rolling around naked with you...*

His appetite gone, Kittredge returned to bed, wondering whether he'd be able to pull off another short-notice contact with the VSS without alerting Quinn and Fredericks.

It struck him that even if the Agency didn't know his precise whereabouts at the moment, they certainly knew the company he was keeping.

Maria was right, he thought as he wrapped his arm around her slumbering form. *This probably won't end well.*

Chapter 12

The "fasten seatbelts" sign went dark, and Sam left her seat on the Airbus. She walked past sparsely populated rows of seats and into the flight attendant's galley.

She lifted her shirt and displayed her bloody abdomen, asking for a first aid kit. The flight attendant turned ghost white at the sight of the bloody mess, but retrieved the first aid kit and handed it to Sam without a word.

Sam stepped into the nearest vacant lavatory, locking the door behind her.

The sickening smell of disinfectant and human waste assaulted her nostrils, and she felt momentarily as if she might be sick.

Her nausea passed, and she steeled herself for the painful process that awaited her. She removed her shirt and set it on the small countertop, taking care to avoid a puddle of water pooled on one side.

Then she untied the ribbon of cloth wrapped around her torso, peeling it away slowly from the wound in her side. The edges of her wound had begun to clot around the paper towels she had used as bandages, and the sting of their removal nearly brought tears to her eyes.

Sam noticed a fresh stream of dark blood pooling in the space carved from her skin by her assailant's switchblade. Stitches were clearly a necessity; otherwise, the wound would never close. *Is there a doctor in the house?*

She set the first aid kit atop the closed the toilet lid and inventoried its contents. Among other items for headaches and minor scrapes, the kit contained a topical disinfectant and analgesic, and a roll of medical tape.

She gritted her teeth, cleaned the wound with a wet paper towel, clamped the edges of her slashed skin together with her fingers, and rubbed ointment over the area. Then she peeled and applied strips of medical tape over a new, dry paper towel. The pain made her sweat, but she was pretty sure the wound wouldn't become infected before she could receive proper medical attention.

Sam had no idea when that might be. She was flying straight into the lion's den.

On the way back from the lavatory, Sam tapped Brock on the shoulder. He followed her, and they shuffled forward to Frank Ekman's seat.

But for Ekman, the row was completely empty.

"Hi, Francis," Sam said. "Let's chat."

She motioned for him to move from the aisle to the middle seat. Brock took the window, and Sam boxed Ekman in by taking the aisle seat he'd just vacated.

"I feel like we hardly know each other anymore, Frank," Sam said with a wink at Brock. "I mean, you hardly had anything to say during our little meeting with Tom. And I feel like that was an important meeting, so maybe you should have had more to say."

Ekman's eyes locked on hers. He was clearly mulling something over. She returned his gaze without blinking.

He didn't say anything.

"I'm sure you saw the cut-rate goon squad waiting for us outside Headquarters," she pressed.

"I did," Ekman said.

She lifted her shirt to show him the bloody wound in her side. "Your doing?"

He shook his head, looking tired. "No, Sam. I thought it was something you might have arranged for my benefit."

Brock's jaw clenched. He shot Sam a look that said, just say the word and I'll clock this jerk.

"But shooting yourself in the abdomen strikes me as an improbable level of commitment, so I'm rethinking my theory," Ekman said.

"The guy had a switchblade," Sam said. "And come again?" Ekman's statement – that *he* thought *she* might be behind the team of heavies they'd encountered outside of Homeland – caught Sam by surprise.

"You've made a big deal out of not knowing what's going on," Ekman said. "For the record, if that's really true, you're not the only one in that boat."

Sam cocked her head at him. "Frank, do you really expect me to believe that? You and Jarvis are thick as thieves."

Ekman snorted and shook his head. "Hardly. But I could accuse you of the same thing," he said. "All of your running around, all of your outrageous insubordination to Jarvis, this business with the cops – it could all be an elaborate act. You two – or you *three*," Ekman looked over at Brock, "could be into something together, and

I could be the odd man out."

Sam was incredulous. "You can't be serious."

"As a heart attack. But like I said, your knife wound has me rethinking things."

"Unbelievable," Sam said. "How about my house getting blown up? Also an act?"

"The bomb landed in your front lawn, not your house. And you were down in your basement stronghold, on the opposite side of the house, when it hit. So if I were going to engineer a ruse like that, that's exactly how I'd do it."

"Are you serious?" Sam bellowed, awakening the slumbering passenger in the row in front of them. She felt herself becoming blinded by anger. She wanted to throat-punch Ekman.

A glance at Brock told her that he was thinking along the same lines. The vein in Brock's neck was bulging, and she could see him working his jaw.

Ekman looked hard at Sam. It appeared to her as if he were trying to decide something.

He arrived at his decision. "You asked something earlier," he said. "You asked, who can you trust when the good guys are out to get you? Well, that's a great question. And here's another one just like it: who can you trust when your boss and your employee are crooked?"

"Francis, I'm not on the take," Sam said through clenched teeth.

"Put yourself in my shoes," Ekman said. "A few things don't smell quite right in the Bolero investigation–"

"Which I haven't heard anything about," Sam interjected.

Ekman looked at her. "There's a reason you haven't heard much from me about Bolero, Sam. Jarvis has it locked down tighter than a frog's ass."

"Irregularities?" she asked.

"If Homeland accounts used to fund foreign activity count as 'irregular,' then yes."

Sam considered this. JIE Associates? Executive Strategies? They had both sent numerous payments to Everett Cooper, the dead Metro cop, and John Abrams, the dead CIA agent. *But who funded the companies?*

"Seriously? Which accounts?" she asked.

"I'm pretty sure of it," Ekman said. "But I don't know for certain, because I've been frozen out of the investigation. I don't know the specific accounts."

"Then how can you be 'pretty sure'?"

"I have a mole," Ekman said. "Don't ask who."

"Your mole didn't give you the account information?"

Ekman shook his head. "Told me I'd have to ask Jarvis directly. Jarvis demanded the reports be delivered to him personally, paper copies only."

"You haven't asked Jarvis about it?"

"I asked. Jarvis played the need-to-know card."

"Frank, I'm having a hard time swallowing all of this. You've been in lock-step with Tom since all of this started last week."

Ekman snorted. "I'll take that as a compliment. I've been working my ass off not to clue Jarvis in on my suspicions."

Is this bullshit? Sam wondered. *Or is there something to Ekman's claim?* It had never occurred to her that Ekman and Jarvis might not be on the same page.

She did the thing that made her a fantastic investigator: she put herself in the other guy's shoes. Sam realized that if Ekman really *wasn't* aligned with Jarvis, or privy to Jarvis' dealings, and if he really *didn't* know whether Sam might be involved in something untoward, his behavior toward her really hadn't been all that unreasonable. Especially if Ekman was trying to tap dance around Jarvis at the same time.

Never attribute to malice what can just as easily be explained by ignorance. She didn't recall who said it, but it had proven true enough in her experience over the years.

Sam looked hard at Ekman. His gaze didn't waver. *Either he's lying very well, or he's not lying at all.* She thought back to all the times she had put him on the spot over the past couple of years, and recalled the way his nonverbal signals – the blush of his cheeks, two blinks in rapid succession, his inability to hold eye contact – inevitably betrayed his discomfort. She saw none of those signals at the moment.

"Suppose I suspend my disbelief," she finally said. "Walk me through your week."

Ekman did. By his account, he hadn't told Jarvis about his trip to the FAA to look over the flight records during the time of the bombing at Sam's house, but Jarvis had somehow found out about the Fatso Minton connection. Jarvis had ordered Ekman not to disclose anything about it, to anyone at all.

"So you hung me out to dry because you were 'just following orders?'" Sam asked, incredulous.

Ekman shook his head. "No way in hell would I do that. Jarvis told me that he would talk to you personally about the FAA development. I took it as further evidence that you and he were working together on something I wasn't privy to."

"He didn't tell me anything."

"So I gathered, based on our conversation this morning," Ekman said. "I must have hidden my shock and dismay pretty well."

"You blended nicely into the furniture."

"I wanted to kick your ass for not standing up for Sam," Brock interjected.

"Again, think about it from my perspective," Ekman said, looking at Sam. "It could all have been an act that you and Tom put on for my benefit."

"Do you still think I'm involved in something shady?"

"Obviously, the Dibiaso link via Brock is problematic."

"Asked and answered," Sam said.

"You blamed it on coincidence. That's a reed-thin argument."

"But it's no less true. You said yourself that there were no other connection points between Brock and Dibiaso. And there's nothing connecting me to Dibiaso at all."

"Except your name and address on Abrams' nightstand, and your picture in the music box."

Sweet Jesus. Sam was stunned. *How the hell does he know about the music box?*

Ekman smiled at her obvious surprise. "I'm not entirely the

inept cubicle-warmer you sometimes mistake me for," he said. "And you forget that I have access to a lot of DHS fiefdoms."

Of course. She shook her head. Her judicious use of numerous burner phones had kept Ekman from locating her, but she should have been more careful with Dan Gable's end of their communications. It was entirely possible that Ekman had tapped Dan's home and office lines.

"And it was such an obvious blunder, not taking better precautions when you talked to Dan, that I thought it was part of the ruse."

Sam blushed, angry and embarrassed. *Such a rookie mistake.*

Ekman looked at Brock. "And your constant pestering was tough to interpret, too."

Brock shook his head. "I'm pretty sure I wasn't ambiguous."

Ekman smiled. "Not in what you said. It was consistent with someone who wanted to dissuade us from connecting you with Dibiaso. But that just made me more confident that you were actually connected with Dibiaso."

Brock arched his eyebrows.

"Until the sixty-ninth phone call," Ekman went on. "Then I started to rethink my theory about your involvement. Guilty people don't usually overplay their hand that blatantly."

"And what do you think now?" Brock asked.

"Jury's still out," Ekman said. "But I'm showing you an awful lot of leg here. You should take that as a positive sign."

Sam looked thoughtful, then nodded. "I do. But as you say, the jury's still out. What about Jarvis?"

"My opinion? He's bent."

"Anything you can pin a warrant on?"

"Nope. Crooked doesn't equal stupid. He's frozen me out of the key information."

"Lending credence to your theory that he's on the take," Brock observed.

"Yep."

Sam looked at Ekman. *Trustworthy? Telling the truth?* Possibly. But maybe not. On the one hand, Ekman had no poker skills, and the absolute lack of his usual "tells" made her inclined to believe his account. On the other hand, trusting him went against Rule Number One: trust no one.

She decided to stir the pot a little bit.

"Dan's submitting warrant paperwork today," Sam said.

"On whom?"

"You and Jarvis," Sam lied.

Ekman didn't blink. "On what grounds?"

"Can't say."

"You mean you *won't* say," Ekman corrected.

Sam nodded. "I won't say," she agreed with a smile.

She watched Ekman carefully. He looked tired, but not worried. That was significant.

"I suppose being named in a warrant was a likely consequence of staying close to Jarvis," Ekman said.

"Or, a likely consequence of getting your hands dirty," Sam pointed out.

Ekman laughed. "Or that. Fortunately, my hands aren't dirty."

Sam was inclined to believe him. Conditionally.

"Tell me more about the thug team in front of DHS," she said.

"Not mine. I'm not even convinced they were pros."

"The guy with the knife was pretty good," Sam said.

Ekman glanced at her side and nodded. "Or maybe you're slowing down as you get older," he teased.

"Me? Never. Still a ninja, even in my thirties."

"She kicked my ass yesterday," Brock offered.

"Where did you go when we split up?" Sam asked.

"I saw you guys dive in to the Agriculture building, and I went back inside Homeland," Ekman said. "I picked up a car from the motor pool and drove to the airport."

"Were you followed?"

"Not that I know of. But my field skills suck right now," Ekman said.

"Too much time behind a desk," Brock said. "I have the same problem."

Sam extended her hand. "Frank, I'm not yet positive, but I think we're in this together. Unless I learn something that takes me in a different direction, I have your back."

Ekman eyed her warily. "Such a resounding vote of confidence." He pondered some more. Then he smiled and shook her hand. "Don't screw me over."

"Wouldn't dream of it. Unless *you* screw *me* over," Sam said. "Then all bets are off, and God help you."

* * *

The long flight finally ended. Ekman, Brock, and Sam all

exited the plane separately to reduce the likelihood of detection.

Brock wore a ball cap he bought from a teenager on the plane. The hat's brim was curled upward at the end, and Brock wore it sideways on his head, along with a pair of aviator sunglasses he never left home without. He strutted off the plane.

Half a dozen passengers later, Ekman deplaned, undisguised.

Sam brought up the rear. She wrapped herself in a blanket, wore a dark scarf over her hair, and asked for wheelchair service. She hunched forward in the wheelchair and kept her eyes low as the steward wheeled her up the jetway.

It didn't take her long to spot the goon: tall, tough, standing against the far wall, staring intently and looking anything but nonchalant. *Clown.*

The spotter looked right past her. It was impossible to tell if he saw her and had simply done a good job of hiding his recognition, but Sam would have been surprised if that were the case. He didn't give off the vibe of a top-tier professional.

The three of them took separate cabs, with separate intermediate destinations, and planned to rally at a popular all-night internet café in downtown Caracas at midnight. It didn't leave them with much time, but the extra precautions were necessary. Caracas was a tough town, and they needed to be careful. Hunters became hunted in the blink of an eye.

Chapter 13

The telephone, loud and insistent, awoke Dr. Javier Mendoza from his slumber. A glance at the clock told him it wasn't yet midnight on a Friday night. Against his better judgment, he reached for the phone.

"Doctor Mendoza," said an authoritative voice on the other end of the line. It was a statement, not a question.

"Who is this?"

"Agent First Class Vicente Monteverde. An officer will arrive at your door shortly. Open the door for him. He will display a badge, and ask you to accompany him. Bring your medical kit."

What Mendoza wanted to say was that he hadn't seen patients in years, that he was a research doctor and was certainly not an emergency physician, and that he didn't have a medical kit to bring along. But Mendoza tended to stammer when he was confused, flustered, or surprised, and he was unable to say those things at the moment. His stream of partial thoughts didn't communicate his concerns well at all.

"Dr. Mendoza, please answer the door," Monteverde said.

On cue, the doorbell rang.

Mendoza collected himself en route to the front entrance. He calmly explained that there must be some mistake, that he wasn't an emergency doctor, that his role as a highly specialized research pathologist was generally incompatible with midnight calls.

The agent calmly explained that Mendoza should shut up and get in the car.

Mendoza glanced at the man's badge, at the sidearm in its holster on his belt, and at the official-looking sedan parked at the curb, and decided compliance would be best.

"Give me a minute to get dressed."

The car ride was short. It ended at a familiar hospital, one Mendoza had visited many times over the years in the course of his work as one of Venezuela's leading hepatic pathologists.

The walk through the hospital's innards was also short, and the agents led Mendoza through a door he had never previously traversed. It led to a well-appointed hallway, still with a hard linoleum hospital floor but flanked by carpeted walls adorned with paintings and pictures, softer lighting, and muzak streaming from overhead speakers.

So this is where the upper crust goes to die, Mendoza thought.

"We would like you to examine a patient's chart," one of the agents said.

"This couldn't have waited until morning?"

A cold glare gave Mendoza the answer.

"Symptoms?" Mendoza asked, their footfalls echoing down the empty corridor.

"Vomiting, fever, abdomen painful to the touch," the agent recited.

Mendoza nodded. "Icterus?"

The agent looked puzzled. "What's that?"

"Jaundice. Are the patient's eyes or skin yellowish?"

"Extremely."

"Dark urine?"

"I don't know. You'll have to check the charts. Turn here." The agent pointed to a smaller hallway on the left, then to an open doorway into what was clearly a physician's permanent office. Medical texts sat strewn atop the desk, and a tired-looking resident in scrubs greeted him, folder in hand.

"Blood tests?" Mendoza asked.

"Si," the on-duty resident said. "Elevated ALT." Alanine aminotransferase was an enzyme; its presence in high concentrations frequently indicated a disease for which Dr. Javier Mendoza's expertise was entirely appropriate, and frequently necessary.

"Budd-Chiari syndrome?"

"Negative. No blood flow obstructions at all."

"CT scan?"

The resident handed still photos to Mendoza, who looked at them briefly before issuing his verdict: "Are his affairs in order?"

"Hardly," the resident said. "You'll understand when you meet him. Come this way."

Mendoza followed the resident down the long hallway, past a bank of vending machines, and into an elevator. They rose two floors, then exited, walking quickly past heavily armed security guards posted at the entrance to a hospital room.

It took Mendoza's eyes a moment to adjust to the dim light in the room, and the patient's face came into focus slowly.

When it finally did, Mendoza's jaw dropped, and the hepatic pathologist found himself stammering once again.

Chapter 14

The all-night internet cafe was still humming at just after midnight when Sam arrived. Ubiquitous connectivity wasn't yet a Venezuelan norm, and there was still a sizable segment of the population whose homes weren't wired, leading to a steady stream of clientele for the cafe. It didn't hurt that they sold coffee around the clock, which made the customers just as wired as the computers.

Sam picked a spot in the back of the cafe and positioned her chair so she could watch both the customer entrance and the employee access to the kitchen, and did her best not to worry about whether Brock and Ekman had encountered any trouble along the way.

Her own journey from the airport had been uneventful, which was a welcome relief. The wound in her side hurt like hell, and she wasn't much in the mood for another altercation.

The internet security routine was familiar to her by now. She was happy to discover the Tor browser already installed on the cafe's computer. Apparently, Sam wasn't the first customer concerned about masking her identity while online in Venezuela.

She double-clicked on the icon, and the ancient computer worked hard to open the browser.

Sam took the opportunity to scan the room for watchful eyes. Mostly strung-out teenage gamers, a few twenty-somethings with books opened near their keyboards, and a token middle-aged woman. Sam saw no telltale signs that any of them were surveillance assets monitoring her movements, but it was impossible to tell. It was unhealthy to assume that all of the people on her tail were as clumsy as the ones she'd witnessed outside DHS and at the Caracas airport, so she remained alert.

Motion caught her eye at the front entrance. Brock. He ambled to the back of the cafe and pulled up a chair next to Sam. He kissed her, tongue and all. "You're hot when you're running for your life," he said.

She smiled and shook her head.

Sam typed in the IP address she'd memorized. It took her to a password page, where she typed FellatioKillsThinThroatedDebutante. *Funny, Dan,* she thought as the page chewed on the password her deputy had chosen.

Moments later, a page full of text appeared. It was complete gibberish.

At the top was a three-digit number, 432. Sam added the digits together to get nine.

Nine was the alphabet offset key. Alphabet offsets were ridiculously easy codes to break. One just wrote the alphabet in a straight line across the top of a page, then wrote a second alphabet beneath it, placing the second "a" beneath the letter corresponding to the key.

In this case, the second "a" would be written beneath the ninth letter in the first alphabet, "i." To read the coded message, one would simply replace all i's in the gibberish text with a's, and so on, to reveal the message.

Except that this particular usage involved a clever twist, designed to slow down any unwanted decryption attempts. Both alphabets contained a space character after the fourth, third, and second letters, corresponding to the three-digit specifier, 432.

The twist would throw off anyone looking for a simple alphabet offset code. It wouldn't stop a decryption algorithm for more than a few milliseconds, of course, but it would certainly slow down a human who didn't understand the trick. It was a little thing, but sometimes the little things added up to make a big difference.

Sam copied the text from the browser window, and pasted it into a text editor. She made a key to translate from code to plain text, and used the find-and-replace function repeatedly until Dan's message finally became legible.

"Time for the juicy stuff," Brock said.

Sam whistled. If Dan's report on Jarvis was correct, her DHS boss was dirty in an outrageous way.

"If you knew someone could read your keystrokes, would you type the same things?" Dan's report began. "I think our guy TJ wasn't paying much attention to the cyber threat updates."

Thanks for the editorial.

"Of note," the report continued, "is an account registered in the Caymans, used to siphon money to JIE Associates and Executive Strategies."

It was a doozie of a find, but Sam wasn't surprised. She'd thought of this earlier during her conversation with Ekman.

Speaking of Ekman, where the hell is he? Sam wondered, glancing at her watch. He was approaching twenty minutes overdue for their midnight rendezvous. She shook her head and got back to the report.

"He studied almost every document under the sun related to Operation Bolero," the report read. "He deleted the report detailing the account linkages between JIE, ES, and the Caymans account."

Evidence tampering. Known under the penal code as obstruction of justice. *That's enough for an arrest warrant,* Sam thought.

"That's enough for an arrest warrant," the next line of Dan's report concurred, "but there's more."

Sam's jaw dropped when she read the next paragraph: "Jarvis contacted Fatso Minton at Executive Strategies and arranged a meeting in private about a matter of national security. Jarvis deleted the emails, but I was able to find them. Minton arrived in DC on Thursday of last week, two days before he bombed your house."

"Bastard," Sam said. "Jarvis took out a contract on our lives."

Brock seethed. "I will kill him with my bare hands."

"Not if I beat you to him," Sam said.

"But why would Executive Strategies bomb your house?" asked Dan's report rhetorically. "I think it's because the Dibiaso coincidence made him think you were CIA."

Sam was puzzled.

"Bolero wasn't a Homeland op," Dan's report further explained. "It was an Agency op. Tom Jarvis accessed the information on the Agency's secure server, using his CIA credentials."

Click. It finally made sense in Sam's head. *Jarvis* is *a*

goddamned mole! All of those rumors were spot-on! But why would his CIA affiliation make him want us dead?

The answer came to her in a flash: *Because he's not just a CIA mole in Homeland. He's also a VSS mole in the CIA!*

Dan's assessment seemed to agree: "It seems clear that the JIE Associates and Executive Strategies payments to dead spy Abrams and dead cop Cooper came at least in part from Tom Jarvis' Caymans account. Abrams' apparent affiliation with VSS made him a CIA target."

They don't much like double agents, Sam thought. *They tend to execute them rather than arrest them.* Ergo, the staged suicide of John Abrams.

All of that had likely made Tom Jarvis extremely nervous. He undoubtedly feared that the Central Intelligence Agency was about to blow the lid on some very central intelligence regarding Jarvis' extra-curricular activities.

Entirely damned plausible, Sam realized.

She recalled the lengthy conversation in Jarvis' office just a few hours earlier. Jarvis seemed to be genuinely confused about Sam's role. She now understood that his confusion was pressurized by the Agency's demonstrated willingness to thump one of their own, John Abrams, for dipping his hand in the Venezuelan cookie jar.

That kept Jarvis awake at night, because Jarvis' hand was in the same cookie jar. Believing Sam to be another Agency mole, Jarvis thought she was getting ready to bump him off.

Which might explain why a milquetoast like Jarvis would do

something drastic, like hiring an Agency asset to kill her.

In reality, Fatso Minton wasn't a CIA agent. But Fatso and his company were employed exclusively by the CIA, which would certainly be a strong enough connection to make the bombing look like an Agency screw-up when the facts came to light.

And she could understand Jarvis' reasoning for orchestrating the attack on her home. If she and Brock *were* CIA agents, as Jarvis apparently feared because of the Dibiaso connection, wiping them out was a terrific way of keeping them from discovering his affiliation with the VSS.

There wasn't a great deal of downside to ordering the attack, Sam reasoned. Even if Jarvis' suspicions turned out to be incorrect, which they were, and Sam turned out *not* to be a CIA asset, which she wasn't, her death would just be a tragic mistake made by an agency known for its rogue actors and brazen disregard for the rule of law. Plus, the diversion might buy him enough time to outmaneuver the Operation Bolero investigation.

Certainly Jarvis knows by now that he had it wrong, Sam thought. That was probably why he spent so much time mulling things over during their recent showdown. The carpool coincidence with Dibiaso was certainly reasonable, if unlikely. Trouble was, it would have given Jarvis something else to worry about: if Sam wasn't the Agency asset closest to discovering his duplicity, and maybe delivering his punishment as well, then who the hell was?

All of that considered, why was Jarvis still coming after Sam and Brock?

It didn't take much of a mental leap to arrive at a reasonable explanation: Jarvis knew that she was likely to discover his culpability in the process of her own investigation.

Which would mean that he would probably feel the need to finish what he started.

Tom Jarvis undoubtedly still had a contract out on her life.

It would certainly explain the DC Metro Police attention she'd garnered since the preceding Saturday. Using the crooked cops to take her out was a risky move, but who was better positioned to cover up a homicide than the police department in charge of the homicide investigation?

Sam continued reading Dan's report. "I've taken the liberty of submitting an arrest warrant for Deputy Director Jarvis," the report said.

Godspeed, Dan. I hope you don't get whacked in the process.

"Another development of interest: the partial prints found on the data disc in the music box belong to Avery Martinson. Orphaned at eleven years old, ivy league school, hired by the Department of the Interior right out of college. In other words, he's CIA."

Jarvis had flinched when she threw Avery Martinson's name at him during their meeting, and now Sam understood how Jarvis knew Martinson: they were both Agency assets.

And Avery Martinson was Arturo Dibiaso. At least, that's how he'd signed into the Pentagon visitor log.

What a yarn ball.

Another piece locked into place in Sam's mind. Jarvis was extremely interested in their relationship with Fatso Minton, and she finally figured out why. It occurred to her that Jarvis was probably probing to determine whether there was merit to his suspicion about Sam and Brock's CIA affiliation, again due to the Dibiaso link. Jarvis obviously knew that Minton's bread was buttered with Agency money, and he wondered whether the personal connection between Brock, Sam, and Fatso would betray a professional connection as well.

But why wouldn't Jarvis know who was on the CIA payroll, and who wasn't? After all, before Tom Jarvis was a Homeland bureaucrat and a VSS mole, he was first an Agency asset.

The answer was obvious, of course. Stovepipes, security, and need-to-know. An agent couldn't divulge what he didn't know, so the Agency only told its people what was absolutely necessary in order to get the job done. That didn't always include the names of other assets.

Plus, CIA was a big place, employing thousands of people. One could spend twenty years as an agent or case officer, Sam figured, and still only know a fraction of the people on the Agency's roster.

Brock interrupted Sam's cogitation. "Looks like that cell phone is still on, and it's still at the same address," he said, pointing to the last line of Dan Gable's report.

Sam read, nodded, and pondered their next move.

"Suppose the warrant comes through, and Jarvis is arrested," she said. "That doesn't remove the threat. He still has people gunning for us."

Brock grimaced. "Looks like we have to fight our way through."

"I'd feel much better about that if we were on our own turf," she said.

"At least there's three of us now," Brock said.

Shit. Ekman. Where is he? Sam looked at her watch: 12:39 a.m. Long after the rendezvous time. She had a sinking feeling that Ekman wasn't just late. He was probably also in serious trouble.

She looked over Dan Gable's message one last time to make sure she hadn't missed any important details, and was about to close out the browser and turn off the computer to cover her tracks when a new page popped up on the secure sight. Dan had just posted something else. Apparently he was still at work.

"This was just sent to Tom Jarvis," said the line of text at the top of the new page.

The rest of the page contained a picture.

Sam scrolled down, afraid of what she would find.

She heard Brock groan.

The picture was of Frank Ekman. He was slumped against a concrete wall, mouth and eyes open, jaw slack, an angry red entry wound near his right temple.

The left half of his skull was missing.

"Oh my God," Brock breathed.

Sam felt her heart sink. *Where does this end?*

She emptied the memory cache, closed the browser, and turned off the computer. She grabbed Brock's hand and pulled him toward the cafe's back door.

"What now?" he asked as they stepped into the cool midnight air.

Sam's face held grim determination. "I see no way out but through," she said.

Chapter 15

Peter Kittredge climbed into the taxicab as the sun peeked over the Caracas skyline.

Saturday morning.

Maria had awakened before dawn, fucked him goodbye, showered, dressed, and left.

"When will I see you?" he had asked as she prepared to leave.

"Not soon enough," she'd said.

"Where are you going?"

She held her finger to his lips. "You frighten me with your questions." She kissed him one more time and walked out the door of the apartment.

Kittredge felt an unreasonable sense of loss at her departure, as if the air had left the room with her. He couldn't help but wonder whether he'd see Maria again at all. Hers was a brutal, deadly business, and she lived her life with the kind of abandon that could easily lead to problems.

He was unable to fall back asleep, and decided to head home, hoping to finish cleaning up the mess left by the unknown intruders who ransacked the flat he and Charley Arlinghaus shared together.

The streets were largely deserted, and the cabbie was making good time.

Kittredge dialed the number of the Washington, DC hospital in which Charley was convalescing. A brutal attack in the airport parking lot had left him with a fractured skull and a swollen brain. A tired nurse answered the phone, asked Kittredge for his phone password – Boilermakers – and proceeded with an update on Charley's condition.

He was improving, apparently, and the doctors expected him to regain consciousness any day.

That was good news.

But Kittredge's stomach tightened. He knew that Charley's awakening portended a conversation with a number of difficult topics. In the week since Charley's attack, Kittredge had learned that their life together was unequivocally not the life that Charley had cast it to be, or the life that Kittredge had previously believed it to be.

Evidently, Charley was a CIA agent. A no-shit spy.

And Charley's gentle manipulations, applied over weeks and months, had eased Kittredge's journey toward a very precarious and ultimately untenable position. It was Charley who had introduced the notion that there might be money to be made by providing economic information to Exel Oil. It was Charley who had introduced Kittredge to Arturo Dibiaso. It was Charley who had shepherded the chain of events that ended with Kittredge selling secrets to Exel.

So what the hell was that all about? Did Charley know that would be the outcome? Was that the goal all along – to forcibly recruit Kittredge into the Agency ranks by engineering a situation where he had no other alternative?

Kittredge didn't blame his own failings on Charley. But he was beyond angry at Charley for skillfully manipulating him into a situation where the darker elements of his own nature were far more likely to manifest themselves.

So the conversation with Charley wouldn't be a pleasant one.

Assuming Charley can even have a conversation at all, Kittredge thought grimly. It was entirely possible that Charley might have suffered life-altering brain damage. That possibility could simplify things moving forward, Kittredge thought – he certainly wouldn't be able to live a fulfilled life with a man who was a mere vestige of Charley, and he wasn't sure that a purely homosexual existence was still in the cards for him.

But if Charley's cognitive function was indeed compromised, Kittredge thought, it might prove exceptionally difficult to obtain the many answers he sought.

Kittredge's phone vibrated, interrupting his thoughts. He glanced down at the screen.

His blood ran cold. Adrenaline slammed his veins. He felt slightly panicky.

A text: "Need a drop tonight. 6:30."

The sender was Arturo Dibiaso.

Kittredge's hands shook as he typed his reply: "Hard to do on a wkd."

"Important."

He considered. He would have to badge in to the embassy, retrieve the classified information from his office, sneak it out through security, and take a taxi across town to the drop location.

He would also have to notify El Grande. The contact procedures were convoluted and would add a couple of hours to his day.

So much for cleaning up the apartment.

"OK," he typed as the taxi pulled to the curb in front of his apartment building.

Kittredge paid the cabbie, walked into the building, took the elevator to his floor, and wandered toward his door, completely lost in his thoughts. He barely noticed the cleaning lady, hunched over her bucket.

He faced his door, hunted in his pocket for the key, and reached to unlock the deadbolt.

A hand clamped around his mouth.

He felt a hard blow to the back of his knees, and his body twisted as he fell to the floor.

Kittredge landed hard on his chest. The wind fled his lungs in a loud grunt. He felt his arm being wrenched behind his back; pain shot through his forearm and shoulder, and he feared the bones would break.

The hand remained clamped over his mouth, pulling his head to an awkward angle, and he wondered in a panicked millisecond whether this was the end of his life.

"Stay quiet," said a husky voice, speaking close to his ear, "or I'll break your neck."

Kittredge complied. He wouldn't have had the leverage to struggle, even if he had the will.

He heard footsteps, then a deeper voice: "Now?"

"Quickly," said his assailant.

Kittredge felt the sharp pain of a needle penetrating his right buttock, and a burning sensation followed.

Strangely, Kittredge began to feel as if he didn't give a shit about the wrenching pain in his neck, the awkward, painful angle of his arm, or anything at all. The discomfort felt further and further away, stars appeared in his vision, and a smile crept across his face.

Kittredge's eyes focused lazily on the tile pattern on the hallway floor, and he thought it seemed beautiful, sublime even. Why hadn't he noticed this lovely, amazing tile work before? He really needed to slow down, and take time to enjoy the little things.

That was his last conscious thought.

Chapter 16

This must be a dream, Kittredge thought to himself as he opened his eyes. Fiery green eyes blazed back at him, close to his face, staring intently.

She's beautiful, he thought. *A sign from the heavens to give up boys forever?* He chuckled. He heard maniacal laughter, which couldn't possibly be his own, but it stopped as soon as he stopped chuckling to himself.

The woman said something, and the words were unintelligible but very funny-sounding. He laughed, and heard the maniacal laughter again, obviously from someone else, but once again it stopped when he stopped laughing.

He felt a couple of sharp slaps on his cheeks, bringing focus to his consciousness, and the woman's sexy, husky voice began to form recognizable words.

"What's your name?" she asked.

He lolled groggily, until another sharp slap made him alert and fully awake.

"Name," she repeated.

Not this again, Kittredge thought to himself.

He formed the intention to stand and walk away. It was then that he realized he was hogtied, his hands and feet tied together behind his back. He thrashed momentarily, but each tug of his arms or legs caused ligature burns on his wrists.

"Tell me your name," the woman repeated again. He looked at her, noticing her flame-red hair for the first time, thinking again how beautiful she was. Her face wasn't angry, but neither was it patient.

"Peter Kittredge," he said, surprised at the way his voice croaked. "Where am I? Who are you?"

"Nice to meet you, Peter. I'm Special Agent Sam Jameson. Who is Avery Martinson?"

Kittredge felt disoriented, but less frightened. He'd never heard of a CIA agent going by the title "Special Agent," so he felt the odds of having to endure another torture routine were reduced significantly.

"My head feels terrible. What did you inject me with?"

"A little over-the-counter cocktail from an all-night pharmacy. Nothing to worry about," Sam said. "Avery Martinson. Who is he?" she asked.

"I've never heard that name."

Kittredge saw her nod at someone outside his field of vision. He felt a large boot press down between his shoulder blades, then felt a violent tug on the rope binding his wrists and feet together. He yelped as his back arched too far in the wrong direction.

"No time for games, Pete," Sam said.

It's déjà vu all over again, Kittredge thought. "My name is Peter. And I've never heard that name."

"But you've talked to him on the phone," Sam said.

"I really doubt it."

"There's a cell phone inside your apartment. It's still turned on at this moment. You used that phone to talk to Avery Martinson."

"I think you're mistaken. I carry my phone with me everywhere," Kittredge said.

She nodded again to the person behind him, and Kittredge heard the rustling of feet on pavement, then felt a hard pull on his rope again.

"Come on, people. Take it easy," Kittredge said after the pain subsided. "I'm on the payroll at the State Department."

"Interesting," Sam said. "But I don't see how it's directly relevant to the phone call to Arturo Dibiaso."

Holy shit, Kittredge thought. *Dibiaso.*

"Nice poker face," Sam laughed. "Tell me about your friend Arturo, and your recent conversation."

"I've never spoken to Arturo Dibiaso."

Sam looked dubious, and nodded to the person behind Kittredge again.

"Wait!" Kittredge said. "Don't pull on that rope again. I'm shooting straight with you."

"Sure doesn't sound like it," said a man's voice from behind Kittredge's back.

"Go on," Sam said.

"I've never met Dibiaso, but we've corresponded by text."

"Frequently?"

"Don't you have my phone records?"

"No. I have records for a burner account. And it was definitely a phone call, not text messages. The call was from one disposable phone to another one, owned by Dibiaso."

Charley, Kittredge realized. *She must be talking about* his *burner.* Kittredge had found it during one of his many attempts to return his apartment to some semblance of order. He was sure the phone was an artifact from another relationship in Charley's life, but Kittredge had assumed it was a sexual relationship.

"I think you're on to my boyfriend's phone," Kittredge said. "Get my phone from my pocket, and you'll see that I've only texted Dibiaso. We've never spoken."

Sam thought about it. "So both you and your boyfriend have a relationship with Arturo Dibiaso?" she asked.

"Yeah. Charley worked with Arturo."

"What does Charley do now?"

"Huh?"

"You used the past tense. You said that Charley *worked* with Dibiaso. You didn't say that they work together now."

Kittredge grew quiet, pensive.

"Peter," Sam said, "you have the look of a man who's thinking about telling a lie. I'd recommend against it."

He looked at her closely. "You said you're a special agent. What agency?"

"Homeland."

"Doesn't Homeland own the CIA?"

Sam laughed. "One can be forgiven for thinking that. We own just about everything else. But no, Homeland doesn't own the CIA. Honestly, I don't think anyone in the government actually 'owns' the Agency."

"I belong to them," Kittredge blurted. He wasn't sure why, but he felt he could trust the hot redhead, even though she was currently giving him a wire-brushing.

Sam looked at him, squinted her eyes, and cocked her head to the side. "That was an interesting choice of words. You mean you're on the payroll?"

"In a manner of speaking," Kittredge said.

"Split the hairs for me," Sam said.

"I'm not getting paid. But I've struck a deal."

"Kiss your soul goodbye," said the man's voice.

Kittredge strained to see the voice's source. He glimpsed a tall, athletic frame and a handsome face.

"You make me nervous back there. Can you untie me?" Kittredge said. "I'm playing ball and I won't go anywhere."

Sam shook her head. "Sorry. We're not sure we have all the players straight, and we always hedge our bets. Tell me more about the Agency. What do you do for them?"

"I just started working for them. I don't do anything, really."

Sam looked dubious. Kittredge saw her shoot a glance at the man behind him.

"I mean, I had to do this briefing, but that was really just part of my job at the embassy."

"Do tell."

Kittredge told them about the recent meeting between the US ambassador and President Hugo Chavez. They pressed him for details on Fredericks, Quinn, and the nature of Kittredge's relationship with them.

"So you're their bitch, for free?" Sam asked.

Kittredge grimaced. "Pretty much."

"So you're in trouble."

"I'm not in trouble. I have immunity."

"From prosecution?"

Kittredge nodded.

"For what?" Sam asked.

It was getting very uncomfortable. Kittredge had no desire to admit his involvement with Exel to another federal agent. He thought the immunity letter from the Deputy US Attorney General would prevent prosecution by *all* federal agencies, not just a couple of them, but he wasn't anxious to press his luck.

"Seriously, Peter, you need to tell me what they have on you," Sam said. "If they haven't already made you do nasty things, you can bet your ass that they will very soon. The Agency doesn't play around, and they don't pay much attention to the law, ours or anyone else's."

"I'm painfully aware," Kittredge said.

"Spill it."

"I sold a few files to an oil company."

"Embassy files?"

Kittredge nodded.

"So they've got you for espionage."

Kittredge grimaced. "Sounds much worse than it was."

"Usually does." Sam looked away, shook her head, and gnawed her lip as she thought about the situation. *It's still all about Dibiaso,* she thought. *He keeps popping up.*

"Where's your phone?" she asked.

"Front pocket."

She retrieved it.

Kittredge found the feeling of her hand in his pocket to be mildly arousing, despite being tied up. Or maybe even because of it.

"Password?"

He told her, and she typed it in.

She scrolled through the text messages on Kittredge's phone.

"Arturo Dibiaso was your handler," Sam observed.

"That's right."

"Do you realize that you've been selling State Department secrets to the CIA?"

"No I haven't." Kittredge felt a flash of anger. "Dibiaso works for Exel Oil."

Sam laughed. "Man, you are wet behind the ears, aren't you? Dibiaso is an alias used by Avery Martinson. Martinson might not be his real name, either, but he's definitely an Agency guy."

Sam wrote Dibiaso's phone number from Kittredge's cell phone. "Different account than the burner he used when you guys carpooled together," Sam said to Brock.

Another thought struck Sam. "What's your boyfriend's name?" she asked.

"Charley Arlinghaus."

"I know him," Sam said.

Kittredge looked at her. So did Brock.

"We sat through a class together a few years ago. Charley's Agency, too."

"So I gather," Kittredge said.

"You didn't know that before?"

"Something did seem a little off," Kittredge said.

Sam laughed. "You're a train wreck."

"You don't know the half of it."

"I'm all ears."

Kittredge clammed up. He figured he'd said too much already.

Sam tried a long shot. "Some people thought that we worked for the Agency, too," she said, motioning toward herself and Brock. "They tried several times to kill us. Yesterday, most recently. We think they had Venezuelan ties."

She watched Kittredge's face very closely. She saw worry and fear flash in his eyes. "You know something about that, don't you?" she asked.

Kittredge blinked several times.

"You've already told me the answer," Sam said. "May as well just skip the games and tell me the details."

"Charley's in a coma in DC. I think because he's CIA."

"How'd that happen?"

Kittredge told her everything. But he didn't tell her that he knew who'd done it.

"You know who's responsible, don't you?" she asked when he'd finished his account.

"No," Kittredge lied.

"I think you do. Otherwise, you'd have told me all about how inept the police are, about how in the age of ubiquitous airport video surveillance there must be at least one tiny little lead they could follow up on. Something along those lines. That's what you would have said, if you weren't hiding something from us."

Kittredge closed his eyes.

Brock spoke up. "Dude, these people are trying to kill us. If you know something, we'd love it if you just told us. But we have all day, and Sam has a mean streak. And I don't think anyone will hear you scream."

Kittredge looked around, becoming aware of his surroundings for the first time. He saw nothing but scrub brush.

He felt utterly exhausted.

He certainly didn't care about protecting the CIA, and he barely cared about protecting the VSS.

He really only cared about protecting Maria. And himself.

But he didn't want to fight.

"The VSS," he said quietly.

"Who?"

He told them about El Grande and Maria and their burgeoning guerrilla war against the gringos.

Sam let out a long breath. "Peter, it seems to me that you're in a bit of a predicament. Honestly, I don't know how that's going to work out for you."

He nodded. His eyes looked weary.

"Does our little chat mean that Homeland has their hooks into me now, too?" Kittredge asked.

Sam shook her head. "Not necessarily. I'd prefer you to consider me an ally. I think you could use a friend without an agenda."

Kittredge chuckled. "People keep offering me their friendship. Hasn't worked out terribly well so far. And everyone has an agenda."

"Have it your way. Just the same, you should probably consider my offer. I'm one of the good guys."

Kittredge snorted. "Just like the CIA."

"Hardly," Sam said. "And whether you realize it or not, you're very much in need of an exit strategy."

Kittredge shook his head, his expression tired and downcast. "I've been informed that there is no such thing."

"Bullshit. There's always an exit. It's just not always pleasant."

"Or healthy," Kittredge observed morosely. "There's really not any room in my life for another secret relationship."

"Your call. Take care of yourself, Peter." Sam and Brock got up to leave.

"Wait a minute!" Kittredge protested. "You can't leave me here!"

"Wouldn't dream of it. A hundred paces south is a silver sedan. You probably don't remember, but you hot-wired it, at least as far as the fingerprints are concerned. Good luck with that."

With that, Sam stuffed a phone number into Kittredge's pocket, untied one of the loops binding Kittredge's hands and feet, and walked away, Brock's hand in hers.

Chapter 17

Dr. Javier Mendoza's weekend was well on its way to being ruined. He'd been awakened in the middle of the night, brought under armed guard to the Hospital de Clinicas Caracas, and asked to assess a patient with a very particular disease, one which Dr. Mendoza had studied for years.

Hepatitis.

He'd thought the entire ordeal was highly unusual and extremely unnecessary, until he had met the patient.

President Hugo Chavez.

"El Presidente has extremely advanced hepatitis, resulting in cirrhosis." Dr. Mendoza's own words sounded surreal and otherworldly even as he spoke them to the crowd of medical and security personnel gathered around the jaundiced leader's hospital bed.

The room felt horribly closed-in to Mendoza, which was yet another byproduct of his barely-controlled anxiety. The effect was certainly exacerbated by the blackened windows and the dim light.

"How long?" asked His Excellency.

"I have never seen such a virulent strain. My most conservative estimate of its reproductive efficiency is over a million times greater than a normal hepatitis virus. I've never even read about anything like this before. Ever."

"How long do I have?" Hugo Chavez repeated.

"Señor Presidente, we will do everything in our power to slow the progress of the disease. There are drugs we can try, and we will have to see how your body and the virus respond."

"Of course, Dr. Mendoza. That's why you're here. But I want to know how long I have, if you can't kill the virus."

Mendoza wasn't skilled at delivering bad news to patients. The extreme discomfort was one of the reasons he built his career in an entirely different direction. He didn't enjoy working with patients, and he certainly didn't enjoy telling them that they were about to die.

He shifted his weight, and closed his eyes several times. "At this rate of reproduction, we have only days," he said.

Chapter 18

Brock and Sam headed back into town from the deserted field where they'd taken Peter Kittredge for a chat. Brock drove the pickup truck they'd stolen from Kittredge's apartment complex, and Sam rode shotgun.

They'd left Kittredge in possession of the proceeds of their second larceny, a silver sedan, and figured that by now, the somewhat hapless would-be spy had likely worked his way loose of the rest of the ropes tying his hands and feet together.

"What now?" Brock asked.

"Great question. I think we need to phone a friend," she said. She turned on the disposable phone she'd purchased in the international terminal in DC. She'd turned it on just once before, to text a contact number to Dan Gable in case of an emergency.

As the phone timed in, Sam ruminated.

Arturo Dibiaso was Avery Martinson, an Agency asset.

Also in the CIA lineup were Tom Jarvis, Charley Arlinghaus, and the late John Abrams.

Reluctantly orbiting the CIA periphery was Peter Kittredge. He wasn't on the Agency's varsity team, that much was certain, and he was double-dipping. Sam wasn't sure whether or not Kittredge had taken money from the VSS, but she got the sense that his ideological leanings were certainly more sympathetic to the Venezuelans than the Agency goons who'd roughed him up and invaded his life.

Charley Arlinghaus was in a coma, byproduct of the Agency's sub rosa war against the Venezuelan Special Service.

John Abrams was extremely dead. He had unsuccessfully hidden his VSS affiliation from his Agency coworkers, which had proven hazardous.

Everett Cooper was also dead. He was the Metro DC cop who had attempted to kill or kidnap Sam at the Abrams crime scene. He was also the guy whose brains had been splattered all over her wall by the Metro Internal Affairs officers. IA was wise to his illicit additional employment. Cooper was working for the Venezuelans, alongside Abrams.

And that brought her to Tom Jarvis. Behind the dull bureaucratic exterior was one hell of a crooked guy. He really worked for the Central Intelligence Agency. The Agency had planted him inside Homeland as their resident mole, to keep an eye on developments in the world's fastest-growing bureaucracy, to protect Agency turf and funding from being overrun by the zealots atop Homeland.

There was also a second layer of duplicity. Tom Jarvis paid Everett Cooper and John Abrams on behalf of the Venezuelan Special Services. And, wearing his CIA hat, Jarvis had hired Fatso Minton to destroy Sam's home – with her and Brock inside.

She didn't think Minton would willingly kill a friend for any amount of money, so her working theory was that Tom Jarvis had lied to Fatso Minton about the nature of the target he was being asked to bomb.

The pay had to have been outrageous, as undertaking such a bold, violent, brazen operation on American turf would have grievous consequences. It would take just one leak to a congressman, and Fatso could find himself facing jail time.

Jarvis must have sold it pretty damn well. Maybe he told Fatso it was an Al Qaeda cell, that they needed to send a stronger message than simply arresting them.

There was also the possibility that Fatso was moonlighting for the VSS as well, but she figured he was smarter than that. The Agency had made him a rich man, along with many of his employees at Executive Strategies, and it would have been beyond foolhardy to step out of line.

Guess we'll never know for sure. Fatso Minton had been sliced to ribbons. He'd been tortured and killed by a madman.

Which led her back to Jarvis. He'd undoubtedly arranged to have the junior spy league chase them around outside of Homeland headquarters before their flight to Caracas. Hell, the guy with the switchblade might even have been the same guy who killed Minton.

She shivered at the thought.

And Frank. Ekman was the latest victim. Half his head had been blown away just minutes after arriving in Caracas.

She was pretty sure that Ekman wasn't on the take. He was a true believer, a God-and-country kind of guy. She believed the account he'd given on the plane ride down to Venezuela, that Ekman distrusted Jarvis, and wasn't sure whether Sam was in league with the wrong side, so Ekman had kept his head down while trying to figure out what was really going on.

Ekman's likely neutrality meant that his death could have been orchestrated by either the Agency or the VSS. He was a potential threat to both sides. The Agency might have feared he was a VSS guy, and vice versa.

But Jarvis had him killed. Sam knew it in her bones. It was just a theory, in the same way that gravity and evolution were just theories. *It's fact enough for me,* she thought.

A sickening thought struck. *Dan Gable's in trouble.* Her deputy had been working his ass off to keep her alive over the past week, and he was in the process of walking a warrant for Jarvis' arrest through the Justice department. She thought about Ekman's revelation that he'd been monitoring Dan's communications, and she wondered whether Jarvis was doing the same thing. She was suddenly extremely worried for his safety.

She had punched the first four digits of Dan's number into her phone when it began to ring.

DC area code.

She was using a disposable phone, and she had no names programmed into it, but she'd only given the number to one person: Dan Gable.

"Hi, Dan," she said.

She heard a familiar laugh on the other end of the connection.

But it wasn't Dan Gable's laugh.

"Surprise, Sam. I hope you're having a good weekend. I hear it's nice down there this time of year."

It was Tom Jarvis.

Chapter 19

Peter Kittredge entered his apartment for the first time in two days. It was only slightly less of a disaster than when he'd first discovered it ransacked, six days earlier. He'd barely had time to move the big piles of broken glass and strewn clothing around during the ensuing week, in which he'd made the acquaintance of Venezuela's quasi-official guerrilla resistance to oil-thirsty American overtures in the region.

He'd also made a dead drop for Arturo Dibiaso on Monday, and was about to do the same thing again.

Except things were different now.

Now, Kittredge knew the score. Dibiaso was Agency, and so was Charley.

So the Agency had induced him to spy, and had then played the other side of his espionage transactions.

Then they'd captured and tortured him, made him sign away his soul in exchange for immunity from prosecution, and coerced him to continue risking life and limb by stealing secrets from his employer, the State Department.

What a complete, unadulterated mess.

Now, Homeland had shown up on the scene. Over the past two hours, he'd been kidnapped for the second time in the last week, and interrogated for the fourth time. The redheaded DHS agent hadn't used a belt sander to extract the information she'd wanted, but neither had she been entirely cordial. She and her companion had almost broken his arm and his neck, then drugged him, then whisked him away to the middle of nowhere in a stolen car. *Then* they'd had a conversation.

He was confused, and miles beyond frightened.

He was also angry.

The Homeland chick seemed okay. It struck Kittredge that she was just as screwed as he was, somehow caught between the Agency and the VSS, maybe targeted by both. He wasn't terribly upset with her.

But he was murderously angry at the Agency.

More to the point, he was murderously angry at Charley, the man he'd loved, and Dibiaso, Charley's fellow CIA agent and the man who'd induced Kittredge to commit espionage.

Kittredge would have liked nothing better than to shove it up the Agency's backside. He wanted to see them burn, to watch the smug smile wiped off of their faces, to watch them *hurt*.

He had agreed to notify El Grande of his next meeting with the CIA. He would certainly tell them about the Agency's demand for an evening dead-drop, but El Grande wasn't forthcoming about what he and his VSS compatriots intended to do with the information.

Kittredge knew what he *wanted* the VSS to do. He wanted El Grande and his men to show up at the dead-drop armed to the teeth, and he wanted them to gun down every Agency bastard in the country. He wanted to watch them bleed out all over the train station floor, and he wanted to smile at them and wave a glorious goodbye as the life drained from their bodies.

* * *

Kittredge poured a drink. Pure vodka, from the freezer. The coldness burned his throat, the alcohol burned his gut, and the joyous relief was almost a religious experience. The sensation of the alcohol hitting his bloodstream through an empty stomach felt like an old friend, like comfortable shoes.

He made for his favorite chair, but was only halfway there when he heard a knock on the front door.

Kittredge cursed, then padded softly to the peephole.

He saw a raised middle finger.

"Zip it up, get off your knees, stop whatever perversion you're committing in there and open the door."

Quinn.

Kittredge shook his head and unlocked the dead bolt. He didn't bother opening the door. He knew Quinn would do that on his own.

Kittredge was nearly seated in his chair when the giant CIA assassin walked in.

"Gorgeous day for a drive, don't you think?" Quinn said. "Maybe I'll go steal a car. Wait, maybe I'll just borrow *your* stolen car!"

Kittredge grimaced but said nothing.

"Haven't had enough excitement this week, so you thought you'd try grand larceny too?"

"Quinn, feel free to fuck yourself."

"I don't do that. But sometimes I do make love to myself."

Kittredge shook his head. "What do you want?"

Quinn plopped himself down on the couch, propped both feet

on the designer coffee table, and crossed his arms behind his head. "Just checking in on my rock star new recruit," he said blithely.

Kittredge took a draft of his vodka and looked out the window.

"I don't want you to get arrested by the locals before your big dead-drop tonight," Quinn said.

"Why don't I save all of us the trouble and just hand the thumb drive to you?"

Quinn looked surprised. "What makes you think I want it?"

"You could hand it to your boy Arturo. Or to Fat Fredericks. Or whichever Agency asshole wants it."

Quinn smiled. "You're more than just a pretty face, aren't you? You're a bona fide sleuthy spy! A real-life James Bond!"

"And you guys aren't as sharp as you think you are, if a half-assed State Department economist like me can figure out your scheme in less than a week."

Quinn laughed. "I know, right? I keep telling Fredericks how much he sucks. But he doesn't seem to take my advice to heart. I don't feel very empowered."

Kittredge found Quinn's schtick annoying.

"Listen, Quinn, I'd really like you to get out of here."

Quinn feigned a hurt expression. "I'm just here to help, making sure you don't need anything for the big dead-drop tonight, and this is the thanks I get?"

"I'm all set, thanks."

"Actually, you could use a few pointers, I think. You look stiff and nervous when you're putting the bag into the locker at the station. You should really loosen up a little bit, and stop looking

142

around. Makes people think you're up to something."

"So you're really just here to remind me that you're still watching me."

"Something like that." Quinn rose and walked toward the door. "Maybe get a little drunker before today's drop. The booze will relax you."

Kittredge flipped Quinn off.

Quinn blew a kiss on his way out of the apartment. "Have a nice day, partner."

* * *

Kittredge heard the door shut. He felt besieged, watched, violated, and compromised. Again. And he felt completely alone.

He flipped on the television for company.

Headlines in Spanish scrolled along the bottom of the news channel screen, and the talking head stood in front of a Caracas hospital.

Kittredge's Spanish wasn't perfect, but it was good enough to get the gist. Apparently, someone very important was dying an unexpectedly fast death. Cancer, the reporter speculated, or maybe some other liver problem, judging by the jaundiced skin and eyes of El Presidente.

Hugo Chavez.

He was perfectly healthy only yesterday, when he'd told the US Ambassador to get lost. Kittredge had seen him with his own eyes, shook hands with him even. The man was anything but frail, ill, or weak. His grip was strong, his eyes were clear, and his speech was never less than stentorian. He looked like he could've been the

Venezuelan head of state for fifty more years. He certainly didn't look like a man nearing the terminal stages of a liver disease.

Jesus Christ. It snapped into place for Kittredge suddenly, inexorably. He felt a crushing weight in his stomach. Rojo's assessment had been absolutely correct: a great many things had happened during Friday's seemingly-innocuous meeting.

We've assassinated Hugo Chavez.

With trembling hands, he turned off the television.

He longed to talk to Maria. She would know what to do. He wished he had the first clue about how to get ahold of her. He realized that she had been an anchor for him during the crazy events of the past week. It was also clear to him that he was far more than attracted to her. He felt the overpowering urge to cling to her like a drowning man to a life raft.

Because he was definitely drowning.

Tears streamed down his face. *I am party to murder.*

He rose, paced.

There was only one thing to do. *I need to talk to El Grande. Right now.*

Chapter 20

"Hello, Tom," Sam said, looking meaningfully at Brock in the driver's seat.

"Dan gave me your number," Jarvis said.

Bullshit. Not willingly. Sam was sure that Jarvis had either intercepted Dan Gable's communications, or he had squeezed Dan directly to get the information.

That meant that either the warrant hadn't been signed and served yet, or Jarvis had somehow slipped through the trap and avoided being arrested.

It wasn't a good development, no matter how she sliced it.

Brock mouthed something silently: *play dumb,* he was saying.

She gave him a questioning look.

About Ekman, Brock mouthed, using his hand to mime a gun pointed at his head.

She nodded. She understood what he was saying. Giving away their knowledge about Ekman's death would surely put Dan Gable in even greater danger.

"We're following up on that lead we talked about," she said with as much nonchalance as she could manage.

"I'd like you to stop what you're doing and head to the embassy as quickly as you can," Jarvis said. "I have reason to believe that there's a contract on your life."

"You think?"

"I'm serious, Sam. We found agents outside of DHS headquarters. We haven't made any arrests yet, but we're pretty sure they were following you guys."

No shit. You hired them, asshole.

"We saw them," Sam said. "We thought they were part of a security team," she lied.

"They're not, at least not one of ours," Jarvis said. "Hurry, Sam. The embassy is expecting you, and they're arranging a diplomatic flight back to DC tonight."

The hell they are.

"Okay. Thanks, Tom. We'll call you from the airport when we land."

"Do that. We'll have a car there for you. Be careful, Sam."

Jarvis hung up.

Sam exhaled. "Crooked as a stick in water."

"What did he want?"

"He wants us to walk into a bear trap."

* * *

It was ironic that the most important thing for a car thief to do in order not to get caught was to steal another car. Driving the same stolen vehicle for too long was a great way to spend time in jail.

In Sam and Brock's case, driving the same stolen vehicle for too long was a great way to end up dead.

So they pulled into a parking garage, parked in an open space adjacent to a reasonable-looking mid-sized sedan, and got to work.

"You scare me sometimes," Brock told Sam with a smile, while he wiped the first car clean of their fingerprints. "Kidnapping, assault, and now grand theft auto. *Three times.* Sometimes I think if you weren't playing for the good guys, you'd definitely be playing for the bad guys."

"I'm glad you can tell them apart," Sam said. "I sure as hell can't."

She jimmied the door lock open. A car alarm sounded briefly, but it was a cheap one, and Sam disabled it within seconds.

Two minutes later, she had worked the steering column cover free, exposing the ignition wires. She found the right ones, stripped the insulation using a pocket knife, and twisted the ground wire together with the ignition lead. The spark plugs would now have current to fire at the right time.

Then she touched the starter motor wire to the other two exposed leads. The starter motor engaged, and the engine sputtered reluctantly to life.

"Hop in," she told Brock.

"Now for the difficult part," he observed.

He was right. Stealing a car in Caracas was really no big deal. It happened a hundred times a week in the lawless city.

But getting ahold of significant amounts of cash, and a couple of weapons, would be tricky. They weren't worried about the *policia,* or what passed for police forces in Caracas. There was little discernible relationship between the rule of law and the various competing police departments operating in the world's most dangerous city. The cops were woefully underfunded and highly entrepreneurial, which meant that they operated much more like a protection racket than an actual police force. Their major function was extortion, accepting bribes in exchange for a laissez faire approach to almost everything.

Sam's major worry was the hardcore and pervasive criminal element. There were no safe neighborhoods in Caracas. Murders, theft, and home invasions took place daily, and in broad daylight. Even in relatively affluent neighborhoods such as Baruta, Chacao, and El Hatillo, violent crime was a constant worry. Caracas' murder rate was four times higher than Colombia's, and six times higher than Mexico's, even at the height of the so-called drug wars.

For this reason, guns weren't for sale in stores. Getting their hands on a couple of sidearms meant they'd have to use cash, and buy them on the black market.

But they didn't have much cash to speak of.

Finding guns and working capital meant that Sam and Brock would have to deal directly with the violent criminal element, because criminals controlled the city.

In fact, Sam thought, the most adept criminals had risen to national political prominence. Thuggery wasn't a problem in Venezuela. It was a way of life. They'd have to be extremely careful to avoid being kidnapped and murdered.

A few automated teller machines were scattered throughout the city, but they were almost always empty. The banks simply couldn't afford to stock them with cash that would undoubtedly be stolen. They also couldn't afford to pay armed guards enough money to keep them from robbing the machines they were supposed to be guarding.

So there were precious few remnants of the failed experiment, which meant that Sam and Brock had to find another method of obtaining cash.

There weren't many good options. Banks required an established account before honoring withdrawal requests, and the currency exchanges were in league with the criminal element. Customers leaving with any appreciable amount of cash – the kind of cash Sam and Brock would need to extricate themselves from their shitty situation – wouldn't make it half a block before being mugged. The exchange clerks had gangsters on speed-dial. In fact, the gangsters paid them more than their employers did.

There was yet another problem. Because they were obviously American, anyone who would be willing to do business with them would undoubtedly want payment in dollars. That was wildly inconvenient, because Venezuela's particular flavor of socialism, which was much more delusional than average, had created one of the world's most lucrative currency arbitrage environments. There was a booming black market for dollars, and the "street" exchange rate was several times higher than the official exchange rate.

And there was a dire shortage of greenbacks in Venezuela to support this demand, so much so that Venezuelans paid exorbitant sums for plane fare to foreign countries with fully-stocked ATMs. They'd empty their life savings to pull out a few thousand dollars at the official – and artificially low – exchange rate, then fly back home to Venezuela to sell their dollars on the street for a huge profit.

Finding weapons to protect themselves would be a problem as well. While everyone had a gun in Caracas, nobody was *allowed* to own one. At least not legally.

"I wish we'd been able to check a bag on our flight down here," Brock said. "You could have brought a couple of pistols."

Sam shook her head. "They'd never have cleared customs."

"So what are our options, then?" Brock asked.

"I think we're going to have to go old school," Sam said.

"What do you mean?"

"I'll show you. Head south toward downtown."

* * *

Venezuelan pawn shops didn't look like the pawn shops Americans were used to seeing. In fact, almost every shop was a pawn shop of sorts, as unofficial barter economies sprung up everywhere in response to the pervasive, grinding poverty endemic to the region.

They stopped at a jewelry store, which sold a few new pieces, but was mostly stocked with consignment items.

Sam knew the jewelry industry was one of the most heavily gang-infested businesses in the city. How could it not be? No legitimate jewelry business could stand up to repeated gang attacks and robberies. Smart owners capitulated early; dumb ones died.

They didn't relish walking into this environment as a pair of bright-eyed gringos, but they needed to solve their currency problem.

They planned to use a five-thousand-year-old currency to get what they needed.

Sam used her Tricia Leavens credit card to buy two gold necklaces. It was enough gold to be meaningful, but she hoped the quantity would be small enough not enough to mark her as a juicy target for a mugging.

Brock bought a couple of gold pieces as well, and they moved on to the next jewelry store.

"This is going to take all day," Brock observed as they made their way back to the stolen Toyota.

"Probably. But I don't have any better ideas," Sam said.

The second jewelry store was equally uneventful, and the third.

They grew increasingly wary with each stop. Because there was no practical way for them to lock their stolen car, it made no sense to store the gold anywhere but in their pockets.

By the time they left the fourth jewelry store of the day, finally loaded down with what they figured was enough gold to secure private passage back to the States, they had grown downright worried.

Their fears weren't unwarranted. Word had evidently gotten around. The thugs were aware of the two gold-hungry gringos, and two toughs stopped them just a few steps from their car. One brandished a baseball bat. The other wore a jacket despite the warm, muggy weather, and held his hand in his pocket. Sam assumed he had a gun.

Baseball Bat spoke in Spanish. Sam pretended not to understand.

Jacket spoke more loudly in Spanish, with the same result.

It's the same everywhere, Sam thought. *If the foreigners don't understand you, just talk louder.*

"Empty your pockets!" Jacket was suddenly red-faced, and

spittle flew from his mouth.

Sam started sobbing.

Brock looked at her in amazement. She was the toughest person he'd ever met. He'd never seen her wilt in the face of a challenge, particularly not one like this.

He was even more bewildered when she began pleading with the two goons.

"Please, don't hurt us! We'll give you anything you want!" Sam said between sobs. She doubled over in fear.

What the hell is happening? Brock wondered. *This isn't the Sam I know.* He felt the responsibility of solving the situation fall on him, but he knew he didn't have the martial arts skills to handle it.

Jacket stepped forward, hatred in his eyes, one hand reaching for Sam while the other fidgeted in his pocket.

"Listen, asshole—" Brock started to say.

A blur of motion and a sickening crack interrupted him.

In an instant, Jacket fell in a heap, clutching his crushed trachea. Sam's fist had destroyed his voice box and collapsed his airway. He had moments to live, and they would be miserable, painful, panicked moments.

The blur continued, and Brock saw Sam's arm swing in a narrow arc, connecting with the side of Baseball Bat's neck. Sam's blow knocked the goon off-balance. She took one step toward him, planted her left foot, and swung her right foot. It flew with lightning speed toward the young gangster's nose. The top of her foot crushed his face. Brock heard the bones crack. Blood erupted everywhere.

But she wasn't finished. She wrenched the bat free from his

slack grip as he fell to the street, unconscious.

"Wait, Sam!" Brock yelled.

But she didn't wait. She swung the bat down on the gangster's head. Brock averted his eyes, but heard another sickening thud, then a gurgling sound.

Two dead gangsters.

"My God," he said, stunned and sickened. "You're a fucking animal."

"Hardly," she said. "They're obviously foot soldiers. We'd never make it out of here if we left them alive to talk. Help me throw them in the trunk. No use leaving evidence behind."

"Jesus, Sam," Brock repeated. "I don't know what I think about this."

"Think later," Sam said, using the driver's side lever to open the stolen car's trunk. "There was no choice. Help me deal with the situation right now."

They loaded the two corpses into the sedan's trunk, retrieved a 10mm pistol from Jacket's front pocket, and made their way out of the city.

Sam drove. It looked to Brock like she was lost, but she was merely taking precautions to avoid being followed. She'd have preferred to swap cars again, but time wasn't on their side.

The gangs wouldn't be sophisticated enough to organize a disciplined multi-car surveillance procedure, of course. But Sam knew that they weren't running from just the street thugs.

They were also running from at least one state security agency, and maybe two. And if Jarvis wasn't yet under arrest, then the number might be as high as three. CIA, VSS, and Homeland.

Brock rode along silently, white as a sheet.

"Not always a friendly business," Sam said.

"You killed those two dudes. One of them with your bare hands," he said, still incredulous. "You didn't just knock them out. You *smoked* them."

She nodded grimly.

"Was it really necessary?" he asked.

"Only if we wanted to survive."

Chapter 21

Hector Yosue Alejandro Javier Mendoza – El Jerga, The Shiv – was unaccustomed to failure.

He took it personally.

Against his wishes, he had been ordered to kill the woman in broad daylight, and to kill the man whenever possible.

But she was quick, much quicker than she should have been. She squirmed away. His stroke had connected, and he had felt the familiar sensation of flesh resisting the glorious tearing and slicing of his blade, but he had missed. Instead of dying a nearly instantaneous death, as she would have done if his blade had found her heart, she had broken free, broken his nose in the process, and dashed to safety somewhere.

He had been forced to deal with all of the repercussions of a public, daylight assault. But he hadn't achieved his objective. She had run away.

El Jerga had narrowly escaped arrest. Indeed, he had narrowly escaped further bodily injury trying to break free from the bus full of angry passengers. He'd been forced to brandish his blades to get them to back off. Even then, it was a close thing. There was a lot of latent anger in DC, and the passengers seemed willing to take it out on him, an armed assailant.

El Jerga's conversation with the gringo go-between was not a pleasant one. Neither would the chat with El Grande be congenial.

Both of El Jerga's handlers knew the risks of a public, daylight assault on the redhead and her boy-toy. It was far too difficult to control circumstances in a situation like that, and the probability of failure was high.

Still, they had insisted. So El Jerga had demanded payment for the attempt on her life, not just for successful completion of the assignment, which had mitigated his financial risk.

But the personal risk was now extremely high. He would no longer have the same freedom of movement throughout the gringo city, because surveillance cameras had undoubtedly caught his assault on the bus. The gringo security agencies wouldn't likely be after him, he knew, but the local police certainly would be. *We didn't buy every Metro officer,* he thought. *Some of them are still on the job.*

These things would complicate his job considerably. He would mention this to El Grande, of course, and he wouldn't be shy about the impact of the added risk on the price of his services.

El Jerga would also place another demand on them: he would execute the pair at the time and location of his choosing, and in the manner of his choosing. No longer would he allow El Grande and his gringo shill – the bureaucrat whom El Grande had bought, the man who was stashed somewhere in the bowels of an American security agency, the name of which was still unknown to El Jerga – to exert operational or tactical control over the operation. El Jerga would demand absolute field authority.

This would produce another windfall, one that was even more important to El Jerga than money. Having control over the manner of the woman's execution meant that he could kill her as slowly as he wished.

He could enjoy her as thoroughly as he wished.

The demon inside of him would drink its fill. This knowledge made El Jerga almost giddy with anticipation. The rush was visceral, animal, sexual, and he felt his body tingle with eagerness.

He would enjoy the real thing soon enough.

But he would need help finding her again. For this, he was beholden to El Grande, and maybe to the *puta* gringo. It was distasteful, but unavoidable.

He sat down in the coffee shop in the subterranean shopping mall, carved beneath the Crystal City office complexes full of bureaucrats, contractors, and other supplicants to the state. He impatiently awaited the arrival of his contact with an update on the woman's whereabouts.

El Jerga's broken nose throbbed painfully, and he adjusted the sunglasses to a more comfortable position. He felt silly wearing them in an underground shop, but they served an important purpose: hiding the two black eyes that the woman's blow had caused.

She will suffer tenfold for this indignation, he vowed as he watched his contact order a medium Americano and amble nonchalantly toward his table.

The Metro DC policeman sat down across from him, with his coffee in hand and a slightly obsequious smile on his face.

This had better be good news, El Jerga thought to himself as the cop delivered the predetermined opening line.

El Jerga croaked his response, then listened intently to the cop's whispered update.

Chapter 22

Sam took an offshoot from the main access road to El Avila National Park, then took a sharp left onto a jeep trail a few miles inside the nature preserve. The stolen sedan wasn't designed to navigate trails with deep, muddy ruts, and it wasn't long before Sam concluded that she'd driven as far as possible into the woods.

She parked at the base of Mount Avila, the large mass of vegetation-covered rock that separated Caracas from the Caribbean, and popped the trunk.

With a grim set of his jaw, Brock helped her remove the two dead gangsters from the car, carry them to a thicket of dense underbrush, and wedge them as deeply into the vegetation as possible. With any luck, the wildlife would find them before the park rangers did.

They threw handfuls of dirt and mud into the trunk of the car to absorb and obscure the pooled blood from Baseball Bat's crushed face and skull.

Lacking the space to turn around, Sam drove in reverse back toward the paved road. Brock was impressed with her driving skills. "You're much more than just a pretty face," he joked. "If I had to be party to manslaughter, I'm glad it was with you."

She chuckled as she guided the car back onto the paved road of the national park. "Self defense, baby," she said. "It was self defense."

"I'd agree with you completely, if it wasn't for that last swing of the baseball bat."

She nodded, turning back onto the main road and driving toward the national park's exit. "You would have a perfectly valid point, except that we're not in Uncle Sugar's America. It's a different world down here. If we had left either of them alive, we'd never get out of Venezuela."

Brock smiled wanly at her. "This is me, deciding to trust you on that."

She returned his smile. "Stick with me, kid," she teased.

She really wanted to talk to Dan Gable, to figure out what the hell was happening with Tom Jarvis and the arrest warrant, and to find out whether Jarvis had kicked up any trouble for Dan.

But it was a risk. Turning her phone on meant that Jarvis would be able to track her precisely. More importantly, the VSS thugs he was working for could track her movements, set a trap for them, and end the cat-and-mouse for good.

It was also a risk to leave the phone off. She knew that she and Brock would need some help getting out of Caracas undetected. Their aliases would undoubtedly be blown, and Jarvis and the VSS would certainly have alerted every monkey in a uniform at passenger embarkation points all throughout Venezuela.

Sam took a deep breath and hit the phone's power button.

A voice message awaited her, from a number she didn't recognize. She hit the speakerphone option and listened.

Dan Gable's voice crackled over the cheap headset. He'd bought a burner, too, his message said.

160

Smart, Sam thought. *They're all over your other phone lines.*

He said that the arrest warrant for Tom Jarvis had been signed, and an FBI team was being dispatched to take him into custody.

That's one fewer bastard running around, Sam thought.

Dan also said that there had been an attempt on his own life, by a DC Metro cop, who'd pulled even with his car and drawn a pistol.

It's the wild west.

"Sam, I think you need to get out of Caracas," Dan entreated. "You're not going to learn anything more down there. And you're a canary dancing on the cat's tongue."

Sam rolled her eyes. Dan had an annoying penchant for dramatic metaphor.

But he wasn't wrong. Sam had come to the same conclusion.

But how? Booking an airline flight would be suicidal. They'd be rolled up by the VSS instantly.

As usual, Dan had a plan. "Freedom Air Charter International," his message said. "Their business is illicit air traffic to and from North America. Cash plays, and no questions asked. I found them on our watch list; you'll have to make a stop somewhere else down there to launder the flight plan, but you'll be back Stateside in no time. They'll be expecting you. Good luck, and I gotta run."

"That dude's worth his weight in gold," Brock said after Dan's message ended.

Sam nodded her assent.

"Let's get the hell out of this miserable country," she said.

*　*　*

Simon Bolivar International Airport wasn't much to look at. The passenger terminal building was relatively modern, certainly by South American standards, but to practiced North American eyes, it had a distinct not-quite-right vibe to it. Plus, it was a terrific place for a corrupt customs official to detain two gringos and hand them over to the highest bidder.

Sam figured there'd be no shortage of bidders.

Fortunately, they weren't headed to the passenger terminal.

They drove around the long arc to the south and west of El Avila National Park, turned north along the park's western border, and made their way to the coastal region.

The Autopista, Venezuela's Interstate Highway equivalent, bypassed the difficult mountainous terrain on El Avila's western slope, then curved lazily to the northeast, exiting the park at the southeast corner of the airport.

Sam got off the highway, entered the airport's grounds, and turned in the opposite direction from the majority of the Saturday afternoon airport traffic. She headed east toward the private hangars, and kept a weather eye peeled for a particular hangar belonging to Freedom Air Charter International.

Sam hoped the gold in their pockets would be sufficient to secure their passage.

The Bureau had sent a team to arrest Jarvis, but it was clear that he'd already set things in motion. He'd intimated during their eerie phone call that he wanted Sam to head to the American embassy, but that was surely a head fake. Every American embassy was a CIA stronghold, and if Sam's reckoning was correct, Jarvis was soon to be *persona non grata* in Agency circles. His covert association with the VSS had suddenly become extremely overt, likely in response to the Agency's Operation Bolero investigation coming ever closer to exposing his duplicity.

He was in a desperate situation, but he wasn't a desperate man, Sam reflected. He'd use every one of the resources available to him.

Those resources undoubtedly included the Caracas heavies who had assassinated Ekman twelve hours earlier. Sam was on the VSS's home turf, and it was only a matter of time before someone from the home team caught up with her.

"This better work," she muttered as she parked the stolen sedan across from a freshly painted hangar. The letters FACI were painted in bright gold, with a sparkling silver border.

They stepped into a posh, plush, modern lobby. "Business must be pretty good," Brock observed.

"May I help you?" the clerk asked, in flawless English.

"I sincerely hope so," Sam said.

* * *

The whine and rumble of the Cessna Citation business jet's engines filled the cabin. Sam did her best to relax. She was more successful than Brock, who appeared extremely nervous.

With good reason. The FACI receptionist had sent them into the back room to negotiate the terms of their transportation, and they'd ended up paying every ounce of their gold to two men who could only be described as thugs.

"That was like a mob movie," Brock said after they'd

emerged.

"It isn't over yet," Sam said. "I wouldn't be surprised if we get to our first stop in Panama, and have to do some renegotiation."

"At least you've got the pistol," he said.

"For the moment."

They'd boarded the plane wordlessly. The pilot and copilot seemed cordial enough, but the fat security man, with greased hair and greasier armpits, was nothing short of surly.

Sam had no doubts that she'd be able to win any sort of a physical confrontation with the fat man. But she wasn't sure how many reinforcements might join him when they landed in Panama.

"You think these guys might warn the VSS?" Brock asked.

"Anything's possible. I'm pretty confident they're not directly involved with the VSS right now, because we're on the plane. If they were less independent, they'd just have held us up and handed us over to them directly."

"After they took our gold," Brock said sullenly.

"Of course," Sam agreed. "But I think they're probably shopping the information around right now, looking for a juicy offer."

"Wouldn't that be bad for business? 'Fly with us, end up dead.' Not exactly a catchy sales pitch."

"Right," Sam said. "But it depends on how big an offer they get. And we're not exactly their ideal customers, so they probably won't care much one way or the other."

Brock chuckled grimly. "Guess we'd better bring our A-game from here on in."

Sam nodded her assent as the aircraft took the runway, accelerated, and lifted off to the west.

The coast of Venezuela receded in the distance behind them.

Part 3

Chapter 23

It was a lazy Saturday afternoon, but Tom Jarvis wasn't the lazy type. He reclined in a plush leather chair in the downstairs study, one of two exquisitely furnished offices in the museum-sized house in Wolf Trap, Virginia, while the desktop computer saved its files and whirred to a stop.

Jarvis stared out the window, lost in thought.

It was unraveling. It had been for a while. There wasn't much he could do about it, and he'd been forced to take drastic steps. They were extreme measures, and he hadn't felt good about them in the least, but a quarter-century in the clandestine services had left him somewhat inured to the pangs of conscience, mute and fleeting as they might be after so many years.

Blowback was always a strong possibility. He was perched precariously between two federal behemoths and a ruthless little band of third-world thugs. He happened to dislike the Venezuelans a little less than he disliked the other two agencies that paid him, but he had never expected things to become quite so messy.

So it was time. He was as ready as he would ever be.

He inserted a small key into the locking mechanism on the computer's face, gave it a quarter turn, and slid the hard drive out of its receptacle.

Life or death, he thought, looking at the small metal box full of silicon. CIA would execute him, no questions asked, if they got their hands on the files.

If Homeland found the disk drive first, the result would be the same, but it would take a decade longer. There would be an arrest, and a trial with a foregone conclusion, and then they would take ten years to let the appeals run their course before sending him to meet his maker.

Neither was an acceptable end game, Jarvis had decided.

He'd been extremely careful. He hadn't ever connected his computer to the internet. He accepted only CD ROM files, scanned them for malware, then smuggled them to work to be shredded and incinerated with the rest of the classified waste he and his fellow Homeland bureaucrats generated every week.

Each time a new transaction appeared, Jarvis repeated the process. He received the payment details, fed the account information through the one-time encryption algorithm on the computer in his study, copied down the encoded results in a place so obvious that it would never be discovered, and destroyed the disks.

It was extremely dangerous. Death was the best he could hope for. Imprisonment for life would be worse.

But it was necessary. What good was an account full of money if you couldn't access the account? It was like a lost wallet full of cash.

So he had contained the evidence as neatly as possible. He had taken precautions, at least those precautions that were within his wherewithal to comprehend.

Other, more effective measures likely existed, Jarvis knew, and he also knew that the electronic security game moved at a blindingly fast pace. This knowledge gave him the vague awareness that he had likely developed a form of complacency over the years, a psychological inability to recognize the vulnerability inherent in his habits. Yet, despite the stakes, he was unable to break the momentum of those habits.

Probably a damn good time to get out of the game. It wasn't healthy to linger past one's prime, particularly when so much of the clandestine world had become focused on the movement of little ones and zeroes.

I'm a walking coelacanth, he thought, making his way over to the large gun safe positioned against the exquisitely carved oak bookcase.

He entered the code and the lock yielded, revealing a second safe nestled inside. This one required a key, which he produced from his pocket. The smaller safe contained a duffel bag.

He checked the bag's contents, adding the hard drive full of fatal information to the cash, passports, credit cards, and 9mm pistol inside.

Jarvis reached back into the safe-within-a-safe, feeling along the bottom until his hand found the small piece of paper.

On it was written his goodbye to a wife who barely spoke to him, to kids who never called. In characteristic fashion, the goodbye note said everything except what was important. Sorry I had to leave on such short notice, it began. Urgent business at work. People might ask after me, it went on, so feel free to pass my cell phone information to them. I'll be checking messages regularly, and hope to return home soon.

A fitting end to a life spent going through the motions.

He set the note on the vast granite counter in the kitchen, and walked out the back door. He followed the cobblestone path through the backyard to the detached garage full of restored vintage sports cars. Ferraris, Lamborghinis, and even a Bentley or two sat in climate-controlled elegance.

The dehumidifier hummed in the background, and the familiar, comforting smells of motor oil, gasoline, and fine handcrafted machinery greeted his nostrils.

This had been the hardest part for Tom Jarvis. Choosing the one car he would take into his new life, knowing he would have to say goodbye to all of the rest. Heart-rending.

He ran his hands along several of his cars, feeling their curves, indulging in a maudlin moment. He'd bought them for pennies on the dollar and painstakingly rescued them from dilapidation, raising them again to their proper glory over months and years of tireless work. To the extent that Tom Jarvis loved, he loved his cars.

The 1984 Testarossa. He had made his choice long ago, anticipating the need for haste when the time came, knowing that his inevitable indecision would prove tragic unless he prepared himself properly in advance.

Jarvis tossed the duffel bag into the passenger's seat, pressed the button corresponding to the appropriate garage door opener, folded himself into the driver's seat, and turned the key. The engine purred to life, adrenaline surged, and Tom Jarvis drove away from his home, looking back only to ensure that the garage door had descended behind him.

A wistful feeling came over him as he drove for the last time down his street, his many recollections of a mirthless and joyless marriage suddenly awash in the pleasant sepia of nostalgia.

The moment passed quickly, and Jarvis returned to the *pathological detachment* – her words, probably first uttered by that marmot of a psychologist she was seeing, and probably sleeping with – which had served him so well over the years in what could be a very distasteful line of work. She had once told him that she could smell the rot of his amoral core, a declaration that encapsulated their uneasy union better than any other he could think of.

She blamed his employers for turning him into an unfeeling monster, but Jarvis knew better. His employers had merely given him the means and the opportunity to fully become what he always was. Her role had been to make him apologize for it, over and over again, in more ways than he could count.

He turned left at the bottom of the hill, exited the affluent subdivision, and headed toward the Dulles Airport Access road, reflecting on the irony of it all. It was his moral desuetude, the same unflinching response to nothing but the exigency of the moment, which had enabled him to achieve the results so cherished by his Agency handlers over the years. It wasn't lost on him that those same characteristics might also have made his handlers mad enough recently to kill him on sight.

Pathological. She probably wasn't far from right.

Certainly there was some pathology to the way he had simply migrated entrepreneurially toward interesting business arrangements, heedless of the underlying ideologies at play. He was always aware that ideology strongly motivated his employers. All of them, at some level, had sworn fealty to some god du jour; the strongest oaths were sworn to The Republic, and he, Agent Tom Jarvis of the Central Intelligence Agency, had mouthed those same words along with everyone else, all those years ago, acutely aware of the awkward vacuum he felt inside as he did so.

But he'd rarely thought of those ideas since, other than to recognize them for their utility. Ideology was a form of leverage, one that he applied whenever necessary or convenient, profiting at each step of the way, ruthlessly cutting ties or fading deftly into the background when the dogma became too prominent, too shrill.

He viewed it as a running joke he was playing on the rest of the world: he worked for people who did unspeakably horrible things to other people, in the name of liberty and freedom. Most recently, the VSS, but their impassioned cries weren't any more or less compelling than many others he'd heard over the years.

Tom Jarvis didn't do unspeakably horrible things in the name of a greater good. He didn't believe there was such a thing.

Rather, he did unspeakable things because he found it useful to do them.

But he wasn't delusional. It was obvious that his demented indifference – another clever turn of phrase his wife had brought home from the marmot's office one day – was precisely the character trait that had landed him in his current predicament.

One more quick little stop, he breathed.

One hard drive, and one surprise.

He would reduce the former to rubble and ashes, and toss it

into the river.

The latter, he would leave for his pursuers.

Doing so wouldn't bring him joy or pain. It would simply be useful.

Chapter 24

Dan Gable turned on his new burner, and checked for messages. There were none. He turned it off again, feeling his chest constrict.

Dan rode shotgun in the FBI sedan. He looked at the driver. Special Agent in Charge David Phinney seemed competent enough. Dan had never met him before, which wasn't unusual in the gigantic US federal system, but the guy had an air of confidence and alacrity about him that Dan found professionally appealing. That was a relief.

But not hearing from Sam made him uncomfortable. They should have landed by now.

Just a delay, he told himself. He'd hated having to entrust them to hastily-made third-world travel arrangements with an outfit he hadn't thoroughly vetted. It was tenuous at best, and he worked hard not to imagine her and Brock being thrown into a ditch somewhere in Caracas with their throats slit.

There hadn't been much choice, though. Sam and Brock had to get out of VSS territory. They had no other US assets on their side in Caracas, and the considerable risk of being double-crossed by the charter service was nothing compared to the inevitability of a long, painful death at the hands of the state-sponsored Venezuelan guerrillas. So he'd done the best he could, and he'd just have to hope for the best.

He focused on the task at hand. Phinney guided the big, nondescript sedan to the Wolf Trap subdivision, just west of the Beltway. Jarvis didn't live too far from Langley, a convenient fact that saved them some time. The Bureau wasn't keen to let Dan tag along, but he'd sold them on his utility as a fellow federal agent, and as someone who knew Jarvis personally, just in case the arrest didn't go smoothly.

Dan felt the familiar surge of adrenaline he always experienced during field operations. They were rarer now than when he had started out as a young agent, and most of his "heavy lifting" these days was done at a computer keyboard. *Feels good to get outside,* he thought.

His next thought was completely unrelated: *I need a pay raise.* Jarvis lived in the lap of luxury. How the hell was he pulling this off?

Dan chuckled at his momentary stupidity. Jarvis could afford to live in such a posh neighborhood because he was being paid by three separate state security services. *Maybe my little duplex isn't so bad after all.*

The procession of vehicles approached the Jarvis residence purposefully, but not in too big a hurry. Two vehicles at the tail end of the pack peeled off at the cul de sac entrance and formed a road block to prevent anyone else from entering or exiting.

Phinney parked the sedan in Jarvis' driveway, and two more vehicles flanked him on either side. "Wait here," Phinney told him.

Dan protested, but Phinney held up his hand. "A deal's a deal."

He waited impatiently in the car.

* * *

Ten minutes later, Phinney emerged, a frown and grimace on his face. "Too late?" Dan asked as Phinney plopped into the driver's seat.

The Bureau man nodded unhappily. The baseball game was on TV, and he didn't want to spend all weekend chasing a fifty-something turncoat around Northern Virginia. He picked up the radio microphone inside the sedan, depressed the talk button, and held the mic too close to his mouth as he spoke: "Wolfpack, Tango Fox Four Seven, request status update."

"Update available. Request secure line," came the terse reply. Phinney hassled with his secure cell phone, finally connecting after several false starts and a stream of curse words.

The dispatcher read an address. Phinney punched it into the sedan's navigation system.

The trip would take forty minutes. Dan sighed heavily and settled back into his seat.

"Know any jokes?" Phinney asked as he led the convoy back out of the subdivision.

Chapter 25

El Grande's expression was sad, haggard, and weary. "You couldn't have known," he told Kittredge. "And if you knew, what could you have done?"

Kittredge took little consolation in El Grande's words. "It was murder."

"El Presidente is not dead. Gravely ill, but not dead. Tell me again how it happened?"

Kittredge obliged, covering the details of the previous Friday's meeting between the US ambassador and the Venezuelan president, their respective entourages in tow. He'd recounted the events enough times now that his memory was becoming tainted by the act of recollecting.

He wasn't sure how Hugo Chavez had become infected, but he was sure that Fredericks and Quinn were somehow behind it.

"It would have happened without your help," El Grande said. "And from your description, I am not certain whether you helped at all, no?"

Kittredge nodded. He'd merely been the side show, the stooge whose dry, biased presentation on the economic benefits of Venezuelan oil interests selling out to corporate American overlords had served as both pretext and distraction from the main event: committing an act of biological warfare against a foreign head of state.

A long silence hung between them.

"What now?" Kittredge finally asked.

"For us, even though many things are changing, the things at the center are the same," El Grande said, a distant look in his eye. "They advance. We must resist."

He took a long drag of his cigar.

"You must do the dead drop tonight," he said. "It is an important moment for us. We need a victory, however small."

Chapter 26

Sam felt perspiration run down her back, and she fanned her shirt. One glance across the aircraft aisle told her that Brock was just as uncomfortable. Sweat dripped from his brow. The overweight security guy looked like he might have a stroke, but he continued to glare occasionally in Sam and Brock's direction.

The Freedom Air Charter International bizjet had landed without incident at the Panamanian airport more than two hours earlier. The captain had opened the door and deplaned, but beseeched them in no uncertain terms not to leave the aircraft. "It is best not to strain our delicate relationships here," he had said. "If you still want to reach America, that is," he'd added unnecessarily.

They'd given up speculating where the captain had gone – Brock's theory was that he had a Panamanian honey – and did their best to keep their jangled nerves under control. They weren't sure whether the security goon was there to monitor them or to protect them. Either way, his presence and demeanor did nothing to alleviate the feeling that they were extremely exposed, waiting helplessly aboard an idle aircraft while others decided their fate.

A man in a Panamanian officer's uniform boarded suddenly, startling the security guy to his feet. They exchanged words in a dialect Sam didn't understand. The large security man nodded and returned to his seat.

The diminutive Panamanian officer stood in the aisle between their seats, put an officious look on his face, and demanded to see their passports.

Brock looked at Sam, uncertain. Sam shrugged, equally at a loss. They'd paid a small fortune to the crooked little charter agency for the sole purpose of avoiding situations such as this one.

But there weren't many options. Sam produced her Tricia Leavens passport, and Brock gave his fake passport to the officer as well.

The officer looked over their passports carefully. He turned to Brock and Sam, a meaningful look in his eye, and said in perfect English, "I understand you are in somewhat of a hurry. Sadly, it is sometimes difficult to process matters such as this in a timely fashion."

"Passport matters?" Sam asked with false innocence. It was clearly a shakedown. She was inclined to make the little guy work for it, but they didn't have time to mess around.

Brock produced cash from his wallet. Greenbacks. The officer took them without a word, and without thanks, then looked expectantly at Sam. She shook her head.

The officer raised his eyebrows and shrugged, as if to say "I've got all week."

Sam capitulated, paid the bribe, and cursed under her breath as the Panamanian officer left the plane.

Seconds later, the captain returned. "It looks like we are ready to be on our way," he said cheerfully.

Chapter 27

El Jerga opened the hotel room curtains and methodically rearranged the furniture to place the desk within view of the window opening. The aged front desk clerk had looked askance when El Jerga demanded a room with a southerly view – to the south of the cheap hotel was the ass end of a grocery store, picturesquely appointed with overflowing garbage dumpsters and haphazardly stacked wooden pallets – but El Jerga didn't offer any explanation.

He needed the southern exposure in order to provide his antenna with clear line of sight to the geosynchronous satellite positioned over the earth's equator. He attached the antenna to the laptop's USB port, and waited half an eon for the computer to power up, and another epoch for the communications software application to open.

This time he'd cheated and written his password down. He'd reached the limit of his capacity to memorize random strings of numbers and letters. He was aware that some people did such things as a kind of mental sport, but El Jerga had no desire or aptitude to join their ranks.

His password was accepted, and he destroyed the small slip of paper he'd written it on. He opened his browser and a peer-to-peer chat client, logged into another password-protected chat room, and waited.

Two minutes passed. It wasn't like El Grande to be late. Then again, El Jerga realized, he really had no idea whether El Grande had ever truly been the person on the other end of their clandestine computer-facilitated meetings. It could have easily been one of El Grande's minions who'd acted as a transparent go-between.

Didn't matter, really, as long as the money continued to show up in his account. El Jerga's bank was located in the unlikely island location of Vanuatu, a joint British and French protectorate until 1980's Coconut War brought independence – and the freedom to become one of the world's last true bastions of anonymous and private banking. Swiss accounts were for future convicts. El Jerga didn't plan to become one.

A message popped up on the chat page: "Hello, warrior."

El Jerga rolled his eyes and shook his head. *Puta.*

"Hello," he responded.

A string of numbers followed. El Jerga recognized them as geographic coordinates. He used a ballpoint pen to write them on the palm of his hand. No paper trail allowed.

"Understood," El Jerga typed.

"4:48 p.m."

"Understood," El Jerga repeated.

"No mistakes."

El Jerga shook his head again. *Goddamned bureaucrat.* "The last mistake was yours alone," he typed. "I will tolerate no gringo involvement. Full payment due immediately, or I abort."

"Done."

"Verifying," El Jerga responded. He navigated to his anonymous account information, noted the updated total, and nodded with satisfaction.

"Received," he typed, then, "Goodbye." He closed the chat program and browser, turned the laptop off, and disassembled his satellite receiver.

Minutes later, he emerged from his hotel room in shorts, a wife-beater shirt, and flip-flops. He shuffled down the hallway, took the stairs to the ground floor, and made his way to the hotel's business center. As was his custom, he chose the computer furthest from the door, and typed in the coordinates written on his palm.

He studied the street map that popped up, memorizing his route. He paid careful attention to the distance between turns, and he switched to a satellite view in order to study the landmarks around each of the intersections. One couldn't be too careful, and one certainly couldn't have a paper copy of a map in one's possession if things went sour.

He would take the Beltway to the east side of the Potomac River, then exit the highway and loosely follow the riverbank southbound, paralleling the water's meandering journey through the incongruously pastoral region of Virginia just a few miles from the gringo capitol. A second offshoot would take him toward Indian Head, Maryland, and his first destination.

El Jerga called up another set of coordinates, one he had memorized earlier, and familiarized himself with the available routes that would convey him to the evening's second destination.

He thought about what he would do at the second destination. The thought brought a smile to his face, and caused a surge of adrenaline to flow through his body. He buzzed with anticipation. He felt extremely alive.

As was his method, El Jerga planned meticulously, which allowed him to exercise spontaneity in the moment. His preparations enabled him to respond rapidly and with aplomb to any number of contingencies.

He visualized both routes, and several alternatives to each, one more time before cleansing the memory cache and logging off of the hotel computer.

Then he returned to his hotel room, pulled a camouflage-colored duffel bag from beneath the bed, and inventoried its contents: A .45 semi-automatic pistol; a tranquilizer gun; a fillet kit with five blades sharp enough to shave his face, and one dull, rusted blade for special purposes; nylon zip ties; leather straps; a small sledge hammer; two ball gags; automotive jumper cables; two dozen large, metal C-clamps; a power drill; masonry screws; and the *piece de resistance*, an electric transformer with a cord leading to a standard 110-volt wall plug. The transformer had a rheostat on its face to adjust the voltage output. The dial went from zero to deadly.

It was going to be one hell of a party.

El Jerga looked at his watch. His journey would take no longer than half an hour, but he would allot a full ninety minutes. He still had enough time for an hour's nap.

He wanted to be well rested.

Chapter 28

Special Agent In Charge David Phinney, FBI, turned off of the paved road and drove quickly down the gravel lane, following the terrain contours downhill toward the forested bank of the Potomac River. The lumbering sedan bounced on its suspension three times for every bump it encountered. *No wonder nobody but the government buys these cars,* Dan mused. *They really suck.*

The gravel road meandered through gorgeous Virginia forest. It wasn't virgin forest, but it had been managed well in recent years. They crested a promontory, which afforded a view to the riverbed below.

Phinney guided the land-barge to a sloshy stop in front of a large vacation home constructed of logs and river stones. A covered walkway led to a detached garage, almost as large as the home itself. Another path traced a graceful arc to a gazebo with a view of the river, and continued down to a picturesque boat house on the bank.

This is how the other half lives, Dan thought. *I'm still several outrageous crimes away from being able to afford something like this.*

"We're in the wrong business," Phinney observed, obviously thinking along the same lines.

Dan nodded his agreement.

"Recent car tracks," Dan said, pointing to freshly-exposed mud near the garage.

"Saw 'em," Phinney acknowledged. "Sorry, but I need you to wait here again. I'll leave the motor running to keep it cool for you."

Phinney got out of the car, shut the car door behind him, and grabbed a bullhorn from the trunk.

FBI agents encircled the exquisite vacation spot on the river, establishing mutually reinforced fields of fire, looking a bit storm-trooperish in their assault gear.

Dan heard Phinney's voice over the bullhorn, commanding everyone inside the house to come out with their hands up.

Silence answered. More stern direction from the bullhorn, followed by more silence.

Phinney approached the home cautiously, slowly climbing the stairs to the porch. Exquisitely crafted stained glass windows ornamented the front doors, Dan noticed.

He also noticed that one of the doors was ajar.

A sinking feeling settled in his gut, progeny of dozens of similar experiences over the years, many of which had ended very badly for someone.

He watched Phinney ring the doorbell and announce himself again; moments passed without a response, and Phinney rapped heavily on the door.

Dan found himself holding his breath.

Agents flanked Phinney on either side. Dan saw him use his fingers to count backward from three. When his index finger disappeared at the end of the countdown, Phinney opened the door all the way and stepped inside.

Dan saw a flash, and heard the unmistakable report of a

shotgun.

His mouth fell agape. It looked as if Phinney's torso, everything above his sternum, had disappeared completely, replaced by a cloud of pink. The remainder of Phinney's body seemed to linger, suspended upright by inertia, then fell in slow motion to the marble floor inside.

The agents flanking Phinney turned and started a panicked retreat back down the front steps, but Dan knew that they couldn't possibly move fast enough.

The bright flash surprised Dan only with its intensity. The fireball consumed the remaining two agents on the stoop, hurling parts of them onto the front yard and beyond. Gore splattered the windshield in front of Dan's face, and he flinched.

Flames engulfed the front of the house, and smaller explosions erupted in various other spots within the home. The incendiaries burned with incredible heat, and Dan knew instantly that it would be hours before anyone could step inside.

He also knew that by then, there'd be little actionable evidence left.

Dan felt fear, sadness, anger, and weight. He'd never imagined Jarvis could be capable of something quite this venomous. *He's gone way too far,* he thought, watching pandemonium erupt among the ranks of the remaining FBI team.

Now what? The FBI team would be anchored at this site for hours, regrouping, licking their wounds, mourning their losses, picking through rubble with tweezers in a desperate search for leads. All the while, Jarvis would be putting distance between himself and the task force.

He began to feel helpless, staring at the flames licking out from every window within view. He knew he had to move. Jarvis certainly wasn't sitting still, waiting to be captured, convicted, and sentenced to death.

His feeling of helplessness grew, until he became aware of the cool breeze on his face. The air conditioner was on. Which meant the engine was still running.

Dan slid across the sedan's bench seat into the driver's position, put the car in reverse, turned around, and made his way back out to the main road.

He didn't know where he was going.

But he had the beginnings of an idea.

Chapter 29

The Venezuelan bizjet containing Sam, Brock, and the fat, sweaty security guy made its approach over the lush Maryland forest. Brock looked out his window at the Indian Head Naval Support Facility, amazed once again at how ugly military installations tended to be. He was an Air Force snob, and he felt that Navy bases were far uglier than average, possibly because they invariably defiled some of the most beautiful coastal real estate on the planet.

Seconds later, the jet touched down on US soil, and both Sam and Brock breathed audible sighs of relief. They felt fairly certain that Jarvis still had people out trying to kill them, but they felt their odds had improved dramatically following their escape from the heart of VSS territory.

The jet taxied up to a nondescript terminal building. The small rural airport wasn't exactly among the world's busiest, but that suited their purposes perfectly.

The pilots shut down the engines and opened the door, leading Sam and Brock inside the small building. A stylized sign declared the building to be the property of PelicanAir, a name neither of them had heard before. Perhaps Pelican was a US subsidiary of Freedom Air Charter International. Or perhaps it was the other way around. Tough to know who owned whom.

The large security guard positioned himself just inside the

building's entrance. He didn't face out the window, as he would have done if he were guarding the building from intrusion. Instead, he faced Sam and Brock. Her lingering questions about the man's purpose instantly disappeared. The fat guy was there to keep them in line.

"It has been my pleasure assisting you," the captain said, formally and somewhat cloyingly. He looked at them expectantly.

Bucking for a tip, Sam realized. *Relentless.* "Sorry. You guys have already extorted my bottom dollar," she said, smiling sweetly.

The pilot laughed uncomfortably, and motioned them toward the reception desk. "We have arranged ground transportation for you," he said. "My associate has the details."

They approached the desk. "Your car is waiting outside for you," a nubile young clerk announced.

"Thank you," Sam said. "But I'm wondering if there's a car rental place nearby."

The clerk was taken aback, but recovered quickly. "Sure, ma'am. Maybe a mile from here, on the main road. Your driver will be able to take you there, if you wish."

"That won't be necessary," Sam said. "We've been sitting all day, and would like to stretch our legs." *And we don't get in cars with strangers while there's a contract on our heads.*

"As you wish, ma'am. I'll inform your driver." Sam watched her pick up the phone, dial a local number, and dismiss the car.

Brock and Sam watched a black limousine depart the parking lot and disappear down the sparsely-traveled road. Then they set out on foot for the rental agency, walking the fine line between carefully observing their surroundings and appearing paranoid.

Along the way they discussed their strategy. There hadn't been much chance to formulate a game plan during the plane ride because of the presence of the security guard. He'd certainly have eavesdropped, and Sam was convinced the entire Venezuelan charter operation was in the information business just as much as the travel business.

"Should we try to go home?" Brock asked.

"I suppose that depends on what's happened with Jarvis," Sam said.

She turned on her burner, and dialed the contact number Dan had given her. He answered right away. "Damn glad to hear from you," he said.

"Likewise! How are things?"

Dan caught her up on the fruitless search of Jarvis' home, and told her about the grisly scene at his vacation home. "Three dead for sure, maybe a couple more wounded," he concluded.

Sam shook her head. "I'd never have pegged Jarvis for the type."

"That's always the type," Dan said. "Hey, sorry, but I've got to cut this short. I'm working something on the other line."

"If circumstances permit, don't make a move on Jarvis without me."

"Sure. If circumstances permit," Dan said. "Gotta run."

The call ended.

Sam grabbed Brock's hand and broke into a run. Time was suddenly of the essence. She wanted to be there to put a round between Jarvis' eyes in case he resisted arrest.

* * *

The sleepy rental car clerk was anything but swift, and Sam was nearly beside herself by the time they emerged from the office with a set of keys in hand.

Tricia Leavens had sprung for the rental. There was no other choice, but it was a very bold move. If Jarvis or his minions still had access to Homeland systems, he would be able to follow the purchase and pinpoint their whereabouts instantly. And he would be able to use the rental car's embedded tracking device to follow them at will, and strike whenever it suited him.

Their plan was to exit the rental car lot, drive out of sight, and remove the car's locator beacon from its home in the engine compartment, adjacent to the battery.

Another question popped to Sam's mind that she hoped Dan could answer. She thumbed the power button on her burner, bringing it back to life as she pulled up to the rental company's exit kiosk.

Gnarly looking tire shredders deterred anyone from exiting the premises without first receiving the rubber stamp of the bored employee seated in the tiny metal box.

Sam handed the rental agreement and her Tricia Leavens driver's license to the man inside the shack. Something about the man struck her as vaguely familiar, but she couldn't place it.

Something also struck her as wrong. The man was dressed more like a limousine driver than a rental car employee. And he wore black leather gloves, despite the warm fall weather.

It clicked.

This was their "prearranged transportation," courtesy of Tom Jarvis and the VSS.

Sam gripped the shifter to jam the car into reverse.

But she wasn't fast enough. She heard a noise like *ssssip,* and felt a sharp, painful sting in her neck.

She turned toward the man in the kiosk, noticed the strange-looking gun in his hand, and heard the *ssssip* noise twice more as the man fired the gun across her face, toward Brock.

Everything seemed to grow distant from her, and took on a surreal quality. *Something should really be done about this,* she observed, feeling the car door open, vaguely registering the clatter of her phone falling to the floor, the involuntary movement of her body onto Brock's lap, the strong shove that brought her head toward Brock's feet on the floorboard, the pressure of the man's shoulder on her hip to remove her completely from the driver's seat. She barely noticed the acceleration of the car, just before her world faded completely to blackness and silence.

Chapter 30

El Jerga – The Shiv – Venezuelan Special Services operative, killer, deviant, and psychopath, could barely contain his excitement.

But his years of practice and discipline kept him relatively focused and attentive to the very important matters at hand. He left the pimply-faced rental car employee asleep beneath the counter in the tiny kiosk, lowered the tire-destroying barrier, and drove the rental car off the lot.

Two turns and several miles later, he was far enough into the Maryland forest to risk stopping to reposition the two comatose gringos in the passenger seat. He got out, opened the passenger door, and shot each of them with another dose of tranquilizer.

He admired the redhead draped across the man's lap, and ran his hand up her athletic legs and onto her ass, pausing to feel the warmth between her legs. He laughed, tingling with anticipation, then forced himself to get back to work.

El Jerga lifted the woman to his shoulder, popped open the trunk with the key fob, and set her inside. He used one of his many knives to remove the anti-kidnapping latch release handle on the inside of the trunk door. It would ruin his day if the girl awoke early and liberated herself from her temporary imprisonment.

He had big plans for her.

As he drove away, El Jerga suddenly had the feeling that he had missed something important. It was a feeling that struck from time to time, prompting him to take a mental inventory of all the steps he'd taken to cover his tracks. He was more excited than normal – the redhead was an exquisite specimen, and he was beyond anxious to enjoy her – but if he had indeed missed something, he couldn't conjure what it might have been.

He resolved to double-check everything when he arrived at his destination.

Chapter 31

Kittredge retrieved the information from his computer at the embassy without incident. He didn't vary the ritual, and he left the embassy compound with a USB drive full of secret State Department correspondence hidden in a dark body cavity.

He felt anger and guilt.

He hated Quinn and Fredericks, hated what they stood for, and hated the part of himself that had joined in their cause. Coerced or not, he was one of them – an Agency thug, who'd taken part in yet another CIA hit.

Sure, the thing wasn't quite finished yet. Chavez was in deep kimchi, but he wasn't quite dead. But if the news reports were to be believed, it was only a matter of time.

He seethed as he made his way to the train station for the dead-drop. He was ashamed of what his associations made him. He was mad enough to kill, and the irony wasn't lost on him.

Once at the station, he used the bathroom stall to remove the protective cylinder housing the USB drive. He washed it off, removed the drive, tossed it in a duffel bag, and walked to the bank of lockers.

Locker number 69 was already taken.

It was a curveball he wasn't expecting. "Dibiaso," aka Avery Martinson, according to the red-headed DHS agent, had always ensured that locker 69 was free, and Kittredge had nearly forgotten the contingency plan: use locker 96.

He deposited the coins, shut the duffel bag inside the locker, removed the key, and left.

Kittredge had expected something dramatic to happen at this dead-drop. El Grande had hinted that something big was in the works. And the unusual timing of the drop – his handler had insisted on an early evening drop, instead of the normal time in the early afternoon – also hinted that the CIA might have had an ulterior motive as well.

The whole situation is about some ulterior motive. Arturo Dibiaso was a CIA agent. Kittredge had been "selling" State Department secrets to the Agency. The entire thing was asinine, and Kittredge still had no idea what it was really about.

He looked around the train station, expecting to recognize someone from either the Agency or the VSS.

But he saw no one familiar.

Disappointed, he left.

He had it in his mind that he was going to get thoroughly drunk, perhaps even excessively so.

Chapter 32

The large GM land yacht drove horribly, but that didn't stop Dan Gable from keeping his foot on the accelerator. The commandeered FBI vehicle had a decent engine, at least, and he was approaching a hundred miles an hour.

He had just spoken with Ferrari of North America. They'd serviced Jarvis' various Ferraris a number of times, and had recorded the codes embedded in the RFID chips in each of the high-end tires. It was a feature of the new, wired world in which microchips were cheap and ubiquitous.

It had taken a few minutes for Dan to work his way through the tiresome phone answering service, but once he'd spoken to a cognizant adult, Dan got a quick response.

Of course, Ferrari didn't have the equipment to ping the RFID chips from a distance, eliciting an electronic response that could be tracked via satellite. That was something only Homeland could do. And probably the NSA, and the CIA as well, in addition to a few foreign governments, but for Dan's purposes, his own employer would be able to get the job done nicely.

That was a much quicker call, and five minutes later, he had a team of Homeland techs working on pinging the RFID chips in Jarvis' Ferrari tires, and another couple of agents performing similar legwork with Maserati and Lamborghini.

He expected the task to take them half an hour at best, but Dan was surprised when his phone rang just a couple of minutes later. One of Jarvis' vintage sports cars was on the move, apparently a 1984 Testarossa.

The team passed him a set of coordinates to plug into the FBI cruiser's navigation system. The navigation solution resolved on the GPS display, and Dan smiled at his good luck. Jarvis was just seven miles away, still heading south. *We might get this asshole yet,* he thought.

He radioed the Bureau dispatch desk to fill them in and request backup.

He was going to need some help.

* * *

Dan blasted past slower cars on the highway, his foot planted firmly on the accelerator. It had taken him a while to find the cruiser's emergency lights, but once he flipped them on, traffic got out of his way, and he started making much better time.

He was multi-tasking, which was rarely a good idea while driving a car, and an even worse idea while traveling at three-digit speeds.

But it couldn't be helped. He had to coordinate the efforts of two very large federal organizations and a municipal police department, and that was the kind of thing that could take months.

Unfortunately, he had minutes.

His first priority was to scramble the FBI task force in pursuit of Jarvis, who was now much more than just a bad boss. He was now a murderer and a dangerous fugitive. He had booby trapped his vacation home, and the resulting conflagration had taken the lives of three FBI officers. He was sure the Bureau would respond quickly.

As he drove, Dan tried to put himself in Jarvis' head. On the surface, the middle-aged bureaucrat's actions seemed to betray desperation, Dan thought. But his recent investigation into Jarvis' activities told him that there might be more to it than just a panicked response to the mounting pressure of multifaceted intrigues coming unraveled over the past several days.

There was something ice-cold and calculating about setting a lethal trap in a place that would surely be visited by federal agents of one flavor or another.

If Jarvis had any hope of receiving anything other than the death penalty for his crimes, those hopes had certainly evaporated. Spies killing spies was one thing, but blowing up feds on the job was quite another. It was a calling card that begged a jury to fry him.

It was also the kind of move that even made an arrest less likely. Not that Dan or someone else wouldn't eventually find Jarvis – they most certainly would, as it was nearly impossible to stay hidden anywhere on the planet for more than a few months. It was just far more likely that certain *complications* would arise during the attempt to apprehend Jarvis, the kind of complications that would certainly pass muster upon internal review, but that would result in the unfortunate demise of the suspect before he could be tried by a jury of his peers.

Jarvis' deadly treachery meant that he was very likely to receive a de facto trial – and speedy execution – by his *true* peers: the federal agents whom he had betrayed, and the survivors of those he'd murdered.

It was also possible that Jarvis had used the explosion and fire to destroy additional evidence. Based on intimate knowledge of the inside of Jarvis' work computer, Dan surmised that there must be a significant amount of very damning evidence on a hard drive or two somewhere else in the universe.

If that was indeed the case, Dan wondered what kind of information Jarvis could possibly be trying to cover up. Three counts of first-degree murder would be nothing to sneeze at, so the implication was that Jarvis had something even more heinous to cover up.

Another possibility was that the trap at his vacation home was a diversion designed to give Jarvis more time to orchestrate his escape. It had certainly resulted in a solid head start, if the geolocation algorithm Homeland used to find Jarvis' Ferrari was accurate.

Dan was working hard to make up time, but he had a sinking feeling that he was fighting a losing battle. He was chasing a guy who was driving one of the most famous sports cars in the world, after all.

Or, Jarvis could have just gone completely batshit crazy, Dan thought. People came unhinged all the time. Jarvis must certainly be under incredible stress, with the Operation Bolero investigation tightening around his neck, Homeland operatives just a couple of steps behind him and catching up rapidly, lingering and damning financial ties to a rogue state's internal security apparatus, and a CIA problem that had little chance of ending peacefully. He could imagine how Jarvis might believe there wasn't much to lose.

This belief was false, of course. As soon as the Agency caught wind of recent developments, they would descend like a plague of locusts, and they would round up Jarvis' family to use as leverage against him. The CIA employed a particular kind of professional for just that purpose. To Dan's knowledge, no other government agency had the gumption or stomach to employ similar methods. It would get ugly.

The navigation system interrupted Dan's cogitation. "Turn right at the next exit. At the next exit, turn right. Turn right now." He was driving so fast that the computer had a tough time keeping up. He flew up the exit ramp, leaving the beltway behind for a less crowded four-lane country highway.

Gable wondered what was behind Jarvis' decision to exit the interstate. *If I were on the run*, Dan thought, *I would just keep the pedal to the metal.*

But I wouldn't be driving a vintage Ferrari. Only an idiot would try to escape in a high profile sports car like that.

Of course! Could it be more obvious? Jarvis had to be exchanging his car.

Dan cursed at the realization, and stood on the accelerator. There was now even greater urgency behind his desire to locate Jarvis as quickly as possible. Finding the murderous bastard would be exponentially more difficult if he wasn't driving the beacon-red coupe, and the identification chips embedded conveniently in its designer tires.

"Turn right," the navigation system ordered.

Dan cursed again.

The destination was a park-and-ride facility, served by trains and buses every few minutes. Whatever else he might have been, Jarvis wasn't stupid.

It took almost no time to locate the parked Ferrari.

It took much longer for Dan's anger to subside.

Jarvis was long gone.

Chapter 33

Sam awoke. Her head felt dull and groggy, and everything had a faraway feeling. It seemed very difficult to concentrate, but something deep inside her told her that she had to try, that something very important depended on her regaining her wits.

With great effort, she opened her eyes. She discovered that she was looking at a damp cement floor in a dimly-lit room. The air felt musty and close, though the reverberations of a distant mechanical hum seemed to indicate that she was in a very large space.

She couldn't make her eyes focus properly.

I've been drugged, she realized with horror.

She felt the urge to rub her eyes, and wanted her hands to oblige, but they refused. She tried harder, but they refused more.

Curious about the reticence of her own hands, she raised her head to look at them, inciting excruciating pain in the back of her neck.

Apparently, she had been asleep in this position for a while, her neck supporting the weight of her head at an awkward angle.

As the pain subsided, she turned her head to the right, and worked hard to focus her eyes. She wanted to understand what was the matter with her right hand.

It seemed perfectly fine, except that it was fastened very securely to a cement wall by three large, metal loops, one each at her wrist, elbow, and near her shoulder. She surveyed her left arm. Same thing.

She looked down at her legs, noticing them for the first time since consciousness had returned.

She was completely naked, and clamped to the wall by four more metal straps, one each at her ankles and knees. Her legs were splayed, as if she were imitating Da Vinci's famous Vitruvian Man.

Sam felt panic constrict her neck, and an involuntary cry started in her throat, but was stifled by something very large and uncomfortable in her mouth. She tried to shake it loose, but it wouldn't budge, and she became aware of the straps around her head holding it in place. A ball gag.

Panic set in.

She thrashed against her restraints, chafing her arms and legs painfully, but the clamps were fastened securely to the cement cinder blocks. None of them so much as wiggled.

She was bound, nude and silenced, completely helpless.

She looked around frantically. Next to her clothes on the floor sat a small pile of smashed plastic and circuit boards. Her burner phone.

Tears welled. There was no hope of calling for help, and no hope of even turning the phone on, hoping for someone to locate her.

I'm going to die here.

Motion caught her eye, and she looked up. A weak light shone on a nude figure across from her.

Brock!

He was also fastened to a cement wall, perhaps twenty paces in front of her. He was gagged and also naked, but their captor had fastened him to the wall sideways. Brock's head faced to Sam's left, his feet to her right, and his head lolled about as the sedative wore off. Her eyes had trouble focusing on him, but she noticed no obvious signs of injury, and she felt a bit of relief that he hadn't been harmed.

More motion.

A short, stocky figure entered from beyond her field of vision.

Sam shivered uncontrollably, and abject panic threatened to descend on her. *Get your shit together,* she coached herself, remembering her hostage training. *Keep your wits about you. Talk to this guy, become a human in his mind instead of an object, make him like you, find some leverage to use.*

Her diaphragm fluttered as the man walked slowly to Brock. Latino, somewhat short, broad shoulders rounded forward, strong. He was carrying something in his hand, but it was on the other side of his body, so Sam couldn't see what it was.

He removed the gag from Brock's mouth.

"What do you want?" Brock asked, his speech still slurred by the sedative.

The man didn't answer.

He turned to face Brock, his back now to her, and Sam could see what the man held in his opposite hand. A sledge hammer.

The man took two steps back from the wall, gripped the sledge hammer with both hands, and leaned in with his torso.

Sobs formed in Sam's throat.

Then angered, pained, panicked screams, as the man swung the sledge hammer in a wide arc, connecting with a sickening *crack* against Brock's ankle, just beyond the last metal clamp that held the rest of his leg fast against the cement wall.

Brock howled in agony.

Sam screamed in terrified anger, but the sound barely escaped past the gag that was almost large enough to dislocate her jaw. She thrashed futilely against her straps.

Brock screamed, in grievous agony, pulling against his own restraints, his foot hanging by mere sinew at a grotesque angle to his shattered shin. "I will kill you!" he bellowed. "I will fucking end you!"

Still the man said nothing.

Sam saw him push the gag toward Brock's face. Brock jerked his head to the side, and caught the man's finger in his teeth, biting down hard.

The stocky Latino man cursed in Spanish, swung his fist, and connected with a dull thud against Brock's right eye socket.

Dazed, Brock ceased his resistance. Through her enraged tears, Sam watched the man shove the handle of the sledge hammer into Brock's mouth, pry his jaws apart, and jam the ball gag back in, fastening the straps behind Brock's head.

Brock yelled and thrashed, but his words were absorbed by the gag, and each movement jostled the ankle that had just been destroyed by the hammer blow. He slowly settled down, and Sam heard him moaning softly as the analgesic of shock slowly gave way to incredible agony.

The man gave Brock time to get on top of the pain. He waited patiently while Brock's spasms of agony subsided. Then he batted

Brock's foot with the handle of the sledge hammer, sending it swinging grotesquely, shards of bone grinding against muscle and nerves.

Brock passed out.

Sam sobbed, tears of rage and sorrow blurring her vision.

The man turned to face her. He dropped the sledge hammer on the damp concrete floor. He walked toward her slowly, deliberately, as if savoring his approach to her, taking in every part of her naked vulnerability.

He moved out of the shadows and into the light thrown from far above, and Sam shuddered as she saw his face for the first time.

What she saw in his visage was as frightening as anything she'd seen in her life.

She didn't see a menacing scowl, a lascivious leer, or anger of any kind.

Sam saw the placid, joyful visage of pure evil. She saw his two black eyes, and his bandaged nose.

And she saw a horrific scar on the man's throat. It was a scar she recognized.

The switchblade on the bus.

He approached slowly, inexorably, stalking her until his face was within an inch of hers, his eyes brimming with barely-contained excitement.

She thrashed in vain against her restraints, trying desperately to smash her head into his already-broken nose, the nose she had smashed just two days earlier during his attack on the bus, but it was of no use. She couldn't reach him.

He leaned in, inhaling her scent, and placed his lips softly on her neck. She felt his hand travel lightly up her bare thigh.

Sam cried, helpless.

The man violated her with his hand, his eyes closing in pleasure, his hand squeezing, clamping down on her, crushing her, the pain more stark and frightening than she ever imagined possible.

Sam vomited against her gag. She convulsed in torment and terror.

He smiled at her, a terrible, depraved smile of pure malign, then retreated to the shadows.

They would surely die here. She knew it for a fact.

She cried for Brock, for what he had just endured, for the way that she loved him, for the sadness of him having to watch what was going to happen to her, for the sadness of both of them losing their lives, for their shared horror, for the agony of what she knew would be their last moments together.

Chapter 34

Dan heard the chopper overhead. It was either Homeland's emergency response chopper, or the Metro DC police department's ride. Dan couldn't tell for sure, but he hoped it was the former. To the best of his knowledge, Metro IA hadn't yet rounded up all of the crooked cops working for the Venezuelans, and Dan didn't need any more drama.

He dialed the number of Sam's latest burner. It didn't even ring. The call went straight to an automated notice telling him that the user wasn't available.

Helluva time to take a powder, Dan thought. He could certainly use the help.

Dan's next call was back to the local Homeland office's emergency desk. He needed the park-and-ride manager to give him immediate access to the security footage, which meant he needed some top cover. He returned to David Phinney's FBI vehicle and repeated the request with their radio dispatcher. More firepower rarely hurt.

He paced, thinking and cursing. He had no idea how long ago Jarvis had arrived at the commuter parking lot. It was an important thing to know, because it would tell Dan how many trains and buses had stopped since then, which would tell him how many trains and buses the search team would have to stop in order to look for Jarvis.

It was tempting to ask the impromptu task force to stop all

public transportation traffic that had passed through the station in the last half hour, but Dan quickly dismissed the thought. It would demand far more manpower than was on the entire duty shift at the moment.

But he knew that with each passing minute, the odds of finding Jarvis still riding on any one of those buses or trains diminished exponentially. Every stop was another opportunity for Jarvis to step off, change his transportation medium, and gain yet another step on the investigators.

Still no sign of the park-and-ride manager. Dan looked at his watch, shaking his head.

He tried Sam's number again, hoping she might have an idea. Same result: not available. He gripped the phone tightly in his fist and clenched his jaw, the only two outlets for his frustration at the moment. *Where the hell is the station manager?*

Where the hell is Sam?

Evidence rules be damned, Dan finally decided. He couldn't wait any longer.

He went back to Phinney's FBI cruiser, opened the rear driver's side door, and pulled the deceased agent's black jacket from the rear seat.

Then he walked to Jarvis' Ferrari, draped the FBI jacket over the driver's window, and positioned his feet in an athletic stance. He put every ounce of his considerable strength into the blow to the window, which he delivered with his right forearm. His martial arts training had taught him to swing through the target, and he felt almost no resistance as the window yielded.

He heard the muffled but satisfying sound of shattering glass, then reached into the Ferrari to retrieve the parking stub Jarvis had pulled from the automated dispenser at the parking lot's entrance.

6:17 p.m., the stub announced. Twenty-two minutes ago.

It was a start.

He radioed the information back to FBI headquarters.

The duty dispatcher thanked Dan for his effort, then said that the supervisory agent in charge wished to relay to him that the Federal Bureau of Investigation still had the reins for the Jarvis investigation. Dan was to stand down immediately.

"Roger," Dan said, exasperation evident in his voice. It certainly wasn't an unexpected move on the Bureau's part – they had three dead agents, after all. But it was an unwelcome command.

And one that Dan had no intention of obeying.

Chapter 35

Kittredge planted himself in his customary seat at the bar around the corner from his apartment. He'd stopped at home for a shower and a double belt of ice-cold vodka before venturing out for the evening, and was enjoying the onset of the pleasant distance that came with inebriation.

Without a word, the bartender brought him his usual: a vodka and vodka, with a splash of vodka. A drinker's drink if ever there was one.

Kittredge glanced at the television. The news loop was all about Hugo Chavez's sudden outbreak of cancer. The talking heads speculated about the number of days that might be remaining in Chavez's life, based on the frequent comings and goings of one Dr. Javier Mendoza, one of Venezuela's foremost liver pathology specialists. If Dr. Mendoza was involved, the on-scene reporter speculated, the situation must be grave.

Official reports denied that Chavez was experiencing anything other than a minor and temporary health glitch, which did nothing but fuel further speculation about El Presidente's impending demise.

There were vague reports regarding some of El Presidente's family members and close associates also undergoing hospital treatment, though details were sketchy.

We've unleashed a plague, Kittredge thought, tossing back his drink and tapping the bar for another.

We are *a plague,* he thought, with alcohol-enhanced melodrama.

A sharp, painful clap on his shoulder interrupted his thoughts, and a familiar voice in his ear induced instant bile: "Hiya, Petey, partner of mine!"

Kittredge shook his head and sighed. "I like you less each time we talk, Quinn."

"No need to be antisocial!" Quinn said with over-the-top cheer. "I'm here to express my gratitude for all of your help over the past few days. Banner week for the good guys."

Kittredge felt the familiar darkness descend over his mood as he was brought face-to-face with what he'd become: an agent of chaos, corruption, and, now, death.

"What makes you think we're the good guys?"

"I don't. But doesn't it make you feel better to say it?"

Kittredge snorted. "What did you infect Chavez with?"

Quinn laughed. "Me? Why, I was just there to listen to a bright and distinguished economist. I don't know about anything else that might have gone on."

Kittredge shook his head. "Please. I'm not an idiot."

"Then don't act like one. Questions kill."

"So do contagious diseases."

"So I'm told."

"His family is getting sick now, too."

"Whose family?"

"El Cucaracha."

"Don't you mean, 'la cucaracha?'" Quinn corrected. "That

noun requires the feminine definitive article."

"Thanks for the grammar lesson, but I didn't come up with the codename for Hugo Chavez."

"Now you're just being silly," Quinn chided. "No more spy novels for you, partner."

"Don't play games."

Anger flashed in Quinn's eyes. He turned to face Kittredge. "Okay, Kittredge. No more games." There was a malignant hardness in his voice.

"Here's our new deal," Quinn continued. "Listen closely. You shut your hole. If you keep running your mouth about this subject or any other subject you know you shouldn't be talking about, I will stuff you into your shoe."

Kittredge fell silent. Quinn's menace had penetrated his buzz and struck fear into him.

But Quinn wasn't finished. He reached into his pocket and retrieved a digital camera, which he turned on and switched into the "view photos" mode. He flipped through a few photos, then handed the phone to Kittredge. "Arturo Dibiaso sends his thanks. This is what you helped him do today."

Kittredge didn't want to take the camera, and he certainly didn't want to view whatever Quinn wanted to show him.

Quinn leaned in close. "Look at what *you* have done," he hissed. Kittredge saw feral hatred in Quinn's mismatched, wolf-like eyes.

Kittredge steeled himself, then looked at the camera as Quinn held it in front of him. He saw a man lying prone in a pool of blood.

Kittredge's stomach turned.

Quinn advanced to the next photo, a close-up of the corpse's face.

Kittredge recognized the genteel handsomeness instantly. It was Rojo.

His heart sank, and he suddenly felt faint.

Quinn advanced again. El Grande lay slumped, arms tangled awkwardly beneath his torso, face distorted by the exit wound.

"One of the cleanest mop-ups we've ever had," Quinn said. "They were obviously expecting us. But they definitely weren't ready."

Kittredge shook. He was overcome with fear, rage, loathing, and utter disgust.

The camera beeped again. Alejandro this time, but barely recognizable, so gruesome were the injuries to his face and head. Kittredge closed his eyes, and the tears came.

"There's one more," Quinn said. "You won't want to see it, but I'm going to make you look."

The camera beeped one last time, and Kittredge shook his head from side to side, eyes still closed. "No," he said. "Please tell me you didn't. Please."

Quinn waited patiently.

Something within Kittredge compelled him to look. He had to know for sure. He opened his eyes.

His tears distorted the image, but they didn't hide the long, flowing dark hair, mottled by blood, or the exquisite, familiar neckline leading to a beautiful, angelic face, somehow beatific and peaceful after a violent and painful death.

Maria.

Kittredge's world spun. He was only vaguely aware of his own sobs, barely cognizant of Quinn's large frame moving away from him, a hard but understanding look in his wolf eyes, leaving him alone to wrestle hell's worst demon: his own unrelenting guilt.

Chapter 36

Consciousness returned mercilessly. The pain had caused her to pass out, but it was the pain that had awakened her again, sharp and jagged in places, but also dull and deep inside of her. Her body convulsed involuntarily as her mind became aware again of the hideous nightmare.

The metal clamps cut into her skin, but there was a new discomfort, too: something dangled from the oversized gag that was shoved in her mouth and strapped into place. She could feel its tug as she moved her head. It was a cord of some sort.

She surveyed her body, naked and bruised, strapped with metal clamps to a cement wall.

Sam looked more closely at the clamps, and saw that a wire ran between each of them, sealed between the restraints and the metal screws that held them in place.

A sense of foreboding took over her mind, and fear returned with a vengeance.

She looked around quickly for something, anything, that might be able to help her out of the situation, but there was nothing but the pile of clothes, the shattered cell phone, and a duffel bag on the floor filled with God knew what manner of depraved things.

Motion caught her eye again across the room, and she saw Brock struggle against his own restraints, still hanging parallel with the floor, his ruined ankle still dangling at a grotesque angle, sweat glistening on his forehead as he battled the excruciating pain.

Unsupported by restraints around his midsection, Brock's torso sagged toward the floor, and Sam realized that there was another tormentor working its unseen evil against Brock's body: suffocation. His breathing was shallow and labored, the awkward twist of his body forcing his diaphragm to fight against gravity's pull with each breath he took.

Tears of rage and sorrow welled again. Sam yelled to him, hoping the sound would carry past her gag to Brock's ears, and he would know that he wasn't alone in his suffering, that she would be with him to the end.

Their eyes met, and she hoped that the contents of her heart were visible in her eyes from across the room. Tears streamed down her face, and she saw moisture glint across the bridge of Brock's nose as his own tears streaked their way to the damp cement floor beneath him.

She heard a sound coming from deep within the shadows of the large room, and her breathing quickened involuntarily. Her heart pounded, and she felt the sickening crash of adrenaline land in her stomach.

He appeared, walking first to Brock, grabbing his broken foot, twisting with a sadistic hatred that Sam couldn't fathom. Brock howled in agony. Veins bulged in his neck and his face turned red, and she could hear his tortured voice despite the distance and the large metal ball stuffed in his mouth.

This man was the devil incarnate.

He twisted Brock's foot yet again, and Brock's thrashing

intensified, until, mercifully, nature took over and Brock lost consciousness, succumbing again to an agony beyond the brain's capacity to endure.

Satan turned toward her, his face flushed with exhilaration, a vicious smile on his lips. He stalked toward her, and Sam felt her bladder vacate with fear and terror as her body shook uncontrollably.

At least Brock won't have to see this, she thought.

The man stopped at the duffel bag on the floor, rummaged, then pulled out a strange-looking box with a dial on top and a cord protruding from one side.

He disappeared into the shadow beyond the reach of the bright bulbs shining on her naked body, returning moments later with a bright orange power cord.

With dramatic deliberateness, the man made a show of plugging the strange box into the extension cord. He walked slowly toward Sam, and reached his hand out to touch her leg. She shivered in revulsion as he ran his hand up the length of her body, pausing in places that caused her to shake and cry, then abruptly grabbed and yanked on the cord attached to the gag in her mouth.

Her head jerked forward, and she watched the vile little devil of a man plug the cord into the metal box.

With a salacious grin, he flipped the switch.

A pain like Sam had never known coursed through her body. Every muscle contracted, and the force of her thrashing tore her skin against the metal restraints.

It seemed to last forever, and just when it felt that her life was about to end, the current stopped just as abruptly as it had started.

Breathless, she slumped against the clamps that held her body fast, gasping to inhale through her nose.

The man held the device in front of her face, and Sam watched him turn the voltage dial just a little bit higher.

He flipped the switch, and the excruciating pain began again.

Chapter 37

"Mind if I get a closer look?" Dan Gable leaned in and zoomed the park-and-ride security camera monitor to focus on the 1984 Ferrari.

"Gorgeous car," the security guy said. "What does that guy do, rob banks?"

"Worse. Can you print me a screen capture with the time stamp on the bottom?"

"Sure thing. Cost you extra, though."

Dan didn't laugh. "I'll need you to fax it, too." He wrote down two numbers and gave them to the security guard as the printer spit out a near-photo quality picture of Tom Jarvis stepping out of his ostentatious sports car. He had a package of some sort in his hand, and a small backpack over one shoulder.

Dan let the video play, and watched Jarvis walk outside of the camera's field of view, heading east toward the train and bus pavilion. "How do I follow this guy through different camera views?"

Having two things to do at roughly the same time seemed to addle the security guard. "You want me to fax this, or babysit you on that thing?"

"Fax first."

Dan heard the numbers dial and the paper feeder pull the page into the whirring fax machine. "Nice work," he said. "They should promote you. Now show me how to use the video system."

With a couple of pointers, Dan quickly mastered the overly complicated video monitor system. He watched Jarvis walk from his car, drop the package into a nearby trash can, and take the pedestrian walkway across the highway to arrive at the platform for the northbound train.

Jarvis inserted cash into the automated ticket dispenser, retrieved his ticket and change, and nonchalantly took his place among the other passengers awaiting the train. Six minutes later, he stepped onto the fourth car from the front. He reappeared briefly in the camera's view as he took a window seat, then disappeared as the train roared off, heading back toward downtown DC.

"Phone," Dan commanded.

"Are you gonna bust that guy?" The security guard handed the receiver to Dan and slid the phone's keypad toward him on the cluttered desk.

"No, I want to find out who cuts his hair."

Dan dialed, then cursed. The phone was on a closed switch.

"Dial nine to get out," the guard said helpfully.

It rang, and the Homeland response desk operator picked up. "Special Agent Dan Gable, badge 52317. Code orange, repeat orange, Metro park-and-ride at Backlick Road, Springfield."

"Standby," the operator said. Dan heard a click, then elevator music. *Surreal.* He bounced his leg impatiently, replaying the surveillance video to see if he'd missed anything the first time through.

The phone clicked again, and the operator came back online.

"Units rolling, Agent Gable. Please pass details when you can."

Dan described the situation. He took pains to avoid mentioning that the suspect was Deputy Director Tom Jarvis. It was best to sidestep any bureaucratic confusion, and let the operators do their job unencumbered by worries of blowback based on the perp's elevated administrative position.

"Request you direct emergency speed," Dan finished. "The suspect is fleeing from a sabotage and arson scene with three dead FBI agents, and he threw a package into a trash can at the park-and-ride."

Dan heard the operator relay his message to the lead response vehicle via radio in the background. "ETA?" he asked.

"Thirteen minutes, sir."

"Not fast enough. Chopper?"

"That's the thirteen minutes, sir. The cars will be there in about twenty-five minutes."

"You've got to be kidding me. We're a stone's throw from downtown."

"The chopper's departing from Andrews now, sir."

Dan had forgotten that they'd moved the response team's air support arm to Andrews Air Force Base in Maryland. It was just a few miles further away, but it made a difference in this case.

"Okay. I'll try to control the area. Please call the FBI to coordinate. They technically have the lead on this pursuit."

"Then technically, we can't respond without their approval."

"Not true. Life-and-limb clause." Dan was referring to the carte-blanche that allowed all emergency services to operate across jurisdictional lines to prevent imminent public injury or death. "We'll apologize later if their panties get bunched up over it."

"Shouldn't we also involve the Metro PD in that case? Seems like they'd be closer."

Dan cursed. There was significant risk that the Metro cops who responded would be part of the ring of VSS traitors who had spent the week chasing Sam. On the other hand, if he directed the operator not to contact the local police, and something bad happened that could have been avoided with more on-scene manpower, there was no way he would be able to stand the heat. Worse than that, his conscience would tear him up for years.

"Yeah, please call Metro, too," he said reluctantly.

Dan hung up and dashed outside of the security office, sprinting toward the trash can containing Jarvis' package in order to establish a safety perimeter. It was a quarter mile from the security kiosk.

Dan was thankful that the parking lot was mostly empty. If it had been a weekday, the lot would have been filled with commuters making their way home from the city.

But the parking lot wasn't completely abandoned. Dan's heart leapt into his throat when he saw a young mother pushing a stroller near the far corner of the lot, not more than a dozen feet away from the trash can containing Jarvis' package.

"Ma'am! Stop!" he shouted. "Please stop walking! It's not safe!"

He was too late.

A bright flash erupted, followed by wall of heat and a

thunderous explosion. Dan instinctively hit the pavement and covered his head, feeling the lick of flames and the attack of debris shards against his clothing and skin.

The shock wave had barely passed when he leapt to his feet again, charging toward the site of the explosion, hoping against hope that the young mother and her child had somehow survived.

He couldn't help thinking of Sara and his own kids as he dashed down the row of cars toward the source of the smoke and debris. Auto parts, garbage, and shards of glass lay strewn about.

Something caught his eye as he flew past. He turned to look. It was a stroller wheel, still attached to its support, but torn completely from the stroller by the force of the explosion.

Dan stopped running, his throat suddenly burning with grief and choked rage. *Jarvis, I will kill you if it's the last thing I do,* he vowed.

* * *

Dan sped northbound into the city, driving the dead FBI agent's cruiser as fast as it would go, lights blazing and siren blaring.

It had taken him a while to compose himself after the grisly explosion at the parking lot, but he hadn't waited for the cops to show up to secure the scene. He'd simply jumped in Phinney's car, radioed back to the FBI, and used his burner phone to contact the Homeland emergency response dispatcher.

The dispatcher filled him in on the latest in the Jarvis pursuit. Metro PD officers had stopped the northbound train in between two stations along its route, sealed off the cars, and conducted a car-by-car search. The operator mentioned a fortuitous event: there happened to be four Metro cruisers in the vicinity, and it took very little time for them to arrive and begin searching the train.

Handy little coincidence, Dan thought.

Dan wondered aloud when the FBI had arrived to search the train, and the answer was telling: Metro had already searched four of the twelve cars when the FBI response team arrived.

"Let me guess: they found nothing," Dan said glumly. The operator's affirmative response confirmed his suspicions.

So Jarvis has Metro help, he concluded.

But it wasn't a conclusion he was yet willing to discuss openly and indiscreetly. It was best to have found the smoking gun before accusing the police department of such a serious breach of the public trust. He decided to take a different tack.

"Can you tap into the commuter rail security footage remotely from your terminal?" he asked the dispatcher.

"Not directly, sir," the operator said. "But I can conference with the on-call cyber specialist. I'm sure they'll be able to view the footage."

"Have them assemble every second of footage they have on the northbound train that left the Backlick station at 6:29 tonight. And I do mean everything, including things like storefront and warehouse security cameras that might have caught the train passing by, things like that."

"Sounds like a big job," the operator observed. "When do you need it?"

Dan stifled the urge to ask whether the operator was mentally challenged. "With a murderer on the loose?"

"Sorry. I'll have them call the entire team in right away. Is there anything else?"

As a matter of fact, there was. Dan asked the dispatcher whether Special Agent Sam Jameson had phoned in anytime recently.

He was afraid he already knew the answer, and he wasn't wrong. "Nothing from her, sir," the operator told him.

"Write this number down," he said. He pulled his burner phone away from his face, futzed with the call log menu while driving with his knees at over a hundred miles an hour, and shouted Sam's burner number at the operator. "Run a full trace, even more quickly than the video footage."

He ended the call by charging the operator with calling him the instant she had an update. Things had taken an extremely ugly turn over the past hour, and Dan had the feeling that more bad news was on the way.

He drove over the crest of a hill and caught sight of the flashing police lights adjacent to the stopped train. He had nothing better to do than to join the search of the commuter cars, but he already knew the effort was futile.

Tom Jarvis was long gone.

Chapter 38

Sweat poured from Sam's brow, and her hair hung in damp strings across her face. The pain came in waves, and the short, stocky sadist had learned how to adjust the depth and duration of the electric shocks to maximize her pain while preventing her from enjoying the relative respite of losing consciousness.

The current caused her muscles to contract, and painful, bloody trenches formed in her arms and legs where the metal restraints held her fast. In a strangely surreal detachment, Sam heard the sound of her own screams as if they came from someone else, muffled by the oversized, electrified steel ball stuffed in her mouth.

Sam mustered the strength to raise her head and look at Brock, and she regretted it instantly. He had reawakened after passing out from the pain of his broken foot, and he was watching every agonizing second of Sam's torture at the hands of the vicious little man. Tears of helpless rage streaked his face, and she could see him struggle to breathe as his midsection sagged. He was still strapped horizontally to the wall by his arms and legs, and the awkward position of his body forced his diaphragm to fight against his own weight to draw each breath. He would suffocate slowly, she knew, dying only after his abdominal muscles had destroyed themselves trying to keep him alive.

In the meantime, he watched helplessly while Sam slowly met her own grisly demise. *Close your eyes, baby,* she urged him silently. *Don't watch this. Nothing says you have to watch.* She blinked at him, telling him she loved him, telling him it was okay if he had to let go before she did.

Her tormentor stepped in between them, something shiny in his hand. A blade.

Fear penetrated her exhaustion yet again as the man stepped toward her. Her insides twisted, and she wretched as she felt his tongue on her naked body.

Deep and slow, the first cut caught her by surprise. The pain was excruciating, unbearable, intense and horrific in a totally different way than the electrocution. Her body twisted and writhed, fighting against the inexorable strength of the clamps holding her fast to the wall, and the man responded with more pressure. The blade dug ever deeper, and she heard her own otherworldly howl again.

She felt warm liquid dripping in frightening quantity down her leg, then the warmth of the demon's tongue as he lapped at her blood. He pulled away long enough to smile at her, streaks of crimson on his lips and teeth.

Then he brought the knife to her skin again.

She locked her eyes on Brock's, praying for the end to come quickly for both of them, but knowing with grim, apocalyptic certainty that it would not.

Chapter 39

Dan had a conversation with the FBI agent in charge of the manhunt, and he left convinced that the Bureau was more than competent enough to handle all but the toughest fugitive situations.

Unfortunately, Jarvis had proven himself to be far more than just an average fugitive. Dan's earlier assessment of the man – that he was a milquetoast bureaucrat, castrated by his years behind a desk doing everything possible not to make waves – had proven woefully wrong. Jarvis had shown himself to be ruthless, cunning, and brazen.

And frighteningly well prepared. David Phinney's torso had been vaporized by a close-range shotgun blast, and the other two agents had died a fiery death as incendiaries detonated all through Jarvis' vacation home on the river.

Jarvis had then executed a nearly-flawless escape, utilizing the anonymizing effects of public transportation and the stultifying effects of creating multiple crime scenes to cover his retreat into oblivion. Bombs and casualties soaked up manpower, as the task force had to stabilize each new scene he created, leaving fewer agents immediately available to continue the manhunt.

And Jarvis had wisely chosen to hop on a crowded train, knowing that searching each car for clues to his whereabouts would take further time and resources.

And then there was the Metro Police Department connection. Dan had personally processed the computer evidence linking Jarvis to the crooked cops. He was certain that the cops' clandestine duties would undoubtedly include helping to extricate Jarvis from the immediate vicinity, and spirit him away to safety, out of view of Homeland and the FBI. After all, Jarvis himself had paid the Metro guys handsomely.

Dan harbored no delusions that the swarm of agents and police officers that had descended on the train and the two bombing scenes would find a hot lead pointing to Jarvis' whereabouts, and he racked his brain trying to anticipate Jarvis' next move.

Where would I go if the cops were helping me get there?

The answer that popped immediately to mind wasn't a happy answer: *Any damn place I pleased, and nobody would stop me.*

As the DHS chopper circled overhead, Dan concluded that Jarvis was long gone.

The burner phone in his shirt pocket buzzed. He answered the DHS operator's call.

"Two updates, sir," she said. "First, the cyber team has the transportation system video copied and cued up for you to see, but they're still working on gathering the other video feeds with a view of the train or its passengers. That part could take a while, they said, maybe even a couple of days."

"Thanks," Dan said. "I have another tasking for you. Find out how many Metro PD cruisers have departed any of the three scenes, and find out where they went."

The emergency response operator was silent for a while, then said, "I'm not sure how to even get that one started, sir."

"Start with their dispatch desk. Be sure to involve their

Internal Affairs team. Mention something called Operation Bolero. That should get the ball rolling nicely."

Then his stomach twisted as another thought struck. "What about that trace on Special Agent Jameson's phone?"

"That's the second update," the operator said. "Was she in Venezuela? We thought they were spurious hits, but it looks like there were actual phone conversations, and we didn't get anything really steady until a few hours ago."

"What happened a few hours ago?" Dan asked.

"The phone finally came on nice and steady, and stayed on for a good hour or so. It started to look like a normal cell phone record. But it's turned off again."

Oh, no. Dan's heart pounded. Sam would never leave her phone on for an hour.

He took a deep breath. "Listen carefully," he said. "Hang up. Get that chopper to land in the field to the west of the stopped train. Text me the last coordinates on that cell phone record. And call me back in three minutes with the Secretary on the line."

"Got it. Whose secretary do you want me to get?"

Dan shook his head. "The boss. The goddamned Secretary of Homeland Defense. Quickly!"

Chapter 40

The human mind could adapt to almost anything. It was designed to ignore repeated stimuli and pay attention to novelties, new things.

It could even learn to ignore extremely important things. Like pain.

But not the kind of pain that the small, stocky, Latino man had inflicted on Sam over the past hours. That kind of pain caused the brain to howl, to scream, to fight, to detach from itself, to peel away from the reality in which it found itself, running away from the unacceptable glimpse of its imminent end.

Sweat and blood streamed from all over Sam's body. She'd wanted to implore the vicious little man to stop, to bargain with him somehow, to figure out what he wanted and maybe make a trade of some sort, but he hadn't uttered so much as a word, and he hadn't once released her from the stifling, claustrophobic discomfort of the ball gag in her mouth.

She'd broken and swallowed part of a molar, involuntarily clamping her jaw shut against the steel ball as wave after wave of vicious electricity had torn through her. The pain of her now-exposed nerves brushing against the steel ball in her mouth swirled with the competing agonies of electrocution and dozens of bleeding knife wounds around her body, in her arms, legs, and abdomen.

Sam looked again into the ugly little man's eyes, beseeching him to display some semblance of mercy, or even the slightest vestige of human compassion and empathy. But she saw something far more frightening than rage or fury in the man's gaze.

She saw joy.

Her tormentor reveled in her suffering. He wasn't making an example of her, exploiting her for some tidbit of information, using her to send a warning to someone else. He was simply savoring her unspeakable agony, her utter violation.

It was the same look she had seen before. But it was different now. He'd had his way with her for hours. But his demented, joyful gaze told her that her pain and suffering hadn't sated his appetite, but merely whetted it.

In that moment, Sam Jameson resolved to die as quickly as she could.

As he went back to work on her exhausted, bloody body, she barely noticed the low-frequency vibration in the wall that suspended her, the whump-whump that should have been hopeful and familiar.

But the man noticed. He stopped cutting her, and he looked up at the ceiling, as if the noise was somehow coming from the roof of the building. She saw the horrible scar on the man's throat, and wondered if maybe that wasn't somehow the reason for his pure, unadulterated evil and hatred.

The noise and vibration grew louder, until it seemed to come from everywhere at once, and Sam vaguely registered the piercing whine of a turbine. In her exhaustion and terror, she didn't recognize the significance of the noise, but she saw a change in the man's visage, saw him look around quickly and with increasing urgency on his face.

The building rattled with the powerful vibrations, jarring her battered and butchered body, making breathing difficult, and she saw that the man had begun hurriedly throwing things into his duffel bag, as if to leave.

Was he bugging out?

Would it be possible to survive this, to see another sunrise, to hold Brock again, to feel love and joy and happiness?

He stood before her again, the electrical device in his hands, twisting the dial as far as it would go, reaching for the switch with his thumb.

So it ends.

Her heart broke for the loss of herself, for the loss of her days, for the end of her life together with Brock.

She heard the click of the switch. Electricity seared through her consciousness, destroying her body, arching her back once again in horrific, burning agony.

There was a loud crash, the painfully bright intrusion of daylight into the chamber of horrors, rapid movement, gunfire, the shouting of a familiar voice, the appearance of a familiar form running toward her, but Sam comprehended none of this.

While her body continued to thrash in the relentless onslaught of the overwhelming current, Sam surrendered to the blackness.

Merciful and swift in the end, Sam's death ended her suffering.

Part 4

Chapter 41

Today

Sam felt Brock's chest heave with exertion. Her arms were hooked around his neck, and he was still carrying her. Seconds before, Brock had pulled the hospital elevator's emergency stop, and Brock, Sam, and a sobbing nurse shared an otherwise empty elevator car stopped somewhere between the fourth and third floors.

"That bastard is persistent," Brock said, setting Sam down on the floor. "Dan shot him yesterday. I didn't expect him to be on us so quickly."

"Is that what happened?" Sam asked. "I don't remember."

"You were busy," Brock said. *Busy dying,* he didn't say. He shuddered at the thought.

Sam climbed down from Brock's arms. Her legs were still shaky and rubbery, byproduct of the hundreds of volts that had seared her central nervous system.

Movement was agony. Every muscle in her body was knotted and cramped. The current coursing through her body had caused all of her muscles to contract uncontrollably, and there wasn't any part of her body that was pain-free.

She was also covered in stitches. The twisted bastard had sliced into her skin, purely to cause pain and suffering. He could have just killed her, but he lacked the modicum of human decency that simple murder would have entailed. Instead, Sam's killer had relished every shriek of pain and agony he had elicited from her.

And he was just a few feet away from them, gun in hand, trying for the third time to end her life. More precisely, she thought, he was trying to kill her, which would be the third time he'd done so. The doctors said that she had died twice already.

"What now?" Brock asked. He had a black eye and a large cast around his ankle. Sam wore a hospital gown, and nothing else. A stray bullet had killed the orderly accompanying them to the fMRI room, and Sam and Brock were both splattered with gore.

And the nurse wouldn't stop crying. Loudly.

"Do you mind?" Sam asked her. "Tough to think, with all of that noise in here."

"We can't stay here," Brock observed. "He'll pry those doors apart on the floor above us and get in here through the elevator car ceiling."

Sam eyed the nurse, who had an elaborate key ring attached to the lanyard around her neck. "Any of those keys give you access to restricted floors?" Sam asked.

The nurse nodded.

"Make it happen."

"It's the tenth floor though. We'll have to go back up past the floor that guy's on."

"Your key doesn't let you bypass the other floors?"

The nurse shook her head. "A couple of years ago, a patient died while the team waited for an elevator. They took out the override function after that."

"Okay. Got your phone on you?"

She shook her head. "Not allowed while we're on duty."

Sam cursed, then pushed the "call" button on the elevator control panel.

"Who does that call?" Brock asked.

"No idea," Sam said. "But we can't risk unstopping the elevator, because we have no clue where it will take us."

They heard the sound of a phone ringing. It rang a dozen times before someone answered. "Metro Fire Department, state your emergency."

"Thank God," Sam said. "Can you override the controls on this elevator from where you sit?"

"Maybe. Are you stuck?"

"We're stopped between two floors. There's a gunman on the floor above us."

"A gunman?"

"Can you make this elevator go directly to the tenth floor, without stopping anywhere else?"

"Why the tenth floor?"

"It's restricted," Sam said. "The gunman can't get there."

They heard banging above the elevator car, and the groan of metal and machinery.

"Need you to hustle," Sam said. "He's prying the door open on the floor above us."

"Just a sec," the operator said.

"Hurry!"

"Okay, got it."

Nothing happened.

They heard more mechanical grinding from above the elevator car, and then the deafening roar of a gun's report. Several rounds tore into the elevator car, and a ricochet pierced the nurse's foot. She screamed.

During a pause between howls and gunshots, Sam heard the operator's voice shouting over the speaker: "Take off the emergency stop!"

Brock pounded the red button, and the elevator lurched to life, driving upwards.

Several loud thumps on the elevator car's roof told them they were too late. The man had climbed atop the car, and was trying to break in through the ceiling. The nurse's cries intensified as she realized the situation had taken a deadly turn.

"Can we ram him into the top of the elevator shaft?" Brock asked.

Sam looked at the elevator control panel. The tenth floor was the top floor of the building. "Guess we'll find out."

They heard more pounding on the elevator car ceiling, loud and insistent, as the car crawled upward at a glacial pace.

Then more gunfire. Sam and Brock instinctively flattened themselves against the side of the elevator as the rounds ricocheted inside the elevator. The nurse screeched again, a red splotch growing around an entry wound in her shoulder.

The onslaught of flying metal mercifully ended, and they heard a loud thump on the roof of the car, just seconds before the elevator dinged to announce their arrival on the tenth floor. The assassin had apparently flattened himself against the elevator to avoid being crushed between the car and the top of the shaft, Sam thought.

She pulled on the doors to get them to move apart faster.

More gunshots roared, and more screams, but Sam couldn't tell whether the nurse was hit again. As soon as the doors snuck far enough apart, she squeezed through the opening and moved down the hallway as quickly as her battered limbs would carry her. Her hospital gown flapped in the breeze, failing to conceal her nakedness beneath.

Brock followed, the clump of his unwieldy foot cast announcing every other footfall. The nurse staggered behind them, then collapsed just a few feet beyond the elevator. She'd been hit again, but Sam couldn't tell where.

The elevator doors closed, and the car retreated back down the building. Sam had no idea where the attacker had gone, but she hoped he was still on top of the elevator, gliding down to a lower floor.

Sam stopped the first medical-looking person she could find, and pointed to the nurse lying on the floor amidst a growing pool of red. "Help her!" she commanded.

Then she took Brock's hand and continued down the hallway in her halting, pain-wracked dash, looking for an unlocked door to duck into. Twenty paces later, she found one, charged through, and surprised a half-dozen doctors and nurses in a small break room.

"Special Agent Jameson, Homeland," she said. "I need your lab coat," she said to a medium-sized male doctor.

It took some cajoling, but the doctor finally relented, and Sam donned his white doctor's garb. "Thanks," she said. "Which way to the stairs?"

A stunned nurse pointed in the direction opposite the elevator lobby. "I'm not sure what's going on, but should we call the police?" she asked.

"Those are the last people on earth you should call right now," Brock said as they rounded the corner and resumed their dash down the hallway.

"There's an active shooter. Stay here and lock the door," Sam instructed, calling over her shoulder as she shuffled painfully down the hall. "And don't open it until someone lets you out!"

They charged through the stairwell door, and made their way down one flight of stairs as quickly as their injuries permitted. Brock's painkillers had started to wear off, and he winced with every step.

"What's the plan, baby?" he asked.

"Hang on," she said. She peered through the glass window on the door leading into the ninth floor, looking for signs of shooter-induced chaos, but the hallway appeared serene. She opened the door and led Brock into the first unoccupied hospital room she could find, then closed and locked the door behind them.

"We obviously need to get out of here, but we need to be smart about it," Sam said. "Wouldn't do us any good to make it out of the building, just to be gunned down on the street."

She picked up the phone, dialed nine to bypass the hospital switchboard, and rejoiced when her guess was rewarded with a dial tone. She dialed all sevens. She had no idea which cab company she was calling, but one taxi service or another had laid claim to that telephone number since the dawn of civilization.

Five minutes, the dispatcher said. That's how long it would take for the cab to meet them at the hospital's service entrance.

It wasn't much time to make their way through the hospital as carefully as they would need to in order to remain undetected. They were certainly concerned about running across the assassin on their way out, but those were long odds. He wasn't likely to remain in the vicinity for very long.

They were more concerned about being discovered by a Metro policeman. Someone would certainly have called in the emergency to the police department, and the hospital would be swarming with cops in a matter of minutes.

A few of those cops would undoubtedly be on the VSS payroll – just like the assassin, if Sam's hunch was correct.

Brock's foot was throbbing, and the pain was becoming a serious impediment. The surgeons had spent two hours reassembling the bones in his foot, and his cast featured shiny reinforcement bars protruding grotesquely in various spots from his foot. Sweat poured from his face as he fought the pain.

"Elevator," Sam said after just a few steps down the hallway. "It's our only hope of making it out of here."

Brock reluctantly agreed. In the time it would take them to descend the remaining nine floors, the cops would surely have sealed off the stairwells.

Sam pushed the "down" button, and they held their breath as a car approached from one of the floors below.

It finally arrived, full of panicked passengers, who poured out of the car. "Don't go!" one of them shouted. "He's still down there!"

"Which floor?" Sam asked.

"First floor lobby!" someone yelled. "Stay up here where it's safe!"

Sam and Brock looked at each other. "I don't think we have that option," she said.

Brock nodded. "Place will be buzzing with Metro guys."

They stepped into the elevator. "Which floor?" Brock asked.

"Good question," Sam said. They could try their luck on the second floor, but they would still have to get past the first floor on foot. The cops and the shooter would potentially stand in their way.

Brock pushed the button for the underground parking garage, and they waited anxiously as the floor numbers slowly clicked by.

Third floor.

Second.

First.

The elevator stopped.

"Balls," Brock whispered. The doors opened. Sam and Brock flattened themselves against the side of the car, expecting an onslaught of gunfire.

Several eternal seconds passed, and then a few more. But nothing happened. And there were no sounds. The first floor seemed deserted.

The elevator doors closed, and they descended to the subterranean parking garage.

"Let's stay sharp," Sam said. "He might've tried to escape

through here."

Brock nodded grimly as the doors glided apart. Sam held down the button to hold the doors open while they peered out into the dim parking garage. Detecting no motion in front of them, Sam cautiously moved her head from the safety of the elevator enclosure to glance on either side of the elevator.

Nothing.

They listened for a few more seconds to be sure. Satisfied, they made their way slowly and deliberately to the up-ramp leading out of the garage, the pain evident on Brock's face with each step.

"I have no idea where we're supposed to meet the cab," Brock said.

"Neither do I. Hope is my strategy."

It worked. They emerged at the top of the car ramp just as a bright yellow taxi pulled up, with seven sevens emblazoned on its side.

"Mr. and Mrs., uh, Entwhistle?" the cabbie asked, holding the rear door open.

"That's right," Brock said, climbing in gingerly. "Nice to see you. We're in a bit of a rush."

Chapter 42

Peter Kittredge slumped in his window seat, staring out at the ocean, his eyes bloodshot from a night of vengeful power-drinking, and glazed from a morning filled with the same activity.

He couldn't get the images out of his mind. El Grande, Rojo, Alejandro, all dead.

And Maria. *My Maria.*

He tortured himself by recalling the details of her last pose, her beautiful, blood-stained face wearing an improbably placid expression.

It was an image that would haunt him for the rest of his life, he was sure.

After Quinn left, Kittredge had polished off the better part of a liter of vodka. He woke up on the floor, stomach acid and bile in his mouth, his apartment reeking of alcohol-induced sickness.

As the morning sunlight blazed through his apartment windows, Kittredge had found another bottle and managed to choke down a few swallows between heaves. Not all of it stayed down, but in time, the shaking in his hands had stopped, and the pounding in his head subsided.

Disease and cure, in the same bottle.

He had made a quick but deliberate decision to fly back to DC. There would certainly be Venezuelan reprisals for the VSS members' slaughter at the hands of the CIA, he figured, and he wanted to be nowhere near Caracas when the blowback started. The same-day tickets had cost a small fortune, but he would have bought them at any cost.

His head swum as he leaned against the side of the airplane, keeping his eyes open to avoid succumbing to the incipient nausea, but too exhausted and too sick to remain completely upright.

One desire reverberated through his mind despite the self-inflicted misery. Revenge. He didn't know how or when, but he resolved to find an avenue to unleash his smoldering anger at the Agency for invading, and then completely destroying, his entire life.

* * *

A steady, comfortable buzz filled Kittredge's head. A couple more drinks on the airplane had chased away a few more demons and further enlivened him. He drank more vodka with lunch, which had painted a pleasant patina over the world.

It was through this chemically-enhanced, nostalgic verdigris that Kittredge viewed the piercing blue eyes that had so captivated him for all these months. And they still held magic, Kittredge realized, feeling the familiar stirrings within him that had bound him inexorably to Charley Arlinghaus.

"Just south of a miracle, they're saying." Charley sounded every bit like himself. Almost mundanely so, Kittredge thought, given all that had transpired in the last nine days.

"You had us all good and worried," Kittredge said, noticing that he wasn't quite able to maintain the sharp edges on his consonants.

Charley noticed, too. "It's early. Drinking already?"

"Drinking still."

"Stress?"

"You could say that."

"What's going on?"

Kittredge laughed, a harsh, angry, sarcastic bark. "Has Quinn been here yet?" he asked.

"Who?"

"Or Martinson?"

"Peter, who are you talking about?"

But Charley's eyes gave him away. They looked too closely at him, Kittredge thought, searching for information. It was a simple deception he could easily have pulled off under normal circumstances, but the weeklong coma had evidently taken away some of the facile smoothness that normally characterized Charley's deceptions.

Anger flared, but Kittredge restrained himself. He had made a decision. He would certainly let Charley know that he knew the deep, dark secrets, but he would also make nice, to see where Charley led, to see what he could learn.

"Sorry, I just thought you might have known them," Kittredge said.

Charley shook his head.

"I finally met Arturo," Kittredge said.

"Dibiaso?" Charley asked. Kittredge noticed the spark of interest in his eyes and voice.

"Yeah. He's CIA, too." Kittredge said with as much nonchalance as he could pull off.

"Like, *the* CIA?" Charley asked.

"Of course." Kittredge looked at Charley, feeling a potent mixture of affection and anger, but doing his best to appear relaxed and detached.

Charley affected a surprised look, but Kittredge waved it off. "No need for that, Charley. I've known for a little while now."

Charley nodded thoughtfully, the look in his eyes intensifying the way it always did when he was concentrating on something difficult. "What is it that you know, Peter?" he asked, speaking slowly and evenly.

"You're not just an executive assistant for Exel Oil. In fact, Exel Oil may not be a real company at all. I think it might be an Agency thing. But anyway, I know you're a CIA agent, and you're helping pave the way for US oil companies to start drilling Venezuelan crude. And in addition to a vicious comb-over, Arturo Dibiaso has a few other names."

"Who attacked me?" Charley asked.

"Any guesses?"

Charley shook his head. A little too coyly, Kittredge thought. *I know you too well to fall for that.*

He reached up to stroke Charley's cheek, but Charley pulled away, a look of mild aversion on his face.

So that's how it is.

He regarded Charley a moment. "I know you were playing me," he said. "But were you *just* playing me?" he asked.

Charley's eyes hardened. "Of course not."

"The two of us. What were *we*, to you?"

Charley paused, a puzzled look crossing his face. "We were always *us,*" he said. "You know that, don't you?"

A small, tired smile found its way to Kittredge's lips. *A classic Charley non-statement, followed by a classic Charley volley back into my court.* "Sure," he said. "But what *were* we? When we were busy being *us*?"

"Why are you using the past-tense? Tell me what's going on, Peter."

"What's going on is this: I learned what's going on. Your friends are now my friends." Kittredge lifted his shirt to show Charley the scabs and scar tissue on his back, artifacts of his midnight Agency initiation ceremony.

Charley sighed heavily and shook his head. "I warned them not to harm you. I swore I would kill them."

"You were indisposed at the time," Kittredge said. "Which reminds me, why the hell didn't you tell me you were going to be in DC? We could have avoided this whole thing. I wouldn't have gone out chasing boys, which got me kidnapped by Quinn and Fredericks, and you wouldn't have been clubbed in the head."

Charley shook his head. "There was no avoiding it."

"So you know who attacked you?"

Charley sighed. "Yes."

"Then you probably also know that you don't have to worry about them anymore," Kittredge said softly.

Charley was quiet, pensive. "They mentioned a successful operation," he finally said.

"It was my fault."

Charley let out a little laugh. "That the VSS attacked me?"

Kittredge shook his head. "No. That they murdered all of them." He fought back tears.

"Don't you think they deserved it? They were not nice people."

There it is, Kittredge realized. *The infinite gap between us.*

"They were *people*, Charley."

Kittredge breathed deeply to stem the flow of emotion. In spite of himself, he thought of El Grande, fighting to keep gringo hands from stealing the riches beneath his own feet, and again of Maria, who trained and struggled and fought alongside those men, and shared her dreams and her hauntingly lovely self with them, too. *My Maria.*

He held his head in his hands and let the tears spill carelessly onto the hard hospital floor. He felt Charley's hand reach out to him, and felt the familiar comfort as Charley's fingers combed through his hair. For a moment, it was almost like it used to be.

Almost.

Kittredge wiped his eyes. "I need a safe place to stay."

Charley nodded, understanding. "Give me a pad of paper," he said. "I'll write down a number for you to call."

* * *

Kittredge inhaled the cool air. Fall had suddenly arrived, and the chill had a sense of seriousness, of foreboding.

I have to do something, he reminded himself, trying unsuccessfully to replace fear and sorrow with resolve. *People just can't go around killing other people over politics.*

He descended the stairway leading from the street to the subway station. He studied the route map. It wouldn't take long at all to arrive at his destination.

It wasn't much of a plan, but at least it was a start.

Chapter 43

Sam and Brock remained alert and largely silent during their cab ride home. There was much to discuss, but nothing they could say within earshot of the cabbie.

Going home was a terrible option, but they couldn't think of any better ideas. They needed clothes, protective vests, firearms, cash, and transportation, and the most efficient way to obtain all of those items was to simply go home and grab them.

But doing so entailed significant risk. By now, their pursuers would certainly have learned that she and Brock had survived yet another attempt on their lives, and they'd have had plenty of time to regroup for another assault.

Sam hadn't memorized Dan's burner number, and she knew his phone lines had been tapped, so calling him for help was out of the question.

And given the reach and audacity Jarvis had displayed in his spectacular escape, Sam suspected he might have inside help from someone else at Homeland. So calling the emergency response desk was probably a bad idea, too.

She had the cab driver make a slow pass through the neighborhood while she and Brock looked for signs of trouble. Finding none, they directed him to their driveway. They exited the car and made their way slowly and painfully up the driveway to their front porch.

Once there, they discovered a significant problem. Over the past several days, the contractors who were repairing the bomb damage at their house had apparently installed a replacement door.

Neither of them had a key to their own house.

"Ah, hell." Brock said, pain-induced sweat beading on his brow despite the cool fall afternoon.

Sam shook her head. "We can't catch a break."

"I don't want to smash a window," Brock said. "The house will be vulnerable after we leave."

Sam nodded. "And I don't want to leave any evidence we've been back."

"Let's do something, even if it's wrong. I'm sure they have someone watching the place, and I don't want to die on my own porch."

Sam agreed. She stepped off the porch and held her hand out for Brock. "Come on," she said. "Time to violate the golden rule."

"What rule is that?"

"You know the one." *Trust no one.* An old clandestine ops instructor of Sam's used to pound that deeply misanthropic advice into his charges, and it was counsel that she had heeded better than most over the years. But with no secure way to get in touch with Dan Gable, whom she *did* actually trust, there were frighteningly few other options.

They ambled over to the neighbor's house, rang the doorbell, and waited impatiently for the kind old spinster to answer.

"My, aren't you a sight!" The old lady's voice was surprisingly strong and clear, especially given her frail, stooped frame.

"Mrs. Manning, I'm terribly sorry to disturb you," Sam said. "But could we borrow your phone?"

Their neighbor agreed warmly. She showed them inside, fussing over Brock's black eye and broken foot. She put on a pot of coffee and served a plate of cookies, which Sam and Brock devoured gratefully.

"Pardon my saying so," the old lady said, "but you kids look positively terrible. Who did this to you?"

Sam shook her head, washing down the last of her cookie with a swig of coffee. "Can't really say."

"What a world we live in. And to think, you kids got beat up like that with all those police cars patrolling around here all the time."

Sam's ears perked up. "Police cars?"

"Yeah," Mrs. Manning said, obviously perturbed. "They drive by here, real slow, eyeballing everything. Must have been a dozen times today."

Sam gave Brock a knowing glance. They didn't have much time.

Here goes nothing, Sam thought. She took a deep breath, and dialed the number every Homeland agent was required to memorize.

It rang twice, then, "Homeland Emergency Response, please state your name."

"Special Agent Sam Jameson."

The operator was silent for a moment. "Please hold, ma'am," she finally said. "You're on my special instructions list."

Shit! Sam's pulse suddenly pounded, and she felt adrenaline settle uncomfortably in her stomach. Her mind raced. Having special instructions attached to one's name at the Homeland Emergency Response desk was rarely a good thing. Had Jarvis set up an automatic alarm to have her brought in?

She thought about hanging up, but knew it was futile. Unlike in the movies, call traces were nearly instantaneous these days. If they wanted to know her precise location, they would already know it by now. It was probably best just to wait and see what the operator had to say.

The phone clicked, and a strong baritone greeted her. "Sam! My God, what a week you've had!"

It was a familiar voice, but one she couldn't place. "I'm sorry, who is this?"

"How presumptuous of me. I'm sorry. It's Vince Cullsworth."

Holy balls – The Secretary of Homeland Defense!

"Mr. Secretary? I don't quite know what to say," Sam said, shooting a meaningful glance at Brock. His eyes widened.

"I couldn't be prouder of your ingenuity and courage over the past week," Cullsworth said. "What a horrific week it's been for all of us, but for you, especially."

"I can't remember worse," Sam agreed.

"Listen, I'm really relieved you're okay," Cullsworth said. "Dan Gable is here in my office right now. Can I ask you to join us?"

Sam felt relief at the mention of Dan's name. "Sure, sir," she said. "But I have a bit of a transportation problem."

"I'd ask you if you'd like a police escort, but under the circumstances, I think that would be in poor taste," Cullsworth said with a chuckle.

Good - he's up to speed on the situation.

"And probably a bit unhealthy," Sam said. "Could you spare Dan for a few minutes to come pick us up? It'd be good to see a familiar face, if you know what I mean."

"Sure thing. He's on his way."

* * *

It took an agonizingly long twenty minutes for Dan to arrive, during which time Sam and Brock did their best to make reassuring small talk with their concerned and very talkative neighbor, while peering carefully out the front window to spot any police cars that might happen by.

Sam recognized Dan's battered minivan instantly as it pulled into the driveway. They thanked Mrs. Manning and piled into the van.

"You both look a helluva lot better than the last time I saw you," Dan said.

"I don't know if the doctors told you," Brock said, "but Dan did CPR on you for ten minutes before the ambulance arrived."

Sam shuddered, recalling the hellish nightmare of the day before. "I remember way too much from yesterday, but I don't remember that part."

"It's tough to form new memories while you're dead," Dan quipped. He smiled a warm, gentle smile, and grabbed Sam's hand. "Seriously, boss, I'm really thankful you're sitting here right now."

She noticed the moisture in his eyes. "Thank you, Dan. It's good to be alive."

Brock shivered. "Watching you die like that…" he said, shaking his head, struggling to keep control of his own emotions.

She clasped his face in her hands and kissed him, wiping his tears away with her thumbs.

"It was no picnic on my end, either," she said. They shared a tearful laugh, then made their way in contented silence toward downtown DC.

* * *

Vince Cullsworth, Secretary of Homeland Defense, was a tall, grandfatherly man with a kind face and a ready smile. He'd run the Defense Department at one point in the nineties, in between the Iraq wars, and the rumor mill held that he was asked to come out of retirement to replace the Vlad-the-Impaler-type guy who was the Homeland secretary under the previous, markedly more conservative administration.

"We've had our eye on Jarvis for just a little while," he said, his deep, mellifluous voice filling the posh corner office with a million-dollar view. "But I really wasn't aware of how deeply involved he apparently was."

"Bolero?" Sam asked.

Cullsworth nodded. "But it really wasn't pointing at him too directly, from what we could tell."

"Probably just a matter of time, though," Dan offered. "He was pretty sloppy, and it took just a little cyber savvy to figure out that he was eyeballs deep."

"That was terrific work on your part, Dan," Cullsworth said. "And a great computer security lesson for an old dinosaur like me."

"Computers are yesterday's wave of the future," Sam said, smiling.

Cullsworth gave her a good-natured chuckle. "Different world than the one I grew up in, that's for sure. Anyway, there's another interesting angle here."

"Let me guess: Metro Internal Affairs is compromised," Sam ventured.

"Clever girl," Cullsworth said. "How'd you figure it out?"

"It's fairly obvious by the way they still haven't rounded up their internal gang. There's a mountain of evidence IA could've used to arrest them all, yet the thugs are still out patrolling my neighborhood."

Cullsworth nodded. "I'm a former prosecutor," he said. "I've seen much more movement on much less evidence, that's for sure. Their story was that they wanted to make sure they caught everyone involved, but it didn't wash with me."

"Suppose we had been killed," Sam said. "Could the commissioner have stood the heat? It's one thing to gather more evidence, but when there's a clear and present danger..."

"Precisely the point I made," Cullsworth said. "I even considered declaring it to be a federal matter, and having Homeland roll them up."

"I'd have appreciated it," Brock said.

Cullsworth smiled. "It certainly was a very difficult decision. At the end of the day, I concluded that doing something like that would have had troubling Constitutional ramifications."

Something bothered Sam. "Surely, IA wasn't considering *not* arresting the gang of VSS moonlighters, were they?"

Cullsworth shook his head. "I don't know. But that would have been blatantly, patently idiotic, and heads would eventually have rolled."

"No doubt about it," Sam said. "But stalling those arrests was a huge risk to take, especially with all the blood and gore going on. They had to have a reason for taking such an outrageous risk."

Cullsworth's eyes twinkled. "You're exceptionally sharp for a woman who's only recently been dead. Dan and I were mulling that very thing when you called a while ago. We reached no conclusions."

"What about Jarvis?" Brock asked. "Didn't he go Unabomber?"

Dan nodded. He recapped the details of Jarvis' spectacular escape. "It was a helluva diversion, and one of the most outrageous escapes anybody's ever heard of," he finished. "No one has the slightest idea of his whereabouts."

Cullsworth sighed heavily when Dan finished. "I don't know what to make of all that, either."

Sam nodded. From the sound of it, Jarvis didn't just escape. He had made a series of statements in the process. The deadly trap at his vacation home sounded like viciously premeditated murder, and the bomb in the parking lot garbage can was senseless destruction of human life. There were hundreds of other ways to create a diversion, but Jarvis hadn't chosen any of them.

And if a person seriously wanted to disappear, it would be fatally stupid to murder three FBI agents, and then murder a young mother and her child. The Bureau would hunt him down to the ends of the earth.

So the question was, was Jarvis just a pissed off, demented individual with the means and motivation to cause serious harm on his way to an inevitably bad death, or was there a method behind his apparent madness?

He's either rubbing our noses in it, or there's something else brewing, Sam decided.

And where does that leave us? If the events of the past hour were any indication, she and Brock were still very high on the VSS' interest list. They were collateral damage, caught in the VSS blowback caused by the CIA's clamorous and heavy-handed effort to get American wells drilled on Venezuelan turf.

But it was odd that the hit man hadn't bothered asking any questions of them. He hadn't been interested in any information whatsoever. Perhaps Dan's arrival had occurred before he'd gotten around to asking his questions, but Sam doubted it. He'd already had them on the rack for a long, long time by the time Dan showed up. She couldn't vouch for Brock's state of mind, but she would probably have told the sick little bastard anything at all he wanted to know, just to get him to stop inflicting such horrors on her.

They were making another statement, she realized. The VSS thought they'd captured two more CIA agents – byproduct of Brock's random carpool journeys with Arturo Dibiaso, aka Avery Martinson – and they wanted to send a message to any and all

Agency assets involved in the Venezuelan operation that the VSS meant business.

Still, one would think they'd be interested in learning a few operational details, but they hadn't bothered. Perhaps they'd learned through past experience that it was difficult to get straight answers from CIA agents. That probably wasn't because Agency assets withstood interrogations any better than other well-trained operatives. It was more likely because nobody did as good a job of compartmentalizing its information as the Agency did. Most agents simply didn't know enough about any particular operation to be all that useful.

"What do you think, Sam?" Cullsworth's question brought her back into the conversation.

"I think it's our job to assume there's an operation in the works," she said. "It was way too risky for the Metro IA guys to postpone arresting a group of violent rogue cops to have done so without a good reason."

Cullsworth nodded his assent, and Sam went on. "Also, it's possible that Jarvis went completely off his rocker and turned into a murderous psychopath, but I don't think that's what happened. My experience with him is that he's reserved and calculating. In that light, my opinion is that his bombing spree also supports our idea that there's something big brewing."

"I like your assessment, Sam," Cullsworth said. "I agree that it's the conservative approach. Let's think about who we want to assign to work the case."

Sam blinked. She hadn't considered for a second that anyone

else would run point on the investigation. It was her case. She was heavily invested in its outcome. After all, this particular case had killed her twice already.

"All due respect, sir, but I think I need to stay on this," she said. "Dan and I know this landscape better than anyone else, and I think we're close."

Dan nodded his assent.

"Besides," Sam continued, "it's not like I can just go home and watch TV. They're driving by my house every hour."

Cullsworth shook his head. "We've already asked way too much of you. I can't subject you to any further danger, Sam. I would never forgive myself."

Sam frowned. "How would you protect us? We know for a fact that Homeland and Metro PD are both compromised, so where would we go that's out of their reach? Every Homeland safe house is out of the question."

"You'll stay at my home," Cullsworth said. "My personal security detail will see to your safety as if it were my own."

Sam opened her mouth to protest, but Cullsworth cut her off. "I'll hear no arguments. Our department has thus far failed to protect you, and the safety of my agents is my personal responsibility."

Cullsworth's telephone rang, and he picked up the receiver. He listened for a moment, frowned, then cupped his hand over the phone. He looked at Sam. "Someone's downstairs at the desk asking about you. Ever heard of anyone named Peter Kittredge?"

* * *

"Jesus, what happened to you?" Peter Kittredge's speech was

slightly slurred, Sam noticed, and his eyes were glassy and bloodshot.

"I could ask the same," she said, laughing. "You look like a frat party casualty."

Kittredge blushed a little. "Rough day." He looked around Cullsworth's office. "Nice digs."

Cullsworth chuckled. "At least by government standards." The mirth left his face. "Let's get down to business. Tell me how you fit into all of this," he said, looking at Kittredge.

"I'm not sure I do," he said.

"I beg to differ," Sam said. "You're involved with both sides. At least, that was the case a day ago when we talked to you last."

"Ah yes," Kittredge said, affecting a reminiscent pose. "You left me hogtied and stranded in a field, if memory serves."

"You weren't stranded," Brock pointed out. "We left you a car."

"A stolen car. Thanks for that."

"Details," Brock said.

"Tell us why you're here," Sam said.

"Simple, really. I have no place else to turn, and I thought you had an honest face. At least," he added, "that's the impression I got when you kidnapped me."

Sam smiled. "I'm flattered. But I thought you had too many relationships with intelligence agencies in your life already, and you didn't want any more."

"That was before the CIA murdered everyone I knew in the VSS," Kittredge said.

Sam shook her head and frowned. "They do that sometimes," she said. "'Low-intensity conflict,' they call it."

"Not something I can be a part of," Kittredge said, his voice thick.

"Not to be melodramatic about it," Sam said, "but I don't think you have much choice in the matter. It didn't sound like you had much negotiating room, master spy that you are."

Kittredge nodded. "But I can't be party to murder. So you understand my predicament."

Cullsworth leaned back in his leather chair, a pensive look on his face. "And you think we can help you somehow?"

"I don't know," Kittredge said. "Maybe. And *I* had hoped to help *you*. If you think there might be a connection between *that*" – he pointed at Brock's cast and Sam's collection of stitches – "and the 'low-intensity conflict' going on right now."

He pulled a crumpled slip of paper from his pocket. "It's not much, but I hope it leads to something. I hope you stop those bastards."

Sam unfolded the paper and read the telephone number it contained. The area code was local.

"Which bastards?" she asked, handing the paper to Dan, asking implicitly for him to start the telephone trace.

A wan smile crossed Kittredge's face. "All of them."

"I'm not in the business of throwing stones from inside a glass house," Cullsworth said, "and my agency isn't exactly a paragon of human rights and Constitutional rectitude. That's part of the reason I was brought in, as a matter of fact. But if there's criminal or unconstitutional activity occurring on American soil, and that activity falls rightfully under federal jurisdiction, it is my duty to act."

Sam smiled a little at the canned speech, even though she believed Cullsworth actually meant what he said.

"I'm glad to hear you say that," Kittredge said. "Because I led the CIA to the VSS agents." His voice turned maudlin. "I got them killed."

Cullsworth nodded thoughtfully. "And you think there will be reprisals," he said.

"I hope not. But maybe."

"We'll protect you," Cullsworth said. He nodded toward Sam. "Please make the necessary arrangements. After you allow my security detail to take you to my home, that is," Cullsworth added. "I insist that you get some rest and nourishment before doing anything else."

"No argument here," Sam said.

Chapter 44

Dr. Javier Mendoza padded down the now-familiar VIP hallway in the Caracas hospital. He didn't relish delivering his news.

He'd never seen any disease develop and spread quite so quickly and virulently. He felt powerless to help his patient, the most powerful man in Venezuela, who would undoubtedly succumb to the devastating disease in a matter of hours.

Mendoza entered President Hugo Chavez's hospital room. El Presidente was unconscious, machines monitoring his vitals.

Chavez's chief of staff met Dr. Mendoza at the door. "I take it the situation is unchanged?"

"Sadly, no," Mendoza answered. "It is much worse than I feared it might be. I've never encountered a disease as aggressive as this one. Even the most powerful drug therapies have failed to slow its advance."

The chief of staff nodded heavily. "How much time do we have?" he asked.

"Please forgive me if this sounds indelicate," Mendoza said, "but are plans in place, in case His Excellency does not survive the night?"

The chief of staff sighed. "This was my fear," he said. "Yes, there are plans in place."

"My recommendation is that we shift our focus to making El Presidente as comfortable as he can be during this time."

"You're saying there's no hope?"

"In my opinion," Mendoza said gravely, "there is no hope."

"Not even if a donor liver can be found?"

"Even if El Presidente were to survive the surgery, which is not guaranteed given his weakened condition, the virus exists in high concentrations in his bloodstream. It would simply attack the new liver. We would buy him only a few days, in the best transplant scenario I can envision."

"What about a blood transfusion in conjunction with a liver transplant?" Chavez's chief of staff asked.

"Akin to pouring clean water in a soiled vessel," Mendoza said. "There are billions of copies of the virus hiding throughout his organs and tissues. I am afraid there is very little that can be done. Even the most extreme measures are unlikely to prolong his consciousness by a meaningful amount of time."

"Thank you, Doctor Mendoza," the official said. "We will naturally seek other opinions, but I thank you for your diligence and dedication."

"Of course," Mendoza said. He turned to leave, but changed his mind. "There's one more thing," he said, "which may be important to you."

The chief of staff raised his eyebrows, signaling Mendoza to continue. "I am not a forensic biologist," the doctor said, "but I am very familiar with all known diseases of the liver. In my opinion, either we're experiencing a new and utterly unknown natural mutation of the Hepatitis virus, one that makes it suddenly among the most deadly diseases on the planet, or…"

"Or what?"

Mendoza wavered. He was about to make a very serious statement, one with potentially far-reaching ramifications. *Just follow the facts,* he coached himself.

He took a deep breath and continued. "Either we're witnessing the first known case of a terribly unlucky disease mutation," he said, "or El Presidente is the victim of an engineered virus."

"You mean an attack."

"I believe so, yes," Mendoza said. "An act of biological warfare."

Chapter 45

El Jerga fumed in solitary silence.

She was dead! And then, she wasn't.

It was unbelievable, inconceivable even, that anyone should survive that kind of voltage, especially after enduring hours of pain and suffering.

The man was a different issue entirely, El Jerga knew. He should have disposed of the man early on in the proceedings. Now, he was left with yet another loose end.

But killing the man would have had an undesirable effect on the woman. She would undoubtedly have given up much sooner. She'd never have endured half of the suffering he'd planned for her, if she'd witnessed her lover's grisly demise beforehand. It was human nature, plain and simple. It would have taken the fight completely out of her.

The message from the *puta* gringo in the aftermath of El Jerga's second botched attempt on the pair's lives had been unambiguous: *I would kill you myself if Caracas allowed it.* The gringo's orders had been equally clear. El Jerga was to wait in silence until the appointed hour, and check in for further guidance using normal protocols.

El Jerga had attempted to contact El Grande directly, but had received no reply. It wasn't like El Grande to ignore him, and El Jerga interpreted the silence as a change in the value of his own stock with the VSS.

Ephemeral things, success and reputation.

Until three days ago, El Jerga had been deadlier than the plague. But the same victim had survived two of his attacks. *Twice!* And just like that, his fortune had taken a dramatic turn.

It was an outrage and an embarrassment, and El Jerga felt something he hadn't felt in years. He was ashamed. And he could hear in his head what they must be saying about him, that he had finally allowed his passions, his enthusiasm and eccentricity, to interfere with his professionalism.

His face flushed as he pondered the thought. He realized, to his further disgrace, that those voices were absolutely correct. El Jerga's joy was in the doing, not in the outcome, and that weakness had driven him, recklessly and foolishly, to prolong the job beyond what was reasonable. It was needless and selfish, and his indulgence had caused serious problems for his employers.

Yet, if the gringo's message was an accurate indication, Caracas still had need of him. For that, he was grateful. And he took comfort in the knowledge that if they did not have further use for him, he would likely already be dead. El Jerga had no illusions that he was the only competent killer in Venezuela's stable. And he knew that there was such a specialty as a hunter of assassins. There was the distinct possibility that the gringo's message was only intended to relax him, El Jerga knew, to induce him to let his guard down in advance of his death. He resolved to remain more watchful than ever.

And much more sober. No longer would he allow himself the

giddy revelry that had driven him to failure. If the job called for a statement, he would surely make one. But the job would come first. His addiction would come second.

He felt his wounded shoulder, tangible evidence of his failure. The slug had passed clean through, but it had taken a chunk of skin and muscle with it. It needed medical attention if he was to remain useful.

He looked at his watch. It was time. He felt anxious, wondering what message he would receive.

As per his instructions, El Jerga dialed a particular number, using a particular mobile phone, one that had been supplied to him for this purpose alone. He allowed the phone call to ring several times, then ended the call attempt before a connection was even made.

Several seconds later, a notification popped up. Though his phone never rang, he had a voice message waiting for him. He pushed the button to listen.

The message contained no words. It was comprised of a series of eleven tones.

El Jerga sighed. He hated these kinds of messages. He tore the top sheet off of the pad of paper on the hotel nightstand, grabbed a pen, and sat on the bathroom floor to write. Using a table would have left a traceable impression on the wood surface that might later be used to reconstruct his activities, but using the hard bathroom tiles as a writing surface would leave no discernible evidence.

Then he set to work identifying the touch-tone phone key that corresponded to each of the eleven tones in the voice message. It was painstaking work for a man with no musical inclination or training, and it took forty minutes before he was completely confident he had all the right numbers.

He couldn't be too careful. A mistake would be more than just costly for a man in his tenuous position. El Jerga knew that a blunder would likely be deadly. If the enemy didn't kill him, his employer certainly would.

El Jerga folded the paper and placed it in his pocket, tucked his laptop computer under his arm, and walked to the hotel lobby, where he sat in silence while his Wi-Fi antenna synced with the hotel's free service.

He called up a map website, typed in the first six digits of the code he had received, typed a single blank space, and then entered the remaining five digits of the code.

The code represented an address. All that was missing was the street name. But that didn't matter, because the Internet would provide the right street.

The last five digits of the message were a US postal code. And the first part of the message contained enough digits – six of them – to ensure that there was less than one chance in ten million that more than one street address within the same zip code began with the same six digits.

Sure enough, Google returned but a single DC street address.

It was close enough to walk, and El Jerga was thankful for that. He needed to clear his head.

* * *

The doctor sewed the last stitch into El Jerga's shoulder. The old sawbones had kind eyes and spoke softly in Venezuelan Spanish, but cursed like a sailor. It struck El Jerga as incongruous.

"These are grave times," the doctor said. "Tragedies everywhere at home."

El Jerga hadn't heard.

"You've been busy," the doctor said. "So they've asked me to fill you in."

The doctor spoke in reverent tones of the dead in Caracas. El Grande. Rojo. The girl, Maria. Even Alejandro. All dead.

El Jerga didn't attempt to conceal his surprise and concern. "This is catastrophic," he croaked.

The doctor nodded. "Si. Most certainly. But it is not the first time these things have happened in our country." He sighed before continuing. "I am afraid that there is more bad news."

El Jerga felt a heaviness settle in his bones as the doctor relayed the news of El Presidente's almost-certain demise. *Biological weapons?* This was a brazen act of warfare, forbidden by treaties the United States had sponsored and ratified! Was there no end to the gringos' hypocrisy and treachery?

"We must retaliate," El Jerga said, the words exiting his ruined voice box as a harsh rasp.

"Si. We must," the doctor agreed. "And we will. I know this for a fact."

"Where are the girl and her lover?" El Jerga asked.

A knowing smile crossed the doctor's face. "Ahh, I heard there was unfinished business."

El Jerga flushed, surprisingly embarrassed by his recent failure to kill the redhead and her consort.

"No doubt you are eager to finish the job you have been paid for," the doctor said. "But she is no longer your responsibility. In fact, I am to inform you that you are forbidden from pursuing that job any further."

El Jerga protested, but the doctor waved him off. "Not to worry," the doctor said. "They have use for you yet."

He reached into his pocket and produced a small envelope, which he handed to El Jerga. "Vaya con Dios, my friend," he said.

Chapter 46

Sam took a bite of chateaubriand and asparagus and chewed gingerly, taking care not to disturb the broken molar in the back of her mouth. The food was delicious despite the pain. "This is amazing, Mr. Secretary," she said. "Thank you again for your hospitality."

"Of course. Least I could do," Cullsworth said. "And for the record, I had nothing to do with the meal. The staff took care of all of it."

Sam, Brock, Dan, Kittredge, and Secretary Cullsworth occupied just a third of the immense dining room table in the Secretary's Falls Church mansion. It was decorated tastefully but exquisitely. Nothing too ornate, but the Cullsworths had obviously spared no expense.

"Maybe I'd formed the wrong opinion about the upside potential of a government job," Kittredge observed, his face flushed from several glasses of wine.

Cullsworth laughed. "No, I daresay your opinion was likely correct. But I do fit nicely into another stereotype. They say that behind every fantastic fortune lurks a fantastic crime. I am a beneficiary of my great grandfather's, shall we say, *opportunism*."

"Only in America," Brock observed.

"Not quite true," Cullsworth corrected. "But *especially* in America."

"So if the pundits are right, I think that leaves either lust for power or a true believer's heart as the motivation for doing what you do," Sam said.

Secretary Cullsworth smiled. "Guilty of the latter, I'm afraid."

"True believer?" Dan asked.

"I most certainly was."

"Past-tense?" Sam asked.

"Alas, I'm a bit ashamed to admit that it took quite a long while for me to lose my naïveté vis-à-vis the political process and the machinery of government," Cullsworth said between bites of roast beef.

"But you've been a Cabinet member twice now, haven't you?" Brock asked.

"I have. Hence my embarrassment. It took me a frighteningly long time to discover that there is no such thing as a national democracy."

Sam was taken aback. That was quite an outrageous thing to say – and it was tantamount to apostasy for someone who reported directly to the President of the United States. "Mind if I quote you, Mr. Secretary?" she asked with a bit of a wicked smile.

Cullsworth laughed. "Please don't, and I must hasten to add that I am a humble servant of the next-best thing, I think, in the form of the style of government we now have."

"I can't imagine the long hours would be all that tolerable if you didn't believe in what you were doing," Kittredge observed.

"Quite so," Cullsworth agreed. "And speaking of my terrible schedule, I'm afraid I must leave you and go back to work."

"Duty calls?" Sam asked.

Cullsworth nodded. "Testimony at a closed session of the Senate tomorrow. Rather a futile thing, but something I have strong convictions about."

"Do you mind if we ask about the subject?" Dan asked.

"There's a piece of legislation that was enacted several years ago with lingering provisions that are up for a renewal vote in the Senate," Cullsworth said. "The Intelligence Reform and Terrorism Prevention Act. I happen to think a few of those provisions shouldn't be renewed."

"Which ones?" Sam asked.

"Wish I could say," Cullsworth said. "Security, and all that. Suffice it to say that the measures went a long way beyond way too far."

He showed a helluva lot of leg, Sam thought. That kind of candor was unheard of inside the beltway, particularly from the head of a huge department like Homeland.

"When is the vote?" Brock asked.

"Tomorrow, after the kangaroo court," Cullsworth said. "Like I say, it's a fool's errand. The ayes have it by two very staunch votes. It's more about my conscience than anything else. Anyway, if you'll accept my apologies for rushing off. . ."

Cullsworth set his silverware atop his dinner plate and left the room with a smile and a wave.

Then he reappeared, ducking his head back into the dining room to add an afterthought. "You have my full support with your investigation, Sam. Anything at all. I just ask that you keep me informed."

"I will, sir," she said.

* * *

They didn't waste any time getting to work after dinner.

Secretary Cullsworth's home was one of three residences on US soil that contained a SCIF, or Special Compartmentalized Information Facility. It was a specially-sealed and protected room, authorized to hold the nation's most highly classified papers and discussions. The Director of National Intelligence and the President of the United States were the other two earthlings who enjoyed similar access. While Brock and Kittredge had a drink and watched television, Dan and Sam disappeared inside the highly-classified room.

They worked quickly to trace the telephone number Kittredge had given them. They didn't have high hopes that they'd discover anything profoundly useful, but Sam firmly believed that due diligence always paid off.

"This is an Agency number, so they'll have a watch on the information surrounding it," Dan said.

"So we'll IP mask?" Sam asked.

"It's a 'best practice,' as the business school kids say. But we'll take it a step further, and IP hop." Dan outlined the arcane and esoteric steps necessary to remain as anonymous as possible while searching for information online.

"Will it be enough?" Sam asked.

"Definitely not, but it'll take them a couple of days to piece things together." Dan's hands moved across the computer keyboard with practiced speed and efficiency. Various windows opened on both monitors.

"Let's hope it's enough time," Sam said.

"Here goes nothing." Dan entered the telephone number into a database query application. Its simple interface hid an exceptionally powerful spy tool.

"This kind of shit is probably what has Cullsworth's panties in a wad," Sam observed.

"I'm sure it does," Dan said. "Remember all those speeches about civil liberties and Constitutional discipline when he first took over the job?"

"How could I forget?" Sam groaned.

"Here we go. The number's registered to Sally Jane Haynes. It's been hers for twenty years."

"DC address," Sam said. Dan pasted it into a browser window and brought up a Google Earth map of the location associated with the telephone number Charley Arlinghaus gave to Peter Kittredge.

Dan laughed. "Those smug bastards." He zoomed in. "They're not even trying. The address is a vacant lot."

Sam shook her head. "What now?"

"Soft-ping, baby." Dan clicked on the icon for a program called Dominion, and a spartan-looking interface appeared.

"I'm lost," Sam said.

"Simple, really. The Agency undoubtedly has a permanent trace on this number," Dan explained. "Whenever anyone calls or texts, the tracing software notifies a human somewhere. Dominion can tell us which humans get notified."

"Handy."

"But nothing's free. They'll know someone in the US government was trying to look up their skirt."

Sam thought for a moment. "Do it," she said. "I don't see much down side."

Dan continued, clicking on the button to start the search.

It took less than a second. The output showed three email addresses. "So these addresses receive a message when someone calls that phone number?" Sam asked.

"Correct. But they all look like organizational email boxes, so they're probably checked by a low-level CIA admin and passed on to the appropriate case officer."

Sam squinted. "Which basically tells us nothing," she said.

"That's my professional diagnosis. Let's try another toy, though," Dan said. He opened a program called Tracer.

"And this fine slice of geekery does what?" Sam asked.

"Nothing much. Just tells us the location of the telephone that would ring if we dialed its particular number."

"You don't have to actually call the number to do that?"

"Nope," Dan said. "It's pure magic."

"This stuff never fails to freak me out."

Dan smiled. "Glad I'm on the good guys' team."

"Glad you know the difference," Sam said. Dan rolled his eyes.

They waited impatiently while the computer did its work. Just under a minute later, it spit out another telephone number and a set of coordinates.

"Uh huh," Dan said. "Just like I thought. Sneaky bastards."

"Translation, please," Sam said.

"It's a dummy number," Dan said. "The call is automatically re-routed to another phone."

"So what?"

Dan typed the coordinates into Google Earth. They resolved to a familiar spot on the map: Caracas, Venezuela.

Sam frowned, thinking. "I don't know if that tells us much," she said after a while. "I mean, we already know the Agency has assets in Caracas. We already know that Charley Arlinghaus was one of them. It makes sense that he'd give Kittredge a phone number for an Agency asset he was familiar with."

"Could also be VSS," Dan observed.

"I don't think so," Sam said. "Pretty sure the VSS was behind Charley Arlinghaus' skull-cracking. I don't think they would suddenly be friendly with one another."

"So basically, we've learned that a CIA agent probably gave Kittredge the number for another CIA agent."

"Yep. Looks like another dead end."

"Unless the CIA is actually behind this whole mess," Dan said.

Sam looked thoughtful, then shook her head. "I've toyed with that idea about a hundred times," she said. "And each time, I end up concluding that it makes no sense. Why fake violent resistance to your own foreign overtures?"

Dan nodded. "Probably right."

"I think it's all about the VSS."

"Which is another way of saying that we've got nothing," Dan observed grimly.

Chapter 47

Tom Jarvis sat in a dark room, enjoying a cigarette. He'd quit years ago, but suddenly felt the urge, and he saw no reason to deprive himself. *Probably won't be lucky enough to die of cancer,* he thought with a gallows chuckle.

It had been a messy few days. He'd argued against the necessity of it, the explosions and bloodshed, but the boss had been adamant.

And the boss paid very, very well.

And it's the last time, ever, Jarvis thought. He had burned every bridge. It was a conscious choice, designed to remove the possibility of ever finding himself in another situation such as this one. He was tired of ideologues controlling his destiny.

Zealots weren't without their virtues, to be sure. For one thing, they were absurdly committed, at least in a financial sense, to their adored misconceptions. They paid outrageous sums for tasks that required just a little bit of skill, and a willingness to set aside a little moral compunction.

That was the beauty of his own innate nihilism, Jarvis thought. It allowed him to profit handsomely from the misguided ideologues, and to put up with them at the same time.

He returned his focus to the task at hand. He had suddenly found himself back in the tactical game, an unfortunate consequence of the slaughter in Caracas, and something he hadn't done for over a decade. The operation was still moving forward, of course, but the Agency had mowed down all of the intermediate assets. So Jarvis was left to further dirty his own hands.

He dialed a phone number. A funny-sounding guy answered. "Airborne Ads, our flying banners get you airborne, this is Mike, may I help you?"

"Hi Mike. Please go ahead, like we discussed. You'll be there by halftime?"

"Guaranteed."

* * *

El Jerga sat in silence, peering out the car window at the football stadium in Landover, Maryland. He needed to sleep, to prepare for what lay ahead, but an assassin's life was rarely about what was comfortable. It was mostly about what was necessary.

The events of the past few days played over and over again in his mind. His emotions traveled between raw arousal as he recalled the exquisite, animal pleasure he'd experienced at the redhead's expense, and the red-faced shame he felt as a result of failing to kill her.

But his redemption would be swift. At least, he hoped his chance to make amends for his failure would arrive swiftly. It all depended on the contents of the message he was awaiting.

It was a big opportunity, involving important gringos, he was told, and he had no reason to doubt the source.

He heard it before he saw it, a loud, low-flying propeller-driven airplane. He craned his neck to see if it was the right airplane, the one he was looking for.

El Jerga wasn't disappointed. He saw a bright yellow crop-duster aircraft, towing a long, billowing banner behind it, flying toward the football stadium just a mile away. "Cutting Edge Optics, 1-800-PRECISE," the banner declared in large, black letters.

El Jerga smiled. The message contained his activation word, *cutting*. He saw the choice of that particular word as a nod to his unique proclivities, and maybe even as a vote of confidence in his personal abilities.

The word had more immediate pragmatic impact, as well. It was his signal to unleash the demons once again.

Chapter 48

Sam and Brock lay together beneath the covers in Secretary Cullsworth's cavernous guest suite, their battered and broken bodies tender to the touch. Alone for the first time since Sam's brief death, their caresses were tender, almost awe-filled. Their kisses and whispers were soft and reverent.

"I watched you die," Brock said, touching her neck with his lips. "It's hard to express how intense that makes everything feel now."

She smiled. "Nothing like a little death to help you appreciate life."

"That was a lot more death than I care to see again, ever. I'm positive that I'm going to have nightmares for the rest of my life."

"You'll be in good company," Sam said with a shudder. "It was horrible. There was something seriously wrong with that guy."

"I just wish we could send out a task force to find him," Brock said. "But I don't know who we'd send after him, given how few law enforcement agencies we can trust at the moment."

Sam nodded, a sigh escaping her lips. "It makes me tired just thinking about it, but I think we're on our own. Even with Cullsworth on our side, we'd still be at the mercy of whoever he put in charge of the investigation, or whoever showed up on the scene." She shook her head. "Makes you realize how fragile everything is."

Brock agreed. "Weird how trust holds everything together.

Nothing really works without it."

"Speaking of nothing really working," Sam said, reaching for the television remote. "I wonder if the Bureau's having much luck chasing Jarvis down."

She tuned to the 10 p.m. local news, surmising that the regional talking heads would likely devote more air time to the DC manhunt than anything else.

Instead, a breaking story dominated the broadcast: Senator Tom Wharton, a Texas Republican, staunch pro-military and pro-intelligence advocate, and a longstanding member of the Senate Select Committee on Intelligence, was found dead of apparently self-inflicted knife wounds.

Flashing emergency lights visible behind him, the on-scene reporter spoke in grave tones about the length and depth of the slashes on the senator's wrists, of the brief hour between when his wife last saw him, alive and in good spirits, and when she made the horrific discovery of his bloody body in the bathtub.

There was no note, the reporter said, but while the Metro police department hadn't yet ruled out foul play, they had preliminarily classified the case as a suicide.

The reporter wrapped up the piece with a brief homage to the senator's lifetime of public service in regional and national politics, then signed off.

Self-inflicted knife wounds, Sam thought to herself as the newscast shifted to footage of a starlet behaving badly in a DC nightclub. *I wonder how self-inflicted they really were.* Sam recalled the scene of Abrams' death, nine extremely long days earlier. There was no way it was a suicide. They'd held Abrams down and slit his wrists, then subdued him while he bled out.

She couldn't help but wonder whether Wharton's death might have occurred under similar circumstances. One could never trust a newscast for accuracy – every news story that she'd ever been personally involved in was reported with a number of irresponsible and sensational-sounding inaccuracies – but it was interesting that the on-scene reporter made a point of talking about the severity of the wounds in the senator's wrists, as if to convey the depth of the man's despair or his absolute commitment to ending his own life.

Coincidence? Probably. Most things like this had random happenstance as their root cause.

But sometimes not.

Her focus returned to the squawking newscast as the topic finally changed to the Jarvis case. Despite extensive Metro PD and FBI cooperation in what had become the largest manhunt since the terrifying sniper case, the so-called "beltway bomber" was still on the loose.

The police were looking for a single individual – they showed an artist's rendering of someone who vaguely resembled Tom Jarvis, Sam thought, but only if you closed your eyes and thought very hard about Tom Jarvis. Authorities believed that a group of extremists might have been behind the attack. "We haven't ruled out terrorist activity," a Metro PD spokesman said. "There has been a rise in militant Islamic jihadist activities in the district," he intoned, a grave look on his face, "and we are working very closely with our FBI counterparts to bring this matter to a swift resolution. Rest assured that these individuals will be brought to justice."

If anyone noticed any suspicious activity, they were to call a toll-free number listed at the bottom of the screen, the news anchor concluded.

"Looks like they have their best people on it," Brock said sarcastically.

Sam agreed. "I wonder how far up the Metro chain of command the VSS infiltration goes."

"They'll pretend to look hard for Jarvis, and never find him," Brock said. "But won't the Bureau have jurisdiction?"

"Sure," Sam said. "But that won't be much help if a few crooked Metro cops are hiding him. They have resources of their own."

"So you're telling me there's a chance…"

She smiled at the stupid movie reference, kissed Brock, switched off the light, and laid her head on his chest. Sleep overtook them in just a few minutes.

* * *

Sam had no idea how long she'd been asleep before she awoke in a cold sweat. In her dream, she'd been trying to get away from the short, stocky man with the black eyes and the crazy scar on his neck, but she was unable to move her limbs, and each time she squirmed, he hurt her more deeply.

She felt Brock's touch on her shoulders. "Shhh. It's okay," he was saying. "I've got you." She had evidently been thrashing.

Slowly, she relaxed, and her heart rate returned to normal. She was alive. She had survived. Brock's arms were wrapped around her.

The devil of a man had hurt her deeply, repeatedly, and in a disturbingly personal way, and he had even *killed* her. But she was awake, alive, drawing breath, experiencing life.

And she was scared. He was still out there. He'd almost killed her for a third time in the hospital. Tom Jarvis was still on the loose, too, probably bearing down on her and Brock, hoping to finish what he'd started.

She breathed deeply, willing her body to settle down, willing her mind to relax, centering herself. *There is no crisis at this moment,* she reminded herself. *Just breathe.*

She nuzzled closer to Brock. Soon his breathing turned heavy and rhythmic, punctuated by the beginnings of a snore, but Sam couldn't sleep. She couldn't turn off her mind. Snapshots from the previous week full of death, danger, and insanity kept replaying themselves, and she struggled to combine them in a way that made sense.

Suddenly, in a flash, it fit together.

Of course!

She had figured it out.

At least, she thought she had. It was the newscast, combined with the dinner conversation. Together, they formed the right lens, and as Sam peered through it at the week's events, she thought she understood what would happen next.

She looked at the clock. Just before eleven p.m. *It might already be too late.*

But she had to try. If her hunch was correct, there would be more bloodshed. She had to stop it.

Sam slipped out of bed. She toyed with the idea of waking Brock, but decided against it. His broken foot and battered body were likely to make him a liability. And if things went sour, she didn't want him in the line of fire. She wanted him to survive, to live his life, to move on, to grow old and be happy.

She dressed silently and slipped out of the room.

Chapter 49

Homeland Secretary Cullsworth's house was dark and quiet. Only the security detail stirred. Sam smiled at one of the guards as she approached the door leading to Cullsworth's five-car garage. "I don't know how you guys don't lose your minds," she said, "standing here in the dark for hours on end."

The guard smiled in return. "What makes you think we don't?"

Sam laughed as she reached for a set of keys from the holder adjacent to the door. "I'm suddenly in need of some feminine particulars," she lied, choosing the key emblazoned with the familiar BMW logo. "I'll just be a few minutes."

"We're not supposed to let you out of our sight, ma'am," the guard said.

"I know, and I appreciate that. So you'll follow me to the store, then?"

He looked around, uncomfortable. "It would leave a hole in our perimeter, ma'am. I'm really afraid I can't let you go."

She leaned in and lowered her voice. "Mother nature's kicking my ass," she said with the air of a confession. "I noticed there's a convenience store just a couple of miles away. It really shouldn't take that long."

"Couldn't you just, um, *borrow* something from Mrs. Cullsworth?"

Sam shook her head. "Menopause."

The guard nodded his understanding. "There's nothing else you can do about, er, *it*?"

"You married?" Sam asked.

"Yes ma'am."

"Then you know it's not quite life-and-death, but it's damn close."

The guard mulled, spoke into the radio, listened for the response of the team lead – also married, the guard told her – and ultimately relented.

"Thanks a lot," Sam said, stepping past the guard and into the warehouse-sized garage. "Be back in a sec."

* * *

Sam drove fast down the long, wooded road leading out of Cullsworth's exclusive subdivision full of elaborate custom homes. Night's recent descent had quieted all neighborhood activity, which didn't strike Sam as being terribly lively in the first place. It was an older, moneyed neighborhood, with lots of physical space between homes, and even more psychological space between homeowners.

She fished into her jacket pocket to fetch her new burner phone, which she had prevailed upon Dan to purchase during their trip to Homeland headquarters earlier in the afternoon.

Sam dreaded making the call. At this hour, after what she'd put Dan's family through over the past week, she would have preferred to call almost anyone else on the planet. But there was no one else on the planet she trusted.

Sam cringed when Sara answered.

"I was happy when Dan told me you pulled through," Sara

said, "but now I'm rethinking."

Sam laughed. "I can't blame you in the least. I hesitate to make promises, but I think we're getting very close to the end of this little soap opera."

"Doesn't matter," Sara said. "It'll just be something else next weekend."

"God, I hope not. My nerves couldn't handle it."

"Mine either. Anyway, I'm glad you're alive. Mostly." Sam heard rustling as Sara handed the phone to her husband.

Dan sounded groggy and strung-out. "Up for a little adventure?" Sam asked.

"What's wrong with you? Don't you sleep?"

"Nightmares. Anyway, this probably won't be easy, but I need it in the next fifteen minutes. And then I need you to join me."

Sam described her hunch, her request, and her plan.

"Sure thing," Dan deadpanned, after Sam filled him in. "I'll turn water into wine, then whip up that address for you."

"Good plan," Sam said. "As an aside, you should be flattered. I wouldn't have called you if I didn't know what you're capable of."

"Thanks, Sam. No matter what Sara says, we're glad you're still around to ruin our lives."

She laughed, hung up, and made her way into the city. She didn't have the exact address, but she had a good idea of the general vicinity, and she wanted to make good use of the time while Dan worked his cybermagic to find the precise location.

Her route through the city took her north on 14th Street, past its intersection with D Street, two blocks west of the Homeland

Security headquarters. She continued north beyond Independence Avenue, and looked idly at the Washington Monument as it passed by on her left side. It was under renovation, and the entire obelisk was surrounded by a cocoon of scaffolding, strangely beautiful in the light of the powerful floodlights arrayed at the monument's foot. Despite its many, many inconveniences, DC was a gorgeous town.

Except for all the assholes, she reminded herself. If her intuition was correct, and if fortune smiled on her, there might be a couple fewer of them on the prowl when the sun rose.

On the other hand, the odds weren't in her favor. She needed backup – a small army's worth, she reckoned – but that was impossible. The trust problem again. There was nobody to ask for help, nobody who could be trusted not to use their power and access to finish her off, once and for all.

But for Dan, she was alone. He was a capable ally, to be sure, but she still didn't much like their chances.

There was no use crying over the hand she was dealt, Sam knew, and she had long ago resolved to play it well and not worry about much else. But she couldn't help but wonder whether she was enjoying the iconic DC view for the last time.

Despite the obvious danger, it felt nice to finally be on the offensive. She'd been on the run for the last nine days, forced to react to one disaster after another, and Sam was sick of playing defense. Damn if she was going to sit around waiting for some other misfortune – or satanic, murderous bastard – to show up in her life.

Time to change the game up, she thought, feeling a surge of adrenaline flow through her veins.

Her burner buzzed. An address, from Dan. She looked at the clock on the dashboard of Cullsworth's big, powerful BMW sedan. It had taken Dan all of seven minutes to find what she needed.

I really should give that guy a raise. It would be her first priority, assuming they both survived the night.

* * *

Sam parked illegally at the curb of an expensive downtown apartment complex, climbed gingerly into the backseat of big BMW, and settled into her visual scan routine. She loathed this element of investigative work, and often dreamed of assigning these types of surveillance efforts to her various slack-jawed subordinates who were infinitely better suited to endure the monotony and boredom, but the work was too important to leave to the sheeple in the Homeland bureaucracy.

It was the details that mattered, the finer points, the things that the check-collecting dullards would never even notice. Sam solved more than her fair share of difficult cases because she noticed those key details with enviable regularity.

Unarmed and unprotected, Sam awaited Dan's arrival with weapons and other goodies. Her position in the backseat allowed her to take full advantage of the sedan's tinted windows. It was important that she not be seen, by anyone at all.

She worried that she might already be too late, that the Venezuelan bastards and their numerous American errand boys might already have struck a fatal blow against the person she was confident would be their next victim.

It would be a high-profile murder. Another statement. And as the past week had demonstrated, the VSS apparently believed in making statements. They had struck against the powerful American empire with a boldness that bordered on desperation, Sam thought. Dropping bombs on American houses, mutilating prominent government contractors, kidnapping federal agents in broad daylight just a few miles from the heart of America's capitol city…

And the torture, Sam recalled with a shiver.

If she was correct, they'd already added another victim to their list this evening. Senator Wharton, the pro-intelligence conservative from Texas.

Two staunch votes. Cullsworth's words echoed in her head. Though sentiments were sharply divided, the controversial intelligence measures were certain to pass the closed Senate vote, Cullsworth had reckoned.

One down, Sam thought. *And one staunch vote to go.*

She was certain the second vote belonged to Senator Frank Higgs, lifetime hawk and longtime member of the Senate Select Committee on Intelligence, and now the powerful committee's iron-fisted chairman. It was his apartment building entrance she now surveilled.

There wasn't time to debate with herself about the accuracy of her hunch. Besides, such a debate would be pointless. If her suspicion was correct, Higgs' life was in immediate danger. If she was wrong, she had nothing to lose but a night of restless sleep.

Sam's stomach churned. She was concerned that the VSS had already struck, and that Higgs, like the esteemed gentleman from the great state of Texas, was already floating in a pool of his own blood.

There was only one way to find out. Sam had to enter the building.

But before she dared to do that, she had to be confident that no one else was watching the upscale address. Walking into another trap wasn't on her agenda, and she had resolved to take her time and do things the right way.

So she scanned the street in a disciplined pattern, dividing the world into twelve separate thirty-degree sectors, turning her head to dwell for several seconds in each sector. She allowed her eyes to move naturally around the features visible in each of her scan regions, knowing that humanity's hunter-gatherer heritage had wired her to naturally detect movement and other telltale signs of approaching quarry.

Or approaching danger. In Sam's case, the two things were one and the same.

She'd just begun her third full visual sweep of the street when her burner buzzed again. She cursed the flood of light its screen produced, and ducked down in the seat to take the call.

"How far out are you?" she asked.

"Couple of blocks," Dan replied. "I'm in my minivan."

"There's no place to park, but you can block a driveway on the northwest side of the street. I'm in the black Bimmer to the southeast. See you in a sec."

A set of headlights rounded the corner. Definitely not a minivan, Sam thought, watching a large plumbing truck drive slowly down the street. She ducked as the truck approached.

It stopped in the loading zone near the entrance to Higgs'

building, its headlights pointing directly into Sam's front windshield.

Sam lay flat and motionless in the backseat, hidden behind the front seats, until the driver switched off the headlights. She heard the sound of the truck's door opening and closing, and she peeked just above the center console to catch a glimpse of the driver.

Her blood froze.

It was him.

Sam knew that for as long as she lived, she would never forget the man's gait. It was crooked and halting, yet somehow intense, inexorable.

By the dim light of the street lamps, Sam watched as the man who tortured and killed her walked brazenly toward the lobby door and rang the bell.

Where the hell are you, Dan? A girl could use a gun right about now.

Sam saw the shadow of the doorman approach the apartment entrance. Her killer held up a piece of paper and placed it flat against the glass door. The doorman examined the paper, then turned the key to unlock the entrance.

Just as Satan walked inside the building, Dan's minivan passed on Sam's left. *About time,* she thought.

They had seconds to act.

She slid out of the rear driver's side door, then crouched low as she ran, using the cover of the car to hide her retreat across the street. Once there, she ducked behind the row of parked cars along the curb, and hustled to Dan's minivan.

"Dan!" she whispered.

He jumped. "You scared the hell out of me."

"He's here."

"What?"

"The assassin. He's *here*. Just arrived a second ago. You brought vests and weapons?"

Dan handed her a ballistic vest and a government-issue 9mm pistol. Not her preferred sidearm, but it would do in a pinch. She put on the harness containing the shoulder holster, adjusted the strap length, chambered a round, set the safety, and placed her pistol in its holster under her left arm. "Flashlight?" she asked.

Dan nodded, brandishing a billy club full of D-cell batteries with an afterthought of a lightbulb at one end. "I brought the drunk thumper. Are you sure it was him?" he asked.

"Not death-penalty sure, but positive enough to be seriously concerned. What floor is the senator on?" Sam asked, walking briskly back across the street, still in the shadows and out of view of the apartment complex entrance.

"Fourth," Dan said, in a near-run to keep up with Sam's long strides.

"Showtime," Sam said. She stepped up to the door, peered through the glass to the inside of the lobby, and scanned for any sign of the psychopath who'd just gained access to Senator Higgs' residence. Seeing no movement, she rapped on the glass door.

She held her badge up for the doorman to see, and Dan did the same. The doorman pressed a button on the inside of his desk. They heard a buzzing sound, then a click as the latch retracted into the door frame. The door opened.

"You have a universal access key?" Sam asked the doorman.

"Ma'am?"

"A key. Do you have a key that lets you into residents' rooms?"

"Ma'am, I'm not at liberty to say."

"Give her the key, sir," Dan said menacingly, holding his badge beneath the doorman's nose.

"It's all electronic."

"Apartment 401," Dan said. "Code it. Now!"

"Don't you have to have a warrant?"

"Do you want to be responsible for the death of a senator?" Sam asked.

"Mr. Higgs?" the doorman asked.

"Key. Now."

The doorman disappeared behind the counter for what seemed like ages, clicking computer keys.

"Jesus, we're losing time here. Hurry up!"

A shaking hand with liver spots finally protruded from behind the desk, holding out a keycard. Sam snatched the card and ran toward the stairs. "No time to wait for the elevator."

"You'll want to turn to the right when you get up to the fourth floor," the doorman called. "Last door on the left."

Sam and Dan charged through the doorway and bounded up the stairs two at a time. Every muscle in her body protested. She couldn't remember ever being so sore. It was nearly debilitating, and her muscles threatened to cramp at every step, but she kept charging up the stairs as fast as the pain allowed. Dan followed.

Finally, the fourth floor landing appeared. Sam peered through the window into an empty hallway. It was wide, decorated in Modern Filthy Rich, and devoid of movement and people. She pushed on the doorway, but found it locked.

"Swipe the key," Dan offered. It worked. They made their way quickly but quietly to the end of the hallway.

"No cop shit," Sam said in a whisper. "We just use the key and go in. If we give him any warning, he'll slice the senator's jugular."

They listened for a brief second at Frank Higgs' door, but heard no commotion inside. Sam took a deep breath, unholstered her pistol and turned off the safety, swiped the keycard through the electronic reader, and prayed for a quiet lock.

Lucky day, she thought as the door yielded noiselessly. She and Dan entered the senator's posh apartment.

The place was huge. That wasn't unexpected, but it wasn't a welcome development. Searching through all of the rooms in the spacious upper-crust apartment wasn't going to be easy.

They tiptoed through the foyer, which ended at an intersection with a perpendicular hallway. Sam motioned for Dan to take the right, and she veered left, forcing herself to loosen her death-grip on the pistol in her hand.

She snuck toward a gargantuan Schwarzwald cuckoo clock at the end of the hallway, and Sam noticed that its enormous pendulum caught a warm yellow light with each swing. Her pulse quickened. There was a lamp on somewhere in the apartment.

She peered around the corner, and her heart leapt into her throat. Senator Higgs sat in a posh leather chair at a mahogany desk roughly the size of a tennis court, his back to the room, his nose buried in a book.

Behind the senator's head, the assassin was raising a gun.

"Freeze! Hands up!" Sam shouted at the top of her lungs, lunging out from around the corner and leveling her pistol in the direction of the short, stocky demon of a man.

He pulled the trigger.

Sam heard a whisper of a report, saw the senator's arm swing up to his neck, then saw a blur of motion where the assassin had stood.

The killer dove onto the floor, rolled behind an overstuffed leather armchair, and kicked it in Sam's direction. She dodged the chair, leveled her gun, and moved her finger to the trigger as he dashed toward the opposite door, the strange-sounding pistol still in his hand.

Dan appeared in the doorway, directly in the assassin's path, spoiling Sam's shot.

Balls. Sam lowered her gun and watched helplessly as the two beefy men collided in Senator Frank Higgs' study.

Still in a crouch, the assassin's shoulder connected with Dan's chest, and Sam heard all of the air leave her deputy's lungs. He flew ass over teakettle, and the killer scrambled over the top of Dan's flattened body.

The assassin sprung to his feet, raised his heel, and stomped viciously toward Dan's face. Dan moved his jaw out of the way just in time, but the killer's boot connected with Dan's collarbone, and Sam heard a sickening crack. Dan howled in pain.

The assassin moved with surprising quickness out of sight into the dark room adjacent to the study.

She heard a loud thump from the vicinity of the senator, and turned to see that he had fallen from his desk chair onto the floor. Still alive? She had no time to assess his condition. The assassin could easily circle back around through the apartment and shoot them from behind.

Quick footfalls echoed through the ostentatious apartment, lending credence to her fear of an ambush.

She made her decision quickly. "Dan, hang tough. I'm going to get this asshole."

"I'm fine," he said, getting to his feet. "Just a collarbone."

"Hold the fort," she said, rounding the corner past the giant clock and sprinting as quickly as her beaten body could manage.

She saw a flash of something shiny ahead of her in the dim hallway light, and a streak of bright steel moved toward her faster than she could dodge. She felt a searing pain in her thigh, and looked down to see a small dagger buried halfway to its hilt in her flesh.

A dim, gray blur ran toward her. She raised her gun instinctively and fired two rounds at the assassin. He tucked and rolled onto the foyer floor, disappearing around the next corner.

Sam dashed forward to the entryway, narrowly avoiding a second dagger as it flashed toward her at eye-level.

She dove around the corner. The knife protruding from her thigh clanged painfully against the hardwood floor as she rolled, an excruciating distraction that slowed her arrival in the prone firing position.

She got there a second too late. She raised her pistol for another shot at the killer just as the apartment door closed behind him.

Sam clambered to her feet, ripped the knife from her thigh with a bark of pain, and charged out the apartment door.

She looked in both directions down the hallway.

Empty. The killer was gone.

But the stairwell door betrayed the direction of his retreat as it drifted slowly closed in his wake.

You're mine, asshole.

Chapter 50

Sam cursed at the pain as she sprinted down the hallway after the deranged assassin who'd nearly killed her yet again. Dark blood poured from the deep wound in her thigh, and she badly needed to stop the blood loss.

But first, she badly needed to stop a killer.

Arriving at the stairwell door, she planted her good leg to support her body, then winced in pain as she swung her wounded leg to kick open the door.

She charged into the stairwell gun-first, her finger on the trigger, but she heard only retreating footfalls beneath her on the hard tile stairs. He was several floors below her.

Sam gritted her teeth, grabbed the railing for support, and ran down the stairs two at a time, surprised again at how debilitating and painful the electrocution-induced muscle cramps were. The knife wound was no picnic, either.

She heard a door slam shut someplace beneath her in the stairwell. She was certain the killer hadn't exited the stairwell onto the third floor, but she had no idea whether he'd dashed onto the second or first floors.

With backup, she'd have sent someone to search the other floors while she followed the more probable hunch, that the assassin had descended all the way to the lobby in order to make as hasty an exit as possible. But Sam didn't have that luxury. *It's just him and me,* she realized, bounding painfully onto the second floor landing. There was no one to call for help, and nobody she could trust to apprehend the killer if he got away from her.

But he wasn't going to get away. *It ends now,* Sam resolved. She was going to stop the assassin, or die trying.

She swiped through the second-floor doorway, threw it open, and trained her gun down the hallway. It was dark and still. Satisfied that the killer hadn't hidden to ambush her, she charged back into the stairwell and ran down the stairs to the first floor.

As she approached the entrance, Sam saw the doorman lying in a heap on the floor. She saw no blood and no obvious signs of an injury, but he was clearly unconscious. *Strange. Almost like he and the senator had been...tranquilized.* Just like she and Brock had been drugged. Then kidnapped.

Beyond the glass window, the headlights of the plumbing truck suddenly turned on, and she heard the low rumble of its diesel engine grinding to life.

Sam hustled out the door and raised her pistol to take aim at the assassin. The engine revved and the truck chirped its tires, roaring down the street, spoiling her shot.

She mashed the BMW's key fob with her thumb, dashed to the big 7-series sedan, and shoved the key in the ignition as she jumped into the driver's seat. Sam slammed the transmission into gear, spun the steering wheel, and stood on the gas, whipping the car around to follow the plumbing van containing the devil himself.

As she straightened the car and accelerated, she made a disheartening discovery: the van had disappeared.

He had to have taken one of the first two turns, Sam reasoned, probably southbound toward K Street, a major east-west artery through the heart of the lobby district that would afford the killer the greatest speed and anonymity. Sam reefed the big sedan hard to the left and dove down 11th Street, blazing past the Department of Justice. *Irony.*

She saw two cars stopped at the intersection with K Street.

But no plumbing truck.

She cursed loudly and matted the accelerator, hoping to spot the killer's truck before he had a chance to turn again.

A small rise in the road allowed her to see over the queued cars at the stop sign. Sam was certain she glimpsed the killer's getaway vehicle, still barreling southbound on 11th on the other side of K Street, heading toward the center of downtown DC.

Sam smiled to herself. *You screwed up, buddy. There's no good time to drive the Mall.*

She stood on the accelerator and the horn, veered out into the oncoming lane of traffic, which was thankfully devoid of cars at the moment, and held her breath as the big BMW sailed through the intersection crossing one of DC's busiest streets.

Horns blared at her, and she narrowly missed a collision with a delivery truck. She had to swerve into the wrong lane to avoid a car pulling out of an underground parking lot, and she nearly became a minivan's hood ornament in the process.

She caromed back onto the right side of the road just in time to see the plumbing truck make a hard, fast right turn onto New York Avenue. *Is this guy new?* Even at midnight, the traffic around the

White House and the National Mall would be prohibitive. She smiled again. She suddenly liked her chances a lot better.

Something felt warm and squishy beneath her legs as she worked the car's pedals, and she realized that the sticky substance was the blood still pouring profusely from the angry knife wound in her thigh. *Houston, we have a problem.*

Sam guided the big luxury car through a hard right turn onto New York Avenue. Despite its size, the car handled like it was on rails, and Sam was only halfway through the turn when she floored the gas pedal again.

Getting closer! The killer's truck was only half a block ahead of her. The big German engine roared and the speedometer climbed through fifty, and she had closed the distance to just a couple of car lengths when the killer did something exceptionally stupid.

He veered hard left, charging south on 12th Street – a northbound one-way.

Sam gritted her teeth and tucked in behind the killer, following him in tight formation as he swerved the heavy utility truck wildly back and forth to avoid streams of irate drivers heading the opposite direction.

Sam's heart leapt into her throat as she saw the killer try to thread the needle between two oncoming cars. *He's never going to make it.* She slammed on the brakes and braced for the inevitable collision.

She was right. Not even close. The plumbing truck plowed into the side of a large Mercedes that had swerved at the last second to avoid what would surely have been a deadly head-on collision.

The impact spun the Mercedes completely around, and for the briefest of moments, Sam thought she might be able to guide the big BMW unscathed past the twirling wreckage.

No such luck. The Mercedes continued its spin, side-swiping the expensive car she'd stolen from Secretary Cullsworth, throwing her directly in front of an oncoming grocery van.

Sam stomped on the accelerator, torqued the steering wheel, and made peace with the universe, expecting to be crushed at any moment beneath the grille of the big grocery truck.

But the collision never came. The powerful engine rocketed the sedan forward, and she escaped by the narrowest of margins.

She had no idea where the killer might have gone – his plumbing truck was nowhere in sight – but Sam decided she'd had enough fun trying to navigate 12th Street the hard way. She turned the steering wheel hard to the right, plowed the big Bimmer over the curb, and narrowly dodged a signpost on the sidewalk on her way to H Street westbound.

Heart pounding, Sam looked around for the big plumbing van, hoping against hope that the killer had experienced a similar epiphany regarding the difficulty of driving against the flow of downtown DC traffic.

She suddenly found it hard to focus her eyes, and small, colored dots appeared in her vision. *I'm losing too much blood,* she realized as she matted the accelerator.

Sam recalled her many conversations with Brock about not losing consciousness while "pulling G's" in a fighter jet. The trick was to squeeze your abs, ass, and legs, he'd said, to keep the blood from draining from your head.

Sam tried it. More blood poured from the wound in her thigh, but her vision cleared up, and as the stars disappeared from her eyes, she made out the now-familiar form of the assassin's getaway vehicle.

She breathed a sigh of relief for her good fortune at not having lost the killer in the traffic bedlam on 12th Street, but realized she was in serious risk of going into shock due to blood loss. Sam glanced around the car for something she could use to stem the bleeding. Wouldn't do her any good to catch the bastard, only to pass out when she got there.

She found a raincoat lying in the passenger seat floor. She shot her arm down and swooped it up, and set to work wrapping it around her thigh even as she followed the fleeing killer, dodging cars and barreling toward the home of the President of the United States. *This is going to be interesting,* she thought as she cinched the coat tight around her thigh.

H Street veered to the northwest, and Sam saw a line of brake lights stopped at another busy intersection. The killer's truck hopped the curb and drove on the wide sidewalk, careening past cars waiting at the red light. He charged recklessly across the intersection.

Sam followed, hearing the scrape of metal on concrete as the expensive sedan bottomed out on the curb. She stayed close behind the killer as he made a wide, sweeping left turn to join the startled midnight drivers heading west toward downtown DC.

There was an opening in traffic, and Sam mashed the gas pedal to catch up to the fleeing killer. She veered to avoid a turning car, and her eyes were drawn to the blazing whiteness of the most famous residence in America, bathed in floodlights. *The Secret Service guys are going to smoke us both if we don't slow down,* Sam realized as the killer's truck charged toward the end of New York Avenue, where it became Pennsylvania Avenue – practically on the President's lawn.

Apparently, the killer reached a similar conclusion. The top-heavy plumbing truck leaned hard to the right as he threw it into a tight left turn, diving south on 15th Street at the last possible second to avoid the White House area.

Sam nearly didn't make the turn in time to follow him. She clipped the curb just feet from the Treasury building, grinding the BMW's expensive rims before settling back onto the roadway.

She was close enough to hear the big diesel engine roar as the killer gained speed, and she accelerated to keep pace. She peeked the nose of the car out into the oncoming lane to assess what lay ahead, and was relieved to see that traffic was uncharacteristically sparse all the way to the Washington Monument.

If she was going to make a move, now was the time.

She pulled the 9mm handgun from its holster, rolled down the window, placed the gun in her left hand, and squeezed off two rounds at the left rear tire.

Misses.

The killer slammed on the brakes, and Sam was just quick enough to avoid a collision. *Asshole.* If she'd hit him, and her airbags had deployed, she'd never have caught back up to him.

The truck's diesel engine clattered and growled, and the killer was off again, tires squealing.

Secretary Cullsworth's BMW easily kept pace, though Sam followed a bit further away. A stream of crossing traffic caught her eye, and Sam realized that they were rapidly approaching Constitution Avenue.

She tightened the raincoat she'd tied around her thigh, hoping she'd be able to keep her wits about her long enough to put a round through the bastard's tire. And then, with a little luck, maybe also his forehead.

Sam was relieved to see the flow of traffic on Constitution come to a stop. Seconds later, their traffic light turned green, and the killer charged through the intersection, starting the wide arc around the Washington Monument, its lighted scaffolding an eerie, otherworldly shroud draped around the giant concrete obelisk.

This shit has to stop, Sam thought, again bringing the BMW in close for another shot.

She fired two more rounds. One hit the metal above the wheel well.

The other one popped the left rear tire.

The killer's truck fishtailed back and forth in front of her windshield.

He regained control, but Sam accelerated, pulled out into the oncoming lane, and jerked the steering wheel over to slam the BMW's front quarter panel into the left rear of the truck.

The truck spun, and Sam slammed the gas pedal, driving the big, wide nose of the BMW broadside into the truck, ploughing it toward the sidewalk. Sam heard the truck's tires screech and howl as she kept the pressure on the gas pedal, accelerating the truck sideways into the curb.

She braced for the impact, but wasn't prepared for its violence. The curb sheared the truck's right front wheel clean off, and the force of the collision flipped the heavy truck over onto its cab.

The airbag exploded in Sam's face, and she heard the impossibly loud screech of metal scraping over concrete, then felt the damp coolness of upturned sod and clumps of turf hitting her body as the two tangled vehicles gouged deep ruts into the wet grass.

They came to rest a hundred yards from the Washington Monument. The front of Sam's car was propped up on the upended truck, its engine still idling, its rear tires still spinning.

Sam was dazed and disoriented. Her head lolled to the side, and she felt painful abrasions on her face and arms. Miraculously, her left hand still clutched her pistol.

The sound of shattering glass sharpened her focus, and she heard harsh, gravelly grunts as the killer extricated himself from the wreckage beneath her.

Sam clambered to open the door. It wouldn't budge. The car's bent frame had wedged it in place.

She laid down across the front seats and kicked the door with all of her strength. Fiery pain in her heels rewarded her effort, but the door didn't move.

She heard more grunts in the grass below her, more shattering glass, and then the shuffle of footsteps, moving closer to her. The grunts grew louder, followed by the groan of metal, and she felt the entire car move beneath her.

He's climbing up here, she realized.

Sam had no idea whether the killer still had his gun, and she had no desire to press her luck. She aimed her pistol out the window and fired a warning shot.

It had the desired effect – she heard a heavy landing on the grass outside, followed by shuffling footsteps heading off to the west as the killer ran up the broad, green slope toward the giant concrete monument.

Sam reversed her position in the front seat and poked her head out the window. *Holy hell, I'm a long way up here.* The ground was a frightening distance beneath her car, perched as it was on the upturned plumbing truck.

She turned her head and saw the killer shuffling off toward the monument.

There are no good options from here, Sam realized. Any choice she made would have its consequences. Without backup, without the ability to trust the cops, with no one to protect her, and with an alarmingly vigorous leak in her upper thigh threatening her consciousness, Sam made a difficult decision.

She held the gun in her right hand, steadied it on the car door ledge, took aim at the killer's back, and smoothly added pressure to the trigger.

The pistol barked, and bucked in her hand.

The killer pitched forward with a deep, croaking cry of pain. He rolled on the grass, cursing loudly in Spanish, then lay still.

Stay down, asshole.

He didn't. Sam's heart sank as she watched the killer pop back up on his feet, clutching the back of his left thigh, and continue his lumbering shuffle up the hill toward the monument, now zigzagging back and forth to spoil her aim. Before she could draw a bead on him for another shot, he was out of the little pistol's range.

I can't buy a break.

She crawled head-first out of the open window and stretched to grasp the frame of the upended pickup truck, pinned upside-down beneath the BMW. She used the truck's frame to pull her legs free of the car, yelping in pain as her wounded thigh scraped on the doorframe.

Her fingers slipped, and she fell awkwardly onto the grass, landing with a thud.

Sam rolled onto her back. Her arms fell limp by her side, and she gazed blankly up at the stars. Pain and exhaustion wracked her body and her mind, and she was tempted to just close her eyes, to lie there, to let fate run its course, not giving a shit whether the good cops or bad cops showed up, or whether anyone would ever catch the stocky little beast of a man.

But something stirred within her.

She didn't want to die.

And she knew she'd never be free to walk in the daylight, to live her life without looking over her shoulder, unless she stopped the madness once and for all.

It ends now.

Sam stood. It took great effort, and she felt as if she might pass out.

She took deep breaths. Her head slowly cleared, and the stars slowly disappeared from her vision. She fixed her gaze up the hill, and could just make out the killer's form, silhouetted against the powerful floodlights, running toward the base of the monument.

Sam stumbled up the hill toward the giant concrete monolith. She moved haltingly, painfully, but gathered speed with each step. She hoped her strength would hold out for just a little longer.

She prayed for just one more shot at him.

She vowed not to waste it.

* * *

Sam's head swum, and she felt faint from all the blood that had poured from the deep wound in her thigh, but she pressed on, willing her body forward step by step in pursuit of the shadow charging up the hill.

The killer was silhouetted against the bright floodlights that wrapped the Washington Monument in a pale white glow. He was now well out of her 9mm pistol's range, but she was gaining on him despite her halting, pain-wracked gait. All of her fitness training was clearly paying off. *And the slug in his leg probably isn't speeding him up any.*

His shape became harder and harder to discern as he neared the ring of lights, his outline obscured by the blazing wall of light. Sam couldn't fathom why he would be running *toward* the monument, but that's exactly what he was doing.

The stocky assassin dashed into the circle of spotlights surrounding the giant obelisk, his frame suddenly awash in brilliant, blinding light, and Sam could suddenly see him in sharp detail, down to the crimson stain on the leg of his gray plumber's suit, as if to mock her for missing his heart.

He kept running, and Sam kept willing her body forward after him, pouring all of her energy into getting within shooting distance to bring him down once and for all.

Almost there.

The killer limped all the way to the foot of the monument, stepping over the yellow tape restricting public access to the renovation site. Sam saw him pause briefly at the sheet of thick plastic that covered the scaffolding.

Then he ducked down and disappeared inside.

Sam cursed. *This guy's deranged, but not stupid.* He'd forced her to make a choice. She could either guard the monument like a dog with treed game, hoping he would emerge before the crooked Metro cops showed up on the scene, or she could climb into the plastic-shrouded scaffold after him.

It wasn't a choice, really.

It ends tonight, she repeated to herself like a mantra.

But damn if I'm going to follow him through the same hole in the plastic. She approached the base of the monument twenty yards to the south of where the killer had entered, got on her hands and knees, and crawled beneath the plastic covering, pausing on the inside for her eyes to adjust to the relative darkness.

Movement, and clanging.

He's climbing.

The assassin's short, stocky body hung precariously as he scrambled up the metal scaffolding, sliding his feet upwards along the diagonal bars that formed X-shaped reinforcements along the edges of the metal platform.

Sam raised her pistol and steadied for a shot, centering her sights on the killer's chest. Just as she moved her finger to the trigger, the assassin hoisted himself up to the next level of scaffolding, out of view.

She got to her feet as quickly as she could manage, grabbing the steel structure for support, and dashed to the spot where the killer had just climbed up.

Heavy, uneven footfalls sounded on the platform above her. He was running along the second level of the scaffold, and she followed the sound of his footsteps around to the west side of the monument, her pistol trained upwards in case an opportunity presented itself.

Sam felt faint with the exertion, saw stars in her eyes, and felt a fog around her thoughts. She'd lost a lot of blood, and she knew that her time was limited. *Time to put this guy into the ground,* she thought to herself.

She heard the clanging of boots on metal, and realized that the assassin was climbing higher up the scaffolding. Sam pressed her body into the plastic wrapper surrounding the outer edge of the steel scaffold and peered upwards, hoping to spot him.

Sam glimpsed the killer's thick form, making its way quickly up the structure. He had found a ladder on the inside of the scaffold, and was rapidly putting vertical distance between them.

She didn't bother raising her pistol. The assassin's body was shielded by the steel and timber of the scaffolding.

Sonuvabitch. There was no option but to climb up after him.

Sam instantly recognized the method to the killer's madness. She was forced to holster her pistol in order to climb, which negated her advantage. She shook her head, liking her odds much less now. The assassin had gone a long way toward leveling the playing field.

Her body protested with each agonizing upward thrust, but she could tell that her taller frame and better physical fitness were working to her advantage. She was slowly catching up to the killer, despite the intense pain that accompanied each movement of her limbs.

The killer stopped climbing, and peered down the ladder at her. She reached quickly for her shoulder holster, but he disappeared onto the scaffolding two levels above her before she could draw.

This is a problem, Sam realized. She was stuck on the ladder, while the assassin enjoyed the freedom of movement the scaffold platform afforded.

She heard a loud crash, and the protracted clanging of what sounded like dozens of heavy steel rods scattering about the platform above. *He's found a weapon.*

Sam drew her gun to keep it at the ready, but found it difficult to negotiate the ladder with just one free hand. She had to hook her right elbow around each rung while she repositioned her left hand onto the next rung above. It was slow going, and she wasn't sure she was any safer than with her pistol in its holster.

She looked down, and felt a sudden surge of fear. She was thirty feet above the concrete, clinging to a swaying support ladder, trapped halfway between scaffold levels with a deranged killer above her.

Sam looked up just in time to see a long, heavy metal rod leave the assassin's hands, hurled down at her from the platform above. She ducked her head out of the way, but the heavy support rail struck her square across her shoulders and neck.

Pain seared through her battered body, and the force of the impact knocked her off balance. She swung precariously out to the side of the ladder, her left hand flailing desperately to find support.

Both feet slipped from beneath her.

Panic. Her stomach lurched as she fell.

This is how it ends?

Then sharp pain bit the crook of her elbow. It was still hooked around a ladder rung.

It held. Her body swung wildly, then slammed into the scaffolding, knocking the wind from her lungs, wrenching her shoulder as it bore her full weight, dangling three stories above the concrete.

A second metal support rod left the killer's hands and sailed harmlessly past.

But a third one connected, bouncing off her head with a skull-rattling clang that nearly knocked her unconscious. Her body slackened, and she felt her arm beginning to give.

A sound grabbed her attention. An important sound. The clatter of her pistol, free of her slack grip, ending its fall with a bounce and a skid on the scaffolding beneath her. *I'm fucked,* Sam realized, stars still swimming in her eyes.

But she wasn't about to give up.

She grabbed a lungful of air, swung her body, hooked her shin around a rung, and managed a tenuous grip on the ladder with her left hand. Several eternal seconds passed as her muscles strained to right her body.

Finally, she repositioned her left hand, grasped the nearest rung with a firm grip, and pulled herself back in position. She climbed down toward the scaffold floor beneath her as fast as she could make her body move.

She heard another grunt above her, and instinctively flattened her body against the cold steel ladder to dodge another volley of heavy steel reinforcing rods, narrowly escaping a third tooth-jarring impact, one she was sure would have knocked her to her death.

After an eternity of painful scrambling down the ladder, her feet found the hard planks of the scaffold floor, and she immediately dropped to her hands and knees to find her pistol. Splinters dug into her hands and fingers as she moved them around the scaffold floor, searching for the gun.

A loud, metallic clang nearby caused an involuntary screech of fright. Another steel reinforcement rail had nearly found its mark.

Where the hell is the gun? It had to be on the wooden scaffold floor. She would certainly have heard it clatter on the concrete below if it had fallen all the way to the ground. She was sure it was on *this* level, somewhere, but it was lost in the shadow cast by the floor itself, high above the floodlights on the ground below.

She heard the killer's boots on the ladder above her. But her blood ran cold with a stunning realization. His footfalls were growing louder and closer.

He was no longer climbing up the scaffolding.

He was coming down after her.

Sam lifted her eyes toward the ladder. In the cool white light, she saw the same twisted, inhuman grin she'd seen for hours on end as he did vile, unspeakable things to her naked body. She recalled the terror of being clamped fast to a cold cement wall, immobilized and incapable of defending herself against his demonic depravity, forced to watch his horrific, sadistic smile as he drew her blood and her screams, to see the glee in his eyes with each new evil and agony he inflicted upon her.

Anger rose up within her, a rage like Sam had never known, a deep, burning hatred that propelled her upwards to her feet, that willed her forward.

She charged toward the demon on the ladder, her own teeth bared in an atavistic howl, her fists flying in frenzied hatred, her only aim to knock him from the ladder, to hear the wet crunch of his life ending on the cement below.

Her fist connected, driving upward into his balls, a primal roar escaping her mouth as she threw the full force of her body behind the crippling blow. The wind left the killer's lungs, bringing with it a groan of instant agony, and he slumped on the ladder, his descent suddenly stopped by the red rage on the scaffolding below.

Sam watched the wave of pain settle over his body as she reached back to his crotch. She clamped her fist around the soft flesh between his legs, and twisted with all of her might. "You fucking bastard!" she screamed, throwing her body behind the grip on his balls, twisting and torqueing for maximum devastation, feeling the killer's body tense in agony, a terrific comeuppance that brought a vicious snarl to her lips.

"Fuck you!" she howled, bringing her left hand through a ladder rung to the killer's face, her thumb scrambling to find his eye socket. When it did, she drove it into the killer's eyeball, feeling a gooey, satisfying squish that brought another howl of anguish from the stocky assassin, his voice freakish, gravelly, wraith-like.

She torqued harder with her right hand, feeling something give, hoping she'd ripped his nut sack, rewarded by another agonized exhalation. "It's over, asshole!" she raged, digging her thumb deeper into the killer's eye socket, gripping his skull with her fingers to prevent him from twisting free of her devastating grasp. She lowered her shoulder and pushed into his body, praying for his feet to leave the ladder, begging gravity to take him to the death he so richly deserved.

It's working. She felt his foot slip free of the ladder. And a hand.

But he wasn't falling.

His hand disappeared behind his waist, then whipped back around toward her body, a streak of shiny steel reflecting in the floodlights.

His blade founds its mark, cutting her yet again, burying itself in her shoulder, its tip scraping bone. Sam shrieked in pain, and her hand fell away from the killer's face. Her vicious grip on his balls lost its vigor, and Sam staggered back on her heels, too off-balance to dodge the swing of the killer's heavy boot. It connected with her ribs, sending an electric pulse of pain through her body and knocking her onto the scaffold floor.

In a flash, he was on her, his heavy fists pounding away at the back of her head, his knee on the small of her back, pinning her down on the hard planks. The punches came hard and fast, threatening to knock her unconscious, moving toward the vulnerable place where her spine met her skull, each blow beating her forehead into the wooden floor of the scaffolding.

His other hand closed around her neck. Her vision dimmed, and her lungs screamed for air.

The killer's hand drew away, his body coiling for a coup de grace, his weight pushing into her body as he prepared to kill her with his fist.

She felt her consciousness fading, but through the fog and pain, a certainty welled up within her.

Not this time, asshole.

Sam summoned a strength she didn't feel, a reserve she hoped somehow still existed. She drove her left hand and knee down into the scaffold floor with all of her might, rolling her body violently to the right, throwing her head back to dodge the crushing blow she sensed was on its way.

She felt his fist graze her cheek, harmless.

He missed.

She heard the crack of bones and a howl of pain as the killer's fist shattered against the scaffold floor. She continued to throw her body into the desperate roll to her right, pushing harder with her hips, and leading with her left elbow, swinging viciously toward the killer's face.

Her elbow found its mark. His jaw crunched. He fell, dazed,

dead weight, head banging against the scaffold, and Sam continued rolling, scrambling to escape from beneath his bulk. The knife, still buried deep in her shoulder, grazed painfully against the assassin's barrel chest as she squirmed from beneath him, finally extricating herself from his deadly embrace.

She rose shakily to her knees, head swimming, her body held up by pure adrenaline and little else.

Face down on the wooden planks, the killer stirred.

He planted his hands, drew his knees up, lifted his torso, and swung his right arm toward Sam's face.

She dodged.

It ends now.

Sam gritted her teeth and grasped the handle of the killer's knife, protruding grotesquely from her shoulder. With a yell of pain and rage, she pulled the knife out of her flesh and raised it above her head. She drew her body up, grasping the knife handle with both hands, and drove the blade downward with desperate, frantic force, aiming in between the twisted killer's fleshy shoulder and his bony skull, dodging the flailing parry of his arm.

She drove the blade home, feeling the muscle and sinew give way in her killer's neck, feeling his spine sever, feeling the sudden limpness in his body, feeling the slackness overtake him, hearing his last, gurgling breath.

Relief overtook her. She felt the overpowering, ancient joy of survival, the humbling exhilaration of cheating death yet again.

Overcome, she sobbed with exhaustion, with the horror of yet another deadly encounter with pure evil, and with the frightening, accusatory knowledge of the angry, deadly rage inside of her own soul.

She had won, had prevailed against evil incarnate, had killed the walking demon. She had survived.

But a new realization settled.

It's still not over.

Sam felt weight, dread, foreboding. And impossible tiredness.

Below her, she heard someone yelling. It was a familiar voice, yelling her name, with sirens wailing in the background, growing louder.

She found her voice. "Up here, Dan."

"We gotta go, Sam! Metro's on the way!"

Shakily, she rose to her feet and stumbled to the ladder.

Chapter 51

Sam sat alone, enveloped in a plush leather armchair, her legs resting atop an exquisitely carved oak coffee table, watching a growing streak of blazing orange announce the new day's arrival.

Monday.

I hate Mondays.

It had been ten days since a bomb nearly destroyed her house.

Two days ago, she'd been tortured, mutilated, and killed.

Four hours ago, in a flash of rage-driven strength, she'd saved a senator, saved her own life yet again, and sent her twisted, deranged killer to the afterlife.

The time since her exhausting battle with the assassin had been filled with intravenous bags, needles, painkillers, stitches, and other medical care delivered quietly in a flop house in a seedy part of town by a doctor Dan had called.

She was exhausted. She'd slept little more than an hour since the previous evening, when, lying next to Brock in Secretary Cullsworth's guest room, the jagged, uncooperative pieces of the puzzle had finally locked into place in her mind.

That revelation had led her inexorably to the exquisitely-appointed office in which she now sat, watching the breathtaking sunrise.

Important sunrise, Sam thought. *It ends now.*

It was an enormous gamble. She'd staked everything on the

strength of little more than an intuition, a nascent knowing that felt true even before she'd found the words, the logic, and the reasons to explain why.

But she was certain.

Out the window, deep reds turned to lighter oranges and yellows, and a high layer of wispy clouds offered a canvas to the gorgeous colors of dawn. It felt like a moment worth savoring.

It ended all too quickly. She heard mechanical noises, and turned her head to the right of the giant picture window in the enormous office, staring expectantly at the gleaming silver door that concealed a private executive elevator.

The elevator was used by one person, and one person only.

He's the one. She knew it in her bones.

Jarvis' murderous display had been nothing more than a diversion. Psychopathic, unnecessary, disgusting.

She pulled back the slide on her 9mm pistol, chambering a round and setting the hammer for a quick single-action shot, and clicked off the safety.

The mechanical noises grew louder.

Sam's heartbeat grew more insistent. She trained her gun on the elevator door, and forced herself to take deep, calming breaths.

It ends now.

The elevator noise grew to a crescendo, then halted. The doors parted.

Two men?

Of course! How could it be otherwise?

Homeland Secretary Vince Cullsworth stepped confidently

into his office.

Deputy Director Tom Jarvis followed.

"Good morning, gentlemen," Sam said. Both men jumped. Sam saw recognition dawn on their faces, and deepening shock along with it.

"I've had quite a night," she said. "So please forgive me for keeping my seat."

The surprise lasted but a second on Cullsworth's face, and Sam smiled inwardly as she watched the smooth, practiced politician in him rise to the occasion. "Why, Sam, you look like you've been the victim of an attack!"

"You should see the other guy."

"What in the world's happened to you?" Cullsworth asked.

Sam wore an exaggerated smile. "I became reacquainted with your associate last evening," she said, the gun pointed at Jarvis even as she looked at Cullsworth. "The one with all the fucking knives. We met at the Senator's apartment. We all got along swimmingly, as usual, though it seemed like I might have interrupted something. Anyway, he treated me to an insider-only tour of a famous DC landmark." The smile left her eyes and her face hardened. "But then his visa expired."

Jarvis seethed.

Cullsworth shook his head. "Really, Sam, you should see a doctor. Let me call one for you." He stepped toward the phone on his desk.

"Stop!" she commanded. "Stay right where you are."

Cullsworth froze, surprised at the force in her voice.

Jarvis smirked. "There's the Sam I know and despise," he said.

"Always a pleasure, Tom. I have some fun planned for you. In the meantime, I'd like to ask you both to raise your hands in the air, and keep them there for me," Sam said.

Neither man moved.

Sam raised her eyebrows. And her pistol. One or the other did the trick. Cullsworth's arms moved slowly upward. "You must know you're making a huge mistake, Sam," Cullsworth said.

"I think Tom's making the mistake," Sam said. "His arms aren't raised yet."

Jarvis studied her defiantly. "I'm sick of your bullshit, Sam."

"I feel threatened, Tom."

Jarvis sneered. "What are you going to do, shoot me?"

Sam moved her finger to the trigger and aimed. "Left testicle, or right?"

Jarvis raised his arms.

"You're not the average lemming, Sam," Cullsworth said. "So I want you to think this through." His face constricted into a frown. "We cannot stand by while men dismantle the republic that has stood for over two hundred years. We must not run roughshod over every nation on the globe, and ourselves in the process!"

"Spare me the sermon," Sam said. "You're a common criminal."

"Daniel Ellsberg. Edward Snowden. Bradley Manning. Patriots, all of them. Heroes."

Sam shook her head, feeling tired. "You're an idiot and an asshole."

"In troubled times, the greatest acts of patriotism are often against the law. The system goes so far astray that it takes someone with the courage, the vision, the fortitude to step outside the system, to pull it back on track, to save it from itself."

"No argument here," Sam said. "But for one tiny detail. You didn't just leak a few dirty secrets to the press, Mr. Secretary. You're a murderer."

"How many more lives will we save? If we stop just one war of aggression from ever starting, how many countless thousands of lives will be spared?"

"You disgust me."

"This is fun," Jarvis said, "but I've got places to be. Put the gun away, Sam. Really, what are you going to do, kill us? Call the police?" He sneered again.

Sam smiled. "I've got something much better planned. On your knees, both of you."

She stood slowly, unsteadily. She cursed her frailty. Jarvis had certainly noticed, and he had the air of a man who didn't have much to lose by trying something desperate. "Now!" she commanded. "Hands on the back of your head."

Reluctantly, the two men did as she commanded.

"Don't do anything stupid here, Sam," Jarvis said.

She laughed. "I never liked you, Tom, and I'm not going to miss you."

"Seriously, what do you think you could possibly do to us? Call the FBI? Metro?" Jarvis laughed. "Hip pocket. Owned. Mine. They'll show up, alright, but they're going to leave with *you* in cuffs."

"Heavens no, not the FBI, too!" Sam said with exaggerated surprise. "What will I ever do now? I guess you won. I suppose I should surrender." She smiled wickedly.

She circled behind Cullsworth, searched him, zip-tied his feet together, then fastened his hands together behind his back. She gave him a rough nudge, and he toppled over onto his side.

"Actually, I had an even better idea than calling the police or the Bureau," Sam said, making her way over to Jarvis. "Sadly, it doesn't involve shooting both of you depraved bastards, like you deserve. If I did that, I would no longer be able to feel morally superior to you, and that would wreck my healthy self image. So instead, I'm going to phone a friend."

Sam watched Jarvis' face. She could see his mind whirring behind a concerned look.

Suddenly, he connected the dots.

"You bitch!" He leapt to his feet and whirled to face her, fists flying.

She sidestepped the lame, middle-aged attack, then clocked him above his ear with the butt of her pistol. He fell awkwardly, landing on his backside, his legs and arms splayed open. She laughed derisively at him. "Seriously, Tom. You're miles out of your league."

"You can't do this," Jarvis said. "They'll turn on you, too. They'll view you as a loose end, as part of the problem."

"That might be true," she said as she fastened his wrists and ankles together, pressing the barrel of her pistol into his back. Then she leaned in close, her lips next to his ear. "But I can't imagine what they're going to do to you."

She stood slowly and made her way back across the room, settling gingerly into the leather armchair. "Look at you two criminal masterminds," she said with an ironic smile. "Seeing you, lying there like dog shit stuffed in Armani, nobody would believe all the trouble you've caused."

She pulled out her burner and dialed.

"But my new friend certainly believes it," she said, lifting the phone to her ear.

She smiled as a gruff, nasal voice answered.

"Mr. Dibiaso," she said. "They're all yours."

What's next?

Get the **#1 Bestselling Book Three in the Incident Trilogy**:

FALLOUT: A Sam Jameson Conspiracy Thriller

What readers say:

"**The best writing in decades. Move over, Lee Child.**"

"**Some of the best action and spy thriller fiction you will ever read.**"

"**Right up there with Patterson, Baldacci, Forsyth, and DeMille.**"

"**The best thriller I've ever read.**"

"**LOVE LOVE LOVE this series!**"

Get insider deals on upcoming releases

Be sure to join #1 Bestselling Author Lars Emmerich's readers' group. You'll receive insider deals on upcoming releases, and you'll be treated to subscriber-only giveaways and sales.

Just click here to join.

Books by Amazon #1 Bestselling Author Lars Emmerich

The Incident: Inferno Rising

The Incident: Reckoning

Fallout

Descent

Devolution

Meltdown

Mindscrew

Blowback

Excerpt from #1 Bestseller FALLOUT

Prologue

It wasn't like the old days. You couldn't just use a hunting rifle to rid the world of problem people.

Perestroika ruined that for everyone. Satanic Soviets against God's Good Guys used to be a great gig. Simple. Effective. Resonated with everyone's innate xenophobia. The public would put up with just about any amount of gangsterism, as long as you told them it was a shootout between spies over nuclear secrets. And as long as you told them the good guys had won.

The assassin sighed. Bygone days turned a nostalgic sepia in the mind's eye. He knew it was so, yet he was still subject to the illusion.

Could he be blamed? It was a ballsy game, back then. Bullets and blades. None of this biological weapon bullshit, he thought wistfully as he patted the vial of biological weapon bullshit in his suit pocket, shaking his head ever so slightly and tightening his semi-permanent grimace.

They'd have never stood for it, back in the day. No room for hacks and poseurs. It was all about high-velocity cars and high-velocity women and high-velocity bullets.

Highballs, high heels, high stakes, and high times.

Then the goddamned wall came down.

It was tough to find work for a while. People momentarily lost the stomach for permanent solutions.

But statecraft recovered in due course, as did spy craft. The two were inextricably linked, the assassin reckoned.

He was glad he persevered. Glad to have survived. Happy to still be in the game.

Such as it was.

Goddamned drones, goddamned germs, goddamned pencil-necked pencil-pushers, MBA college boys playing at a man's game.

His mark showed up, taking her reserved seat a few tables over from him at the sidewalk cafe on Pennsylvania Avenue, just a block from the White House, saving the assassin from tumbling headlong into another bout of self-righteous self-pity.

He put his gloves on.

Then he felt the vial of biological bullshit again. Hepatitis? AIDS? Bird flu? Mad cow? He had no clue, and he didn't want to know. Sometimes staying alive meant staying dumb. Society lacked a clear enemy, which made people far more sensitive and far more litigious. Hence an even greater need for plausible deniability.

And all those goddamned video cameras these days. One surveillance camera for every ten Americans, he'd read.

It was yet another of the forces driving his profession into extinction. One wrong step and your face would be all over You-view, or whatever the kids called that internet video thing.

His mark's meal arrived. He didn't remember her ordering, but then he remembered that she was a regular, and a wannabe mover/shaker, the kind of person who would put in a standing order at a trendy restaurant, then look too stern and preoccupied and important to enjoy it.

Salad is what they brought her. Twenty-something dollars on the menu, for fifty cents worth of rabbit food.

The assassin humphed. As good a last meal as any, he finally decided after giving it more consideration than it deserved.

He shook his head, annoyed at the wayward thoughts. He was on assignment, after all. No time for fuzzy-headedness.

He was still the best around, as far as he would admit, but he feared he might be hearing the faint thrumming of bat wings up in his belfry. Wasn't getting any younger. Maybe time to remove the semi from semi-retired.

His B-team showed up. Right on time for a change. An elderly couple. Even more elderly than the assassin. They checked in with the hostess, who nodded, smiled, grabbed menus, and walked toward an open table.

Right toward his mark.

Showtime.

The assassin donned his hat, grabbed his cane, palmed the sealed glass pipette in his pocket, stood up, and made for the exit, dodging tables and diners.

He passed the hostess going the opposite direction, then the elderly B-team woman walking behind her. Next was the elderly man.

On cue, vertigo set in, and the old man stumbled into the old assassin, who stumbled into the mark's table, upending glasses and clinking silverware against china.

Lost in the commotion was the sound of the sealed glass vial breaking open over the mark's salad, its clear, odorless contents draining neatly into the overpriced arugula as the assassin's gloved hand searched for a place to arrest his feigned fall.

"I'm so terribly sorry, ma'am," he said to his mark, regaining his balance, setting aright the molested flatware, looking straight into her forty-something-year-old eyes, which registered officiousness and severity and focus and genetically bitchy overtones behind clumping makeup. The assassin didn't doubt that somebody would want *this* particular DC muckety-muck out of the picture. She had that vibe about her, like maybe a few hundred people might like her better dead than alive. But maybe he was projecting.

She allowed a small wave and an unconvincing smile that never made it any further north than her cheeks, and let out a perfunctory "think nothing of it" in a tone that would have been much more at home in the company of a "bugger yourself," then joined her assassin in restoring order to the contents of her table.

Apologies from the clumsy B-team man for good measure, a polite tip of the hat to the mark, and the assassin was on his way.

And that was that.

He walked out of the cafe, took a right, waited for the light, and walked toward the park and the setting sun, just an old man on a postprandial stroll, taking his air, as they used to say.

Hell of a night for it. Beautiful breeze, beautiful sunset. His mind was already long beyond the killer bug already at work on the Justice Department bureaucrat's innards.

Chapter 1

One year later.

Sam Jameson died once. In the line of duty. In the service of a not-terribly-grateful nation. Death by torture. It sucked.

Fortunately, her death didn't take.

But it did rattle about in her psyche, lingering neurotically, prompting uncomfortable questions.

To wit: what the hell am I doing with my life, and why the hell am I getting killed over it?

She lived a pretty full-throttle existence before her untimely but short-lived demise, busting skulls and catching spies as a counterespionage agent at Homeland, which always sounded too much like Fatherland for Sam's liking, with disturbingly similar overtones of xenophobia and aggression and totalitarianism. But beggars couldn't be choosers, and nobody else would employ a pinup girl with a mouth like a sailor and a mean left hook, unless there was first a disagreeable amount of reeducation.

But in her post-death life she'd taken a slightly different tack. She still followed her instinct, but no longer did she take the kinds of unreasonable risks she used to take.

That's what she told the man she loved, anyway, whose voice she now heard, sexy and deep, intellect and testosterone adorably audible even through her tiny cell phone speaker.

"Why you?" Brock James asked. She heard notes of disappointment and anger. Dark clouds brought on by yet another ruined weekend.

Sam shrugged, a useless gesture in a phone conversation, but human wiring predated phones by a zillion eons. Plus or minus. "Born lucky," she guessed.

She heard him let out his breath. Dead giveaway for exasperation, in her experience as his live-in consort. "They're sending you halfway around the globe to view a case file," he said. "Can't they just email it to you?"

She shook her head, again pointlessly, eyes half closing as she let out her own sigh. "It's protocol in cases like this one."

"Like what one?"

"A guy died. Run over by a car."

"In Budapest?" An edge to Brock's voice. "Must happen a dozen times a day. Why do they need you there?"

"Because he was one of ours."

A long pause. The energy changed.

"Shit. Sam, I'm really sorry." More silence. "Anyone we knew?"

"Mark Severn," Sam said, conjuring her coworker's youthful face as she spoke his name.

Ex-coworker, to be completely accurate. As of yesterday.

"The bass player?"

"That's him," Sam said. "*Was* him, I guess." She recalled a few enjoyable evenings watching Mark Severn's rock band play in various Alexandria booze joints. The band was tight and well-rehearsed, and they were becoming kind of a thing around town. Sam and Brock enjoyed hanging out, tapping their feet, singing out of key, half-transported from the usual Washington DC manure for a few hours, overall an agreeable effect.

"Shit," Brock repeated, anger replaced by commiseration. "I liked him."

"Me too. He was going to be a good one." Implying a marked contrast to the rest of them. Sam often complained that the Department of Homeland Security was a behemoth among bloated DC bureaucracies, and she respected precious few of her fellow agents' skill and professionalism. The more ambitious among them were fat desk jockeys playing at cops and robbers. The less ambitious sent emails to each other about cops and robbers. Losing a rising star stung on personal and professional levels.

"Accident?" Brock asked.

"By all accounts."

"I'm sorry you have to go. I made plans for us."

Sam closed her eyes, feeling a tired burn inside her lids that accused her of working too hard yet again. "I'm sorry, baby. Really."

"Forget about it. Duty calls. Will I get to see you naked before you leave?"

An airport announcement blared, making Sam's response both inaudible and redundant. She repeated it after the harangue relented, just to fill the silence on the phone. "There were tickets in the file Davenport gave me," she said. "My flight's in an hour."

More silence on the other end of the line. Brock was an

understanding guy by nature — twenty years as a fighter pilot tended to give one a rather sanguine approach to non-lethal setbacks — but he was obviously several notches south of happy.

"But listen, an idea struck me." The corners of her mouth crept upward. "I have a proposition for you."

It took a moment, but he came around. "I love your propositions," he said, a small smile around his words.

"Join me."

"In Budapest?"

Sam chuckled. "If you're going to join me, then yes, it'll have to be in Budapest."

"Isn't that in Africa or something?"

"Europe, smartass."

"G'day."

"Close."

"Guten Tag."

"Getting warmer."

"I'll see what I can do."

"Just buy a ticket. For Saturday. Two days should be plenty of time for me to finish up the paperwork on Severn. Then we could both really use a week off."

"Strong offer," Brock said.

"I'll pick you up at the airport, and we'll bonk like bunnies on our hotel balcony."

"I'd fly to the moon to get in your pants."

"Don't. I won't be there."

"Europe it is."

"Then I'll see you Saturday."

"I love you painfully," Brock said.

"I love you worse."

Sam dropped her phone in her purse next to her Kimber .45 — being the living, breathing personification of Big Brother wasn't without its perks, which included, improbably, much less infringement on the Constitutional right to bear arms than the average US citizen enjoyed — and trudged wearily to her gate.

She sighed.

Long day behind her.

Long day still ahead.

Chapter 2

His mother named him Nero. She was aiming at power and strength. She got ruthlessness and megalomaniacal insanity instead. She must have been sick on history day.

He went by Jeff. Short for Jefferson, his middle name. After Thomas Jefferson. A philandering miscegenation-prone oligarch, if you dug too deeply. Best to admire the stern visage on the two-dollar bill and not ask too many questions.

He had never seen a two-dollar bill. He had, in fact, seen an insufficient number of bills in any denomination.

He blamed his name, at least in part. Some men got great, powerful, awe-inspiring names, which undoubtedly catapulted them to wealth and notoriety.

He got Nero Jefferson Chiligiris.

Thanks, mom.

He was born in Cleveland, Ohio, circa 1969. The city was deep in Rust Belt ruin by the time Nero came of age. Especially so on Nero's side of the tracks. Nothing to do for money that wasn't illegal.

He was a lifelong Browns fan, which was a perfect metaphor for the pervasive futility all around him. Even the good years weren't very good.

There were plenty of male role models in Nero's life, but none of them were particularly positive. He spent his youth in and out of juvie, mostly for petty crimes related to scaring up enough money to eat.

Then came his eighteenth birthday, a milestone significant in that it meant the end of juvie and the beginning of an adult criminal record. He became intimately familiar with a couple of state correctional institutions.

Then, one unlucky day, he crossed state lines during the commission of a crime. Blam. Federal offender.

Federal prisoner.

Fifteen years. Out on parole after ten.

Scared straight wasn't quite accurate, but Nero saw the wisdom of remaining on the outside.

And strange as it might have been for a tough street kid, he didn't like violence. He was big enough to survive relatively unmolested in prison, but his disposition was anything but outsized. He never picked fights, never intimidated people, and never joined the mutual blood-letting during the turf wars endemic to prison life.

He did his time, worked out at the prison gym, kept his nose clean, and researched opportunities to make a legitimate living on the outside.

Which amounted to jack and shit. Nobody was hiring. Qualified, college-educated workers weren't finding jobs. What hope did a felon have?

There was one industry that embraced Nero's ilk, however. Debt collection. It was an industry made of misfits and unemployables from all walks of life. Buffalo, New York was its capital. Browbeating deadbeat dads and down-on-their-luck homemakers into making just a single low monthly payment to set right all those thousands of dollars of debt wasn't work that anyone else wanted, so the work fell to the ex-cons, and they flocked to Buffalo by the thousands.

And it was one hell of a booming business. All you had to do was hustle. Start dialing debtors in the morning, work your "talk-off" technique all day, and rack up the payments. There was enough cash to insulate your big new house and fill the trunk of your big new Escalade.

But it was the wild west. The criminals working the phones resorted to shockingly criminal measures to extract and extort payments on old and long-forgotten debts.

Nero never had the stomach for that sort of thing, so he was never better than an average collector. But he was thrown out on the streets just like the rest of them when the federal regulators finally woke up to the madness. He had the rug pulled out from under him three times in less than a year.

Nero took it as a sign.

He managed to make a few acquaintances during his stint in the seedy underbelly of America's economic system. One of them was an irascible and almost unbearably arrogant gentleman of nondescript Middle Eastern descent whose real name Nero never learned, but who went by the moniker Money and paid handsomely in cash for services rendered.

They weren't difficult services, either. Mostly courier work, based out of Denver. Locked duffel bags, locked suitcases, sealed backpacks. Always heavy.

The deal was always the same: Nero was allowed to bring no cell phone, no pager, no GPS, no computers or electronic devices, and no weapons. He was always to drive an old car without a GPS tracking system. The exchanges took place in extremely remote locations, and absolutely no words were exchanged between couriers.

Sure, Nero had the vague notion that something slightly untoward might have been afoot. But he was making good money. He had people depending on him. Kids and a girlfriend. Wife, really, but they'd never bothered with a ceremony. Oldest boy starting high school.

He made sure his ignorance was absolute. He had no clue what was in the bags, and he worked hard to keep it that way. Prison sucked, and he had no desire to return. Money's business was no concern of Nero's. He went out of his way to make sure the boss knew it, too. Nero knew his place.

On this day, Nero Jefferson Chiligiris's place was several miles south of a rest stop on I-70 in Eastern Colorado, near the Kansas border. He was driving a Pontiac Grand Am, old enough to have the cheesy plastic bumpers and no On-Star on board.

The air smelled much less like Colorado and much more like Kansas. Nero hated Kansas. The bugs and the humidity got to him. And the bovine slack-mouthed look most Kansans had about them. At least, most of the ones in his tax bracket, which was admittedly less impressive than it might have been had he bothered to report all of his income.

Nero looked around. Not another car in sight. Corn fields on either side, getting on toward the harvest, Nero figured, judging by their size.

Out of habit, he looked overhead as well. Nothing but a couple of birds circling, riding thermals up from the two-lane blacktop road that ran straighter than a laser beam as far as the eye could see.

No traffic, no cops, no bug-smasher airplanes buzzing around. Perfect conditions.

The other car approached from the highway side. Another beat-up old shitbox, ready to give up the ghost if the engine's wheezing was any indication.

Nero found the trunk button, heard a clunk as the latch released, and stared straight ahead. He had long ago mastered temptation, and was no longer even curious about who might have been on the other end of the transaction. He didn't want to know anything about them. Not even what they looked like.

Nero felt the suspension lighten as the other courier lifted the large red duffel from the back of Nero's Grand Am.

Then there was a thunk, the replacement bag, ostensibly the *pro quo* to his *quid*, either greenbacks or goods, Nero didn't know which. And didn't want to know. Not his business.

The trunk slammed shut. Nero stared straight ahead, heard the other courier's footsteps in the gravel, started his Grand Am, and put it in drive.

And all hell broke loose.

Nero heard a low, thrumming buzz. The air vibrated. The sound grew more intense, more insistent. It became overpowering, hammering Nero's chest, battering his car, shaking the earth around him.

The noise grew unbearably loud. It assaulted his ears, robbed him of breath, scared him witless.

A helicopter appeared, impossibly huge and deafening, pounding the air into submission, skidding to a hover just above corn height. Then another, and one more, surrounding him, angry and ominous and in his face.

One blocked the road to Nero's south and a second blocked the north, trapping him on the narrow road.

Nero stared wide-eyed, pulse pounding, insides clenched with fear and dread, adrenaline slamming his veins.

Strapped in each chopper's doorway was a man in a black jumpsuit wielding an assault rifle.

The third helicopter took position overhead and just to the west of the road. It was the one with the loudspeaker, Nero later realized. Get out of the car with your hands above your head. Instructions he'd heard before, but not in a very long time.

So much for the straight life.

Chapter 3

Uncle Sam didn't spring for business class — bad optics, they said — so Sam tried to get comfortable in her coach seat, an obvious impossibility for anyone over five-three. It was one of the low-grade annoyances that added up over time, contributing to the general angriness Sam sensed inside and around her.

She was more acutely aware of those things in her post-death incarnation, because the notion had crept into her mind that peacefulness ought to be a priority on some level, which she thought to be much more related to subtracting things from one's life than adding.

Like airline travel. She could permanently subtract *that* from her existence and be forever happier.

And she would undoubtedly have to subtract work as well. Not entirely, but substantially. It was likely the only way to remedy the constant fatigue that plagued her, and the scowl on her face most mornings, and the preoccupation that had come over her.

She could tell it was taking its toll on Brock. He understood, of course. He'd been awakened in the middle of the night countless times during his own career, sent off to foreign lands to fly circles over petulant dictatorships or dodge surface-to-air missiles and drop bombs on rogue states. But she could see the tiredness in his eyes.

And her death had taken a remarkable toll on him.

How could it not? He had been forced to watch the whole

thing, strapped horizontally to a wall while his shattered ankle dangled at a grotesque angle, his heart and psyche breaking just as completely and painfully, unable to turn away as a deranged killer had his way with her battered body.

And for what? For truth and justice? For good to triumph over evil? Laughable.

Existential questions welled up often from deep in her consciousness, more bitter each time. Justice was a farce. She worked for fools and charlatans.

But she couldn't stop. Trouble had a way of finding her. New bastards presented themselves to her with frightening regularity. And once on her radar, she didn't have it in her constitution to simply look away, to leave them for someone else to handle.

Because they would mishandle it. And the bastard would walk. And that conjured in her the image of her helpless little self, cowering under the hard glare of the biggest bastard she'd ever met, powerless to give him what he deserved and restrained from hurting him by the invisible bonds of a twisted love-hate thing.

To hell with all of them, she thought. Finding and stopping the bastards would be somebody else's problem for a change.

She bounced her knee, restless, wrestling.

Then she decided. She was going to ask for a transfer out of field work. She'd had enough, had given enough. The costs were just too high.

She would ask for an administrative job, put up with bureaucrats and senseless meetings for a few years, then put in for early retirement.

They'd travel. She'd give Brock random and deeply satisfying head when he least expected it. She'd maybe have children with him.

Maybe.

After she exorcised a few more personal demons.

But it would all have to wait.

Mark Severn's death deserved the department's full attention, and she resolved to set her weariness aside and go about her business with dignity and respect.

Then take a vacation.

Then quit.

She looked at her watch. 3:45 pm DC time. Six hours to Brussels, and with the time change it would be 4:50 am by the time she got out of the noisy aluminum tube. Then a two-hour layover, followed by a two-hour flight to Budapest.

Restlessness struck. She got up and walked to the lavatory as much out of a need to move as a need to pee. She chose the far lavatory, the one in the middle of the plane, to afford more time out of her seat. She took her time strolling up the long, narrow aisle, watching with idle amusement as heads bobbed and shifted in unison with the mild turbulence.

She looked at her face in the bathroom mirror. Tired. Older than she wanted to look. Younger than she felt. Red hair and green eyes still blazed back at her. Still the spark of life, still the slightly defiant arch of her eyebrow. Time to figure out what you want to do with your life, she thought.

Business completed, she wandered back down the aisle toward row forty, still contemplating fate and future.

She was miles away when a familiar feeling brought her instantly back to the present.

An uncomfortable feeling.

Eyes.

Someone was looking at her. Studying. Evaluating. It was a sixth sense she had developed over years in the field. It had saved her life countless times. Her adrenal glands were already at work before her eyes darted to her right.

A man. Professional but not very. His eyes lingered on her, even as hers bored through him. A seasoned pro would have smiled, played it off, even come on to her. Maybe even looked down at her figure with a smile. Anything to hide the operational assessment going on behind the eyes.

This guy wasn't that smooth, but he was definitely on the job. His cheekbones were high and Slavic, mouth slightly too small, eyes tilted slightly upwards at the outer edge, containing an operator's interest and an American-style knowingness despite the decidedly foreign heritage.

All of this Sam gathered in an instant.

Then just as quickly she smiled, affecting a look as if she might say something, as if she might have known the man, like maybe they had met somewhere before.

Then she pretended to think better of it, turned her head, and continued onward.

She noted the man's seat number as she walked past. 32A.

She found her seat. As she turned around, she took an extra second to survey the passengers. Tails traveled in pairs. At least, the

serious ones did. Sam wondered where the other guy might be
lurking.

A few more questions popped to mind, the kind that were hard
to answer while trapped on an airplane, smelling-distance away from
three hundred other people.

She looked again at her watch. Still six hours to go, minus
three minutes. A long flight just got infinitely longer.

* * *

She tried to sleep. Nothing doing. Her body needed it badly,
but the sardine-like accommodations and the compulsion to survey
her surroundings kept her awake.

As was often the case during air travel, the hours passed like
months. She took notes on the Severn case to stay occupied. The
captain's cool-guy voice finally announced their impending arrival
in Brussels.

Four millennia later, the airplane came to a stop at the gate.
The seatbelt sign went off, causing nearly everyone on the plane to
stand up simultaneously.

Sam couldn't see the guy in 32A. He was eight rows in front
of her. Might as well have been eight miles.

When she walked up the ramp and onto the concourse, he was
nowhere to be found. She found a quiet corner to pretend to check
her messages while scanning the crowd for any hint of him.

No luck.

Maybe he was more professional than she gave him credit for.

Maybe she should figure out what the hell was going on.

She took out her government-issued Blackberry. She hardly

ever saw Blackberries anymore, except in the hands of US government employees, which made Sam wonder whether the company was being propped up for political reasons.

She did the time-zone math, grimaced, then auto-dialed a number she'd called a thousand times before. It belonged to Dan Gable, the most capable deputy a girl could wish for. It was a quarter to eleven in DC, and she knew he'd be awake.

"I thought I was rid of you for a few days," Dan said instead of hello. A squealing baby was surprisingly loud in Sam's ear.

"I wasn't going to call you at this hour, but then I did," she said.

"No worries. I was just contemplating jumping out the window."

"You make fatherhood sound so dreamy."

"Who's dreaming? That requires sleep."

Sam laughed. Her relationship with her second-in-charge was easy and informal. Strictly business — no overtones or undertones — and Dan was as competent as they came. He was one of two men she trusted, and the only other human at the Department of Homeland Security with whom she'd entrust her life.

To call him a lifesaver was a gross understatement. He'd helped her through countless impossible situations.

And he had brought her back from the dead.

Dan had arrived too late to save her from the madman, but early enough to bring her back to life. He had pumped her heart for her, and breathed life back into her lungs, while Brock watched broken and helpless. The doctors had made clear to her that she owed her continued existence to Dan Gable.

He was five-eight, two inches shorter than Sam, built a little bit like a bowling ball but with very little fat, with thick, beefy arms and stubby fingers that pecked away at a computer keyboard with the best of them.

Dan was beyond competent in the field — rock-steady aim, rock-steady disposition — but his real value was in his otherworldly mastery of espionage via computer. There were very few who could hold a candle to him, and it was those skills that Sam intended to invoke.

"Please give my apologies to Sarah for calling so late," Sam said.

"I would, but it wouldn't do any good."

"Still mad?"

"Perpetually. Mostly at me."

"This shouldn't take too long. It should leave plenty of time to kiss and make up."

"Lay it on me."

"I made a new friend this evening. Bulky guy, Slavic bones, definitely watching me."

"Sure he didn't want to ask you on a date?"

Sam chuckled. "No. He was unmistakably on the job."

"I thought this was supposed to be a milk run, followed by a week's vacation."

"Me too."

"But you do have a long list of people pissed off at you," Dan said helpfully.

"Thanks. I didn't feel exposed enough already. Seat 32A, on Brussels Airlines flight 1850."

"Got it," Dan said. "Do you know who Brussels code-shares with? It'll make the hacking a little easier."

"United Airlines."

"Great. Shouldn't take long. Call you when I have something."

Sam thanked him and signed off.

For the first time in a long time, she wanted a drink.

It was a strange sensation, with a few years of sobriety behind her. She fought the urge, of course. That was one genie she could never let back out of the bottle.

Chapter 4

Nero Jefferson Chiligiris assessed his situation. He'd been arrested by some kind of a SWAT team, bound in chains, and flown to a detention center on the outskirts of Denver.

He had no idea how long ago that had been. They'd confiscated his watch, along with his wallet, shoelaces, and belt, and put him in a windowless holding cell.

It wasn't like a prison cell. There were no bars. It was just a six-by-eight room, no bigger than a broom closet, with concrete walls and a chair and a fluorescent light overhead that hummed and buzzed. There was no switch in the cell, and the light stayed on the whole time. Nero was certain there was a camera in the light fixture as well, keeping tabs on him.

He still had no idea why they'd taken him. Nobody had said a word about it, and all of his questions went unanswered. "You'll find out in due time, Mr. Chiligiris," one of the men in black had said.

Which had Nero thinking. Sure, he didn't work for a great guy. Even the name was a little bit off-putting. Money. Like, I'm The Man. Arrogant to go with it, and a pretty dangerous temper.

Not that Nero had ever given Money cause to lose his temper. Nero was a model employee. He never skimmed, never peeked, never asked questions, never moonlighted, never screwed up. Nero was pretty much a perfect hire for a guy like Money.

And Nero was a model citizen. Family man. Even had a

minivan. He hadn't knowingly dabbled on the sketchy side of the line for eons.

So the current mess had to be on Money.

And Nero's recent rationalization to Penny, who was concerned that Nero couldn't really describe what business Money was in, felt a little bit silly in light of his new circumstances. "Maybe Money's not doing anything illegal at all," he'd said. "Maybe he just doesn't trust bankers and guards. Maybe he just likes to do security his own way."

"And maybe I'm Miss America," Penny had said.

And maybe she was right about Money, the way she was right about almost everything.

Not like him. He was a little bit too stubborn. You could always tell Nero, his mom used to say, but you couldn't tell him much. Good advice usually didn't stick except in hindsight.

This was one of those hindsight-type situations, Nero figured. He alternately cursed his deliberate naiveté, then defended the Money decision by asking himself rhetorically where else he could possibly have found a job that paid enough to keep a roof over their heads.

Anyway, how the hell did they find him? He left his cell phone at home — a serious risk, given that there were no pay phones around for an emergency — and he drove a shitty 1990's car without any GPS tracking on it. Just like Money insisted on. He had no pager. He didn't even use a burner phone. He didn't use a credit card, ever. Way too easy for people to track your movements and stake out your regular haunts. He didn't have anything to hide, but you couldn't be too careful.

He was as clean as clean could be, yet they'd swooped in on him almost as soon as the transaction took place.

Could they have tracked the other guy, the one who showed up to exchange duffel bags near the Kansas border? Definitely a possibility. They arrested that guy, too, but it could have just been for show, to protect the other courier's identity as a stooge. You could never rule anything out.

Still, it seemed weird. He had taken so many precautions to keep his nose as clean as possible, to make himself as hard to track as possible.

Could it be some tax thing? He was a W-9 employee, which meant he had to hire a guy for an arm and a leg to figure out all the wherefores and therefores. And there might be a few stacks of bills — cash bonuses for jobs done well and with minimum fuss — that Nero might have neglected to mention to the IRS.

But the cash was in coffee cans, in holes, often on public land, with nothing but GPS coordinates to point the way, which were themselves on a yellow sticky in a safe deposit box, all of which would have required The Man to have a serious burr up his ass to go after.

And seriously, what did the IRS care about fifty grand? It probably cost that much to send the helicopter team after him.

Besides, wouldn't they need a warrant for all of that, anyway?

And why hadn't they read him his rights?

Which brought him back to where he started: where am I, and why the hell am I here?

The door opened, breaking the unproductive mental loop in Nero's head.

In walked a Special Agent America looking guy. Big barrel chest, veins like a geography map carved in bulging forearms, thick neck, short haircut, 9mm sidearm strapped to his trim waist, clipboard clenched in a beefy paw.

Nero saw a second guy positioned just outside the door. The two agents could have been twins.

Nero stood up. He wanted to be polite. He wanted to be helpful, and get to the bottom of things, and demonstrate that he didn't know the first thing about anything that any law enforcement-types might be interested in.

"Mr. Chiligiris," Special Agent America said. "Please have a seat."

Nero sat back down on the chair.

"Do you know why you're here, Mr. Chiligiris?"

"No, sir. I was hoping you could tell me."

America looked disappointed. "Cooperation is always best, Mr. Chiligiris."

Nero nodded. "Trust me, sir, I'm willing to cooperate. I got a job and a wife and kids to get home to."

"You're married?"

Nero blushed a little bit. "Well, not technically, but me and Penny have been together for years."

America made a note on the clipboard.

"You're a convict, Mr. Chiligiris."

Nero bristled. "Ex-con. I'm past all that now. Like I said, I got a family. Responsibilities. Can I call home?"

"Do you know why you're here?" America repeated.

"Like I said, sir, I was really hoping you could clarify that for me. And maybe you could tell me where I am, while you're at it."

America eyed Nero. The agent's jaw muscles worked. His eyes seemed preternaturally clear. Hard. It had a spooky effect.

"You're in Denver," America said. "In a holding facility belonging to the Department of Homeland Security."

"Can you tell me why I'm here?"

"What do you think, Mr. Chiligiris?"

"What do *I* think? I think I'd like to know how I can help you, so I can get out of here and go home. Has anyone called Penny, let her know I'm OK?"

"No calls have been made on your behalf, Mr. Chiligiris."

"Can I call her, please?"

America shook his head. "Not at this time."

"Am I arrested? Are you charging me with something?"

"You are not under arrest."

"So you're releasing me?"

"No. Your present status is as a detainee."

"Detainee? What the hell is that?"

"Don't raise your voice, Mr. Chiligiris."

"Don't you have to read me my rights? And what about that Habeas Corpse thing?"

"Corpus."

"What?"

"*Corpus*," America said. "It's Habeas *Corpus*. Your right to be brought before a judge and formally charged."

"Exactly! That's what I mean. What are you charging me with?"

America wrote on his clipboard. "Mr. Chiligiris, The USA Patriot Act and the Military Commissions Act set aside Habeas Corpus in cases like this one."

"Case? You have a case against me?"

America shook his head. "Not like you're thinking. Not with clerks and lawyers and a judge."

"Then what?"

America clicked his pen, lowered his clipboard, bored through Nero with those freakishly clear eyes for another long moment.

He rose. "Mr. Chiligiris, you are being detained on suspicion of conspiracy to commit acts of terror against the United States of America."

Nero's jaw dropped.

"You're insane."

"I'm afraid not, Mr. Chiligiris."

"You're absolutely out of your mind."

America shook his head. "Not in the slightest," he said. He rapped on the door. The latch clacked. The door opened. America turned to leave.

Nero rocketed out of his chair. "What the hell? I'm a US citizen! I'm clean! I have rights! I want a goddamned lawyer!"

A giant fist shoved Nero back into the seat. A small smile crossed America's face. "You're not getting it, Mr. Chiligiris. Involving yourself with terrorists takes you off the citizen list. We take the gloves off for cases like yours."

America left. The door slammed shut in his wake.

Nero trembled with fear and rage. His hands balled into fists. He rose, paced, cursed.

He smacked the wall with his hand. Timidly at first, then again with more force.

Then a flurry of fists, flying with an irrational, helpless abandon. He pounded the walls, hands numbing with pain, a howl leaving his throat, like a caged animal

He collapsed back into the chair.

"I'm fucking innocent."

He was certain no one heard him.

Get the #1 Bestselling **Book Three of the Incident Trilogy**:

FALLOUT: A Sam Jameson Conspiracy Thriller

What readers say:

"The best writing in decades. Move over, Lee Child."

"Some of the best thriller fiction you will ever read."

"Right up there with Patterson, Baldacci, Forsyth, and DeMille."

"The best thriller I've ever read."

"LOVE LOVE LOVE this series!"

Made in the USA
Coppell, TX
27 July 2021